Fiddler's Dream

Also by Gregory Spatz

No One But Us
Wonderful Tricks

Fiddler's

a novel # Dream

Gregory Spatz

Southern Methodist University Press

Dallas

This novel is a work of fiction. Names, characters, places, and incidents are either the product of the author's imagination or are used fictitiously.

Requests for permission to reproduce material from this work
should be sent to:
Rights and Permissions
Southern Methodist University Press
PO Box 750415
Dallas, Texas 75275-0415

Grateful acknowledgment to *Shenandoah* where chapter one
of *Fiddler's Dream* appears under the title "Bluegrass Boy."
Cover image: "A Mother Driving Her Child to Richfield for a Violin Lesson,"
by Howard Sochurek, Time and Life Pictures.
Jacket and text design by Kellye Sanford

Library of Congress Cataloging-in-Publication Data

Spatz, Gregory, 1964-
    Fiddler's dream: a novel / by Gregory Spatz.—1st ed.
    p. cm.
    ISBN 0-87074-508-5 (alk.paper)
    1. Bluegrass musicians—Fiction. 2. Fathers and sons—Fiction. I. Title.

PS3569.P377F53 2006
813'.54—dc22

                                                                    2005057606

Printed in the United States of America on acid-free paper

10   9   8   7   6   5   4   3   2   1

For Larry and Alice Spatz—
finest of parents, finest of musicians

Acknowledgments

Thanks to the Corporation at Yaddo, Hawthornden Castle International Retreat for Writers, Washington State Artist Trust, the Michener Copernicus Society of America, the University of Iowa Writers' Workshop, and the Eastern Washington University office of Grants and Research. Thanks to Ann Joslin Williams for always reading and rereading when I needed it, to DeAnna Heindel, and to my wife, Caridwen Irvine-Spatz, for prodding me along, believing in me, and helping me to figure it all out.

About the Chapter Headings:

The letters at the start of each chapter correspond with notes from the scale of G major—G being one of the most popular keys for fiddle tunes (including the tune "Fiddler's Dream"). The Roman numerals are symbols for chords. The chord at the start of each chapter is derived from, or inclusive of, the note it is paired with. Taken together, the chords provide a condensed chart for the harmonic structure of the tune

"Fiddler's Dream." In my mind, they also chart Jesse's progress in the narrative.

—G.S.

(g)–I

Just before leaving, he looks in on her. There are cigarettes on the porch floor beside her, a half-full glass of gin and one unashed cigarette on the lip of the ashtray, so he knows she must have lit up before dropping off. Under the mosquito netting she's younger and beautiful, like someone he doesn't know. "Mama?" he whispers. There's a hitch in her breathing, but she doesn't waken. He leans forward, pulls the netting back, and sees her bare shoulder, the back side of her head—familiar brown-white, waved hair—and the bones of her spine leading out of sight under the sheet.

"Mama, I'm leaving."

She doesn't stir.

He straightens and lets the netting fall into place, enclosing her—goes back inside, through the living room and down the hall. He doesn't stop over the things he loves the most and knows he will miss. The view from the living room window— the valley floor with mist and cloud-shadows moving over it like stains coming through the trees, not like something cast;

the musty, charred pine smell of the fireplace; the plant table by the window; cloth-faced cupboards in the kitchen and the floorboards there worn to silver. He walks right through like he plans on being back later that day.

The road down is rutted from spring runoff, dame's rocket and blackberry blossoms showing through in the bramble alongside. He's known this road so long it isn't like driving any-more—it's more like thinking or being in a dream. Just past the second fork he glimpses two deer in a stand of pines, almost indistinguishable from the surrounding trees and shadows, and he wonders if this will be the spot to remind him from now on—because he's still thinking as if he'll be back—*that dawn, that day I left.* Then the stretch of gradual descent through slen-der moose maple and white birches with slabs of glaciated gran-ite in between, the air softer and sun-scented as if hours more of daylight had passed. At the bottom is the sign, hand painted black and red, next to the state's smaller reflective metal one: Watson Mountain Road No. 2, Proceed at Your Own Risk. Under that are the names of people living here, but not his or his mother's.

He sits a moment at the end of the road, idling.

"Feel something about this," he says aloud, but he has no name for the feeling and can't be sure what it is. Tree shadows flicker onto the lichen-shouldered rocks. He glances once at Genny's letter, open on the seat next to him, her blue felt-tip scrawl, and the map with directions to her place underneath, though it will be two days on the interstate before he needs them.

He takes the east route around the lake, past the driving range and the marina. No one is out yet, and the surface of the water is smooth gray with reflections of the mountains floating deep into it. Outside town the road goes up from the shore, through spruce and tall pines; a few miles farther the pines give way to shiny-leaved oak and poplar. Always, he feels buoyant here, like he's broken free of everything in the world. It's his favorite stretch of the road. He gets glimpses of the water down through the trees to his right, flashes of silver between tree trunks. The air has smells of lake water and leaves and moss-wet stones, so there's a feeling in every breath of being in water and out of it simultaneously. As he drives he imagines stopping one last time to take it all in. But there's no point really. He pictures himself in the cab of his truck with the windows down—or maybe he'd get out, lower the tailgate and sit back there, swatting black flies, waiting for some endlike feeling. All the time he'd be thinking how he needed to travel on.

He remembers a night when he was five or six. He and his mother were in the living room listening to his father's band on the radio—a live radio show taped earlier that year. "Those aren't men," his mother said. "They're angels. Hear how they always know the right thing to play, like they're talking to each other? It's a divine thing, not normal. Do you hear it?" She stroked the hair from his forehead in a way he liked. "Maybe someday that'll be you. Sure. Maybe the two of you together." Her fingers smelled bitter—lime rinds and gin and stale perfume. "Won't that be something?"

He pictured his father leaning into the microphone and moving his eyebrows up and down, crooning. Then he'd step back from the microphone and lift the neck of the guitar, like this was a part of what he had to say in his song—pick a few bass notes and slip up to the microphone again to continue where he'd left off, shaking his hips. They'd seen him play recently, at the club in town, so it was easy enough to imagine. The radio rattled with audience laughter. His mother wagged her head side to side and sang along a few beats.

"This is a happy time for us," she said. She pulled him closer and drew him across her lap. "Aren't you happy?" she asked, and patted his bottom in rhythm with the song. He heard her stomach rumble and creak in his left ear and felt the heat from her lap and legs rising in front of his face like a shield between himself and the radio. It made him woozy with sleep. He was happy for the moment, though he didn't believe she was less lonely or worried than usual, and he knew his father was not an angel.

Soon he's among mountains he doesn't know the names for. They're not unlike the ones he grew up in, caused by the same rents in the earth's crust and drift of glaciers, so the light and vegetation and shape of the horizon are familiar enough. He drives through the morning and into the afternoon, south and west through the only three states he's ever been in in his life—Vermont, Massachusetts, New York—then south again, into Pennsylvania. The light is strong on his face, and the air booms through the open windows. He leaves the radio off and sings away the hours.

At the campsite he pitches his tent in grass so thick and spongy he doubts he'll need the pad to sleep on. From the bed of the truck he gets his cook stove and two tins of canned spaghetti and a bag of carrots. He pumps and lights the stove and empties the cans into a saucepan, stirring with a carrot every few minutes and biting away the leftover sauce at the end until the noodles are sizzling. By now the light's faded to amber and blue, and he eats, barely making out the sweet sauce-gummed noodles and cheese at the bottom of the pan.

Afterward he gets his guitar and mandolin from the truck and sits with his back to the picnic table, playing. The strings bite sweetly into his fingertips—they're hard as feet and blackened and grooved diagonally across with string marks—and there is some stiffness in his left hand to play through. His pick edge floats over the chords and strings of notes. Always his mandolin, '40s Gibson fern with a red and yellow finish, sounds better in the cool, dry air—throatier and with less of a pop to it. He loves the feeling of the neck between his left thumb and palm—how it makes his own throat ache and feel pressed out, like being full and hungry at the same time. And he loves the curve of the scroll too, the dully varnished curly-maple upswelling like a horse's neck, like a sound unfolding, the wood swooping and beveled going down from the scroll into the belly of the mandolin. He hits some G-intervals—thirds, fourths, sixths, intersecting the notes and listening, tuning strings. Hammers the high G a few times and goes straight into "White Horse Breakdown," because it's always what he starts with.

The whole state of Pennsylvania can't be this flat, he supposes—not that he minds the flatness. He feels protected and out in the open in it at the same time, both of which feelings he likes. He saw the mountains at the northeastern side, where he entered, and he knows of other parts where the land is supposedly rolling with hills. Genny told him. It was where she grew up. And he knows people in the surrounding towns and villages can't hear him, yet he imagines them listening. He pictures them coming home from work and heating up their dinners to eat next to open windows and out on back steps with the fading light that carries his notes to them.

He plays and chops chords until his hands are sore and loose, then switches to guitar, leaning from the table now to play. He's better on mandolin, though there's a way his inexperience with the guitar makes playing it more exciting to him. Both his picks are genuine tortoise shell, the guitar pick cut with more of a point and hatch-marked on either side so he can grip it lightly, the mandolin pick rounded to a near-circular edge, slick as skin between his fingers to make him bear down harder for the tone.

"Mr. Monroe," he thinks. He hears it in his head the way he's been told so many times the man likes being addressed—accent on the first syllable and the *o* shut to a soft *u* sound.

His usual fantasy: "Mr. *Mun*roe. I'm here to audition for the Bluegrass Boys." He hits a B chord, whips the pick up and back down on the Five, then the One again, then the G run. "I play all the instruments about equal, sir, and I've got every record you ever made—must've listened to them a million times apiece." He pictures some of the ways this information might register with Monroe. It could please him or annoy him or mean nothing at all. "Some of my favorites are with you and Charlie . . ."

"Heck, let's hear what you got, then," Monroe might say. Or maybe he'd want more conversation first, like an interview: "My brother Charlie and me ain't made a record since nineteen and forty, boy. Do you like any of my newer stuff at all?" No, he'd get right to it. He'd say, "Which one you like best?" Or, "OK, let's you and me sing some of that 'Midnight on the Stormy Deep.'"

He closes his eyes and imagines the fiddle kick in to "True Life Blues" instead, and there he is, hitting the guitar backup and coming in with Monroe on the vocals. "'I hate to see . . .'"

On his way to the shower house before sleeping he passes a lit-up orange tent just off the path. The light is from a flashlight propped against one inner wall of the tent so it shoots through the nylon, striated orange to darker orange. He stops there to watch as a woman inside kneels on the floor and begins undressing, her shadow projected to the roof and side of the tent like she's on a screen. She lifts something off over her head and lets it fall behind her, then lies back to become part of the shadow blur of everything else on the floor of the tent, her back arched a moment, her legs lifted and kicking. Now he makes out the shape of her head moving just above the other shadows on the floor of the tent. Then there's her arm, definitely her arm, swinging back and forth. She's brushing her hair.

He steps off the path and walks quickly across the campsite to be beside her tent. Her light is out before he's come alongside the tent, and now he hears her inside moving around—the zip of the sleeping bag zipper going one way and back the other not as far. He imagines himself lifted in with the air through the open window-mesh and lying beside her, the smell and feel of her against him, whoever she is, and closes his eyes to see it better. The last time—months ago now—was with Michelle, home from college for one of her long weekends. They were in the woods then, and she was on top of him, nothing on but her rings and the garnet-beaded choker he'd given her. He sat up to be closer, and there was the view of the lake running out behind her like a painting.

"The next woman you're with," she said, moving against him, "you'll think of this—you'll think of me." But he had never been with anyone else and didn't know whether to agree or disagree. "Here," she said. She spun a ring from one of her fingers, a stoneless silver circle, and slipped it into his mouth. "Yours."

He turns and heads back up to the path to the shower house.

"Mama," he says, as soon as his feet hit the gravel. He remembers how she was asleep under the mosquito netting when he left. Then the house, the stairs up to his room and the familiar smell in the upstairs hallway, the light on by her chair in the window—how she'll be winding down about now, deciding whether to sleep inside or on the porch. Only she won't be. Tonight nothing will be the same for her.

"Don't think, don't think," he tells himself swinging open the door to the men's room. "Nothing I could do for her anyway."

Ordinarily, he feels some comfort seeing his face in a mirror, but tonight he barely notices. He runs hot water over his hands and rubs them together, more to settle the aches in his fingertips and tendons than to get them clean, then leans to wash his face, plunging his fingers back through his hair and feeling the water on his scalp and neck. His mother would say: "You know everything is all right in the world as long as there's hot water and soap to wash your face at night before you sleep." She said it most nights when he was smaller and they were getting ready for bed.

I'll write to her from Genny's, that's what—tell her how much better off I am, he thinks. Say, "I don't need any more school now, Ma. You got to see. I'm meant to play music. That's all." Something like that. Then he'll write Michelle too, maybe—give her his new address so she knows how to reach him.

"'I got a letter . . . ,'" he sings—Monroe again, "Letter from My Darling"—and the rhythm of it swings through him, lifting him back out of thinking. He sings some more, closes his eyes a second, and feels how strong his voice is, coming through him from his heels to the top of his head.

There's a flush, and a stall door at the other end of the bathroom opens and springs shut. A lanky man in cowboy boots and jeans stands smoothing his mustache with two fingers. The man looks him over, hikes his pants, and then walks out, his footsteps sounding crisply and fading out down the gravel walk.

"Stupid kid," he says to the mirror. "What do you know about the world, anyway?" It's something his mother might say. He doesn't hate himself for sounding like her, though his awareness of it does undercut the feeling. What he means is how did that man look at *him*? What did he see? A nineteen-year-old kid singing to himself, on the way to his destiny? A lost kid missing his mother and his home?

He turns off the taps, shakes water from his hands, and cranks out some brown paper towels from the dispenser.

"You're an idiot," he says to his reflection, and grins. He doesn't believe it, though he supposes it's always been the truth. He wanders back out into the night to sleep.

He was about eight when his father came for the last time. They had no idea then it was his last visit. Two of the men from his band were with him—there were five altogether—both from Texas, both in checked cowboy shirts, boots, and jeans. They were nearly indistinguishable from each other until they were playing. One had knobby knuckles and a moon face with almost no hair; the other was also beardless but sleek-fingered, and he smiled more often, and there was a powerful smell of cologne and sweet new cloth about him. When they practiced their music, the one with knobby knuckles played make-believe drums on the tabletop. He used a coffee can for the high hat cymbal and slapped his foot on the ground for the bass kicks. The other man played fiddle. The fiddle was dull yellow and sat under his chin. When he played he kept an ironic look on his face, like he was trying very hard and not trying at the same time—like he was sad and like he was ready to tell a joke. He swayed subtly forward and back, and sometimes he lifted his right shoulder for emphasis just before drawing the most poignant notes. The boy's father sang and interrupted things now and then to say what was going wrong; and then occasionally they all quit playing and sang together, leaning their faces in toward each other without meeting eyes, adjusting the pitches.

"That's it," his father might say, finishing a song. Chuck-chuck, he'd hit the pick against the guitar strings, his fingers splayed against the neck to mute the notes. "I'll get a high baritone in there and come back on the lead for the verses. Boys, I do believe we'll knock them dead in Montreal."

"What's this?" the boy asked the fiddle player later, when they'd all stopped awhile for cigarettes and coffee. The fiddle lay in its red plush-lined case on the kitchen table. He pointed to the silver thumbscrew at the end of the bow. It was octagonally shaped and had a band of ebony through it and a bit of mother-of-pearl embedded at its end.

"That's my bow. That's what . . . they call that the thumb-screw. It's so you can loosen the bow hair when you're not playing. So you don't strip the arch out of the stick, see?" He lifted the bow to show him. "You want to try?" he asked. The man had engulfed him without his noticing, he was so absorbed in looking at the violin and the insides of its case. Now he was within the strange warmth of him and the man's arms were going around his shoulders, his chin touching him lightly on the top of the head, so close he could smell the coffee and clove and lentil soup and cigarettes on his breath. "You hold it with your chin," the man said, and he realized the fiddle had the same smell as the man, but denser and brocaded with other smells of wood and varnish, case cloth, rosin, and bar smoke. The half-moon chin rest was cold against his cheek for a moment, then warm as flesh pressing back into his flesh. "Good. Good. Now," the man said and spread his bow hand over the boy's hand to show him, "curve your index finger like this, right. Your thumb hooks in here, under the frog. That's what we call them because the damn Frogs invented the violin bow back in whatever it was, two hundred and fifty thousand years ago. No, pull it like this— down first, always a downbow first, and keep your arm straight, and then back up. Good. That's it."

They drew the bow together down and up several times, and then the man stood back, watching. Open E string. *Zing, zing, zing, zing* it roared into his left ear like a fire and went through his temples, filling his head. He drew the bow back and forth, back and forth, more and more pleased with himself.

"Keep your head up," the man said. "It ain't a pillow."

"Kid's got a natural touch," someone said.

"I say he does," the fiddle player said. "Look at that wrist. Limp as a damn rag."

"That's my boy."

Then he became aware of his mother glaring at him from inside the kitchen door. *Don't be too much,* she had said. *You be too much for him, and he won't come back, so remember. He isn't used to being around children.* He wasn't sure, but he thought this might be too much. Then he thought he would just move his left hand around a little to make some notes first, before he stopped, the way the fiddle player did it—slide his fingers up and down the neck of the violin and softly shake his wrist to make the tone come out warbling. In his head he heard some of the notes he wanted to play and pressed his fingers down into the strings. The sound died right out.

The men were laughing, and his mother came into the room. There was the difference in her footsteps, light and ringing. How could she stand it, being that set apart from them always?

His father lifted the violin away from him and said, "Next time, son. When we stop back I want to hear some of that old 'Faded Love,' and then me and your ma can take a turn around the room. That'll be something, hey? What do you say?"

"Sure," he said, not having thought for a second until then, how close his father was to going again.

"You say thank you to Tommy Lee for letting you try his old five-dollar fiddle?"

He nodded solemnly. "Thank you," he said.

It must have been only a year or two later that his father married another woman and took himself out of their lives completely. A few of his songs had been picked up by a country western star. One became a hit, so for a while there was no music allowed in the house—nothing to remind her of his betrayal. The hit was an up-tempo number he'd written just after late Sunday breakfast, slapping his bare foot on the kitchen floor and looking mock-forlornly at the boy's mother over dishes on the table and singing, making her blush and smile scoldingly.

When he came home after school, if she wasn't at work she was in bed with the blinds drawn, sweating and saying things half-aloud. "I'm sick," she'd say.

"Want me to call the doctor?"

She'd raise her head to see him at the foot of the bed. "He was here already today," she'd say, whether or not it was true. Then she'd let her head sag back into the pillows. "I don't know what it is—what's wrong with me."

"What's the doctor say?" He was not scared. He was too attached to her pain, too much a part of it, to fear or wonder about it. His stomach felt knotted and acid from eating canned food every night—soup, beans, corn, spinach, whatever he found to open and cook without her—and there was always the dry taste of tin in his mouth.

"Rest," she said. Her voice was barely audible.

Part of him wanted to believe it was nothing serious. That he could shut the door and walk away and the next time he opened it the blinds would be up and she'd be herself again, singing under her breath, a scarf tied around her head maybe, and her house-cleaning jeans on, because the house badly needed to be cleaned. Another part of him was angry, knowing this wouldn't happen. He wanted to go back in there, right up close to her, and look into the sickness all the way down to where she was herself still, unchanged. Then he'd shake her. "Get up," he'd say, and she'd rise because she'd know he was right, and what had been holding her under the covers was gone.

He couldn't remember how it began, but soon she wasn't working at all, and there were winter afternoons that stretched into evenings, him lying with her on the bed and neither of them speaking. Because there were no words between them he didn't know how to think of what was happening or afterward how to remember. There was her skin and heat and the sweat darkening her hair in his memory. Also, the feeling that parts of his brain were shutting down and going speechless, like before sleep. They slept much of the time. There was nothing in it like sex, really, except they were so close his dreams and the pressure of their bodies together were not always distinguishable. Then one day she was awake downstairs by the fire, and when she drew him to her, into her heat and the smell of the fire, soon after he'd said whatever he had to say about his day in school, he realized he wasn't going to be like this with her anymore. He felt himself going hazy and losing the parts of his mind related to speech again, and he knew he had to be outside, anywhere away from her. She held him close, his head vised to her chest so he could feel her pulse, and said, "Jesse. Jesse." Nothing else. It was the last time he let her hold him like that.

Soon after, he started playing the violin. His father had sent one for his birthday the previous year, just after his last visit, and it was too big then—a cheap Japanese violin with a machine-cut scroll and thick cinnamon-brown varnish and a fingerboard of black-painted pine, not ebony. It was still too big, but less so now, and he was more determined to play. Under his chin the fiddle sounded like it was coming through a phone line, it was that pinched, and it smelled bad—sour and musty and sometimes like tar, depending on how warm the day was. He tuned it how he wanted and tried to remember what the fiddle player had shown him about how to hold the bow correctly.

His mother was awake more and more now—it was spring. By then it was clear his father would never return, and she had begun her moralizing. "Don't place your ideals in another human being," she might say. "Especially members of the opposite sex. It's the worst and most pitiful mistake. You have to remember, because it's so, so tempting to let another person appear to you like all the good things in your life that you've been missing out on. But that's not love, it's . . . I don't know what. Desperation and need. The quickest path to being lost. One of the quickest, anyway." Or, "Remember, honey, baseness and laziness and shame don't fall, because they can't. But the good must fall. This is how we know them." Or, "You must always do what a woman asks you. Nothing will turn out for you otherwise." He didn't know which he hated more, the admonitions themselves or the anger in them he knew was no distance from the sadness that had wiped her out so long. The words were different, but the feelings to cause them were the same.

If he wasn't up in the woods by himself or downtown with

kids he knew, he was in his bedroom or the bathroom holding the violin as the man in his father's band had shown him and trying to make it sound good. He'd slide his fingers around on the strings and improvise three- and four-note melodies. Of course, nothing was right: the sound post was down, the bridge was too fat and put on backward, the strings were mixed up, and the tail-gut was slowly fraying so that sometimes his pitch would jerk down a notch without warning, or a string would go slack under his fingers. All this he found out later that year when the tailpiece came totally unmoored, and he had to bring it in to Genny's shop for repair.

He'd always known he would leave. He knew it from the first time he touched a fiddle—the way those men had looked at him, their voices suddenly changing around him. He knew it again the day of his first lesson, and a few years later still, when it dawned on him that music was a way of putting things he could never say outright—the shape of the mountains and the light slipping down them at the end of the day, and that pulse in his throat when he saw a girl he liked, how her hair fell around her ears, the colors in it reflecting light, and the way she'd lift her chin suddenly, looking right at him.

He hadn't known how or when it would happen, or even exactly *that* it would happen, until the night, three months ago, when he met and played with a singer-guitarist from Nashville named Red Spence. This was at the Lion's Den, a basement-bar in town for tourists staying in the inn upstairs or having a steak and scampi dinner in the inn's popular restaurant—also, a good filler gig for solo musicians and duos on their way through town. They played first in the men's room, the one place they could find to warm up. It was huge as a living room with tinted mirrors lining one wall and a mosaic-tiled floor, the tiles in a repeating octagonal pattern. The stall partitions were marble, and there were marble sinks as well, big enough to sit in, with brass and porcelain fixtures. He watched himself and Red in the mirror reflection, over Red's shoulder, playing, and because of the reverberant acoustics he wasn't too surprised at the seeming confluence of the sound. Jesse had been alone in the audience all night before introducing himself (they had a friend in common), watching and listening, imagining himself into vocal harmonies and instrumental fills. He knew ahead of time how it was going to work.

"God dang," Red said after the first duet. "You want to sit in the rest of the night, by all means. Can't pay you nothing, but if you feel like it."

Red's hands were freckled and surprisingly pudgy considering his speed, and he wore gold rings with stones on almost every finger. His hair was long in the back and short in the front with unnatural gold-red highlights, and too evenly curled—too sculpted. Already there was something about him Jesse didn't like; also something that he did. His eyes were hazel and had an appealing clever humor like his guitar playing. This, Jesse liked.

He watched himself in the mirror, nod and look away, chop a B-flat chord on the mandolin. Chuck-chuck. He'd never played with anyone as big as Red—a legend for having won the national guitar flat-picking championship three times in the '80s—and he supposed the main thing about this was not to think about it, not to play as if he had something to prove.

"How about . . ." Jesse said and started into "The New Camptown Races," easy and loping. He leaned more on the double-stops, paring down the strings of arpeggiated notes to match Red's sparse backup. And then, because of the difference in the way he was playing and the newness of it, for a few seconds he felt as if he'd slipped out of himself through the music, into their reflections in the mirrors—as if he were hearing around everything from the outside. He'd never felt this before, and he liked it. He looked away and back at Red and tried to stay fixed on the light caught in the string ends and bronze tuners on his guitar headstock to steady himself.

At the end of his first pass they met eyes, and Red half nodded, taking the lead. Now Jesse tipped his head to hear the mandolin in his left ear and Red's lead coming off the ceiling in the right one, so he could understand exactly how to balance and color things, where to mute his chop or let it ring or shake in the tensive shuffle beats for a transition. He watched Red's right hand and saw he had a way of syncopating his downstrokes—a pause and an extra hard plant to imply other notes between the ones he hit. Red did so many things at once rhythmically, crossing back and forth between strings, his musical line ended up almost more vertical than straight ahead, each note in a knot of chordal relationships and breaking away.

At the end of his solo Red shook his head, faintly annoyed with himself, and took a step back, then surged in with the backup.

"Lot of Clarence in your leads," Jesse said when they were done.

Red nodded. "Clarence and Doc. A little Tony. Ha!" He shook his left hand out hard and walked away and back in a circle. "Shit motherfucker!" he said. He grinned widely. "I need to do *that* about ten times a day. God damn."

They shook their heads at each other and laughed some more and then went back out into the bar to see about setting up extra microphones.

They sang all the brother duets they could think of: "What Would You Give in Exchange for Your Soul?" "Rabbit in a Log," "What Does the Deep Sea Say?" "Nine Pound Hammer," "Will the Roses Bloom Where She Lies Sleeping?" Jesse watched Red's mouth for phrasing. He wasn't conscious of what it took, doing this, only watched Red's lips, imagining himself into the breaths and syllables and pauses to match things. If he forgot or became distracted—someone at the bar, a face on the muted television across the room, a slipup in his own playing—then he'd come out wrong and they'd end jaggedly on a word or phrase. No one was listening, really, and yet he was concentrating that intensely. Sometimes Red went to a note too hard, overstating his emotion in a way that warded off true feeling. But that could be exhaustion. He'd said he was on the road now ten days; another week before he was home again.

Between songs they punched chords idly and looked up at the ceiling. "Let's see, let's see," Red said, and they suggested songs back and forth, picking out a note or two to remind each other how it went until they hit on something, or a succession of related material they knew in common. They played until last call, never stopping, and at the end of the night got into a medley of old-time D-tunes, "Forked Deer," "Soldier's Joy," "Woodchopper's Reel," "Ladies on the Steamboat," stringing the tunes along one after another like they were trying to outdo themselves or get something out of their systems.

"God dang, where you been hiding all these years anyhow?" Red asked afterward. He had a sip of beer and shifted his right leg so his guitar fell forward slightly in his lap, then leaned out of his chair and laid the guitar on the floor. His face was flushed from playing, and his eyes seemed shallower, pupils enlarged.

"Just up the road. Outside town," Jesse said. "I was mostly into contest material until a few years ago—fiddle contests, you know—so I wouldn't have been much fun to pick with."

Red blinked and his chin came up slightly. "Fuck me, motherfucker. Fiddle contests? You play fiddle too? How old are you anyway?"

"Nineteen. Twenty this summer."

"They just keep a gettin' younger." Red had a last swallow of beer and looked out over the bar, shaking his head. Three people were left—two men in business suits and a woman, silent between them, and the bartender. "Jesus. I was so busy smoking dope, fuckin' girls—I didn't even *start* playing guitar until I was like twenty. A little Stratocaster." He laughed and said something else about sex and his electric guitar-playing days, but there was a burst of laughter from the woman at the bar, which Jesse couldn't hear through. "Well, if you don't mind, I'm gonna go have me one last drink." Red winked. "I'd ask you to join me but that'd be looking for trouble, wouldn't it—you being *under-age* and all."

Jesse nodded.

Red stood and held out his hand. "Been a real pleasure, man," he said. "I tell you what, next time bring the dang fiddle. And like I say, if you get to Nashberg, you be sure and call. Got lots of folks there to pick with." He stepped down from the stage, not looking back, and went to the bar, where he immediately struck up a conversation with the bartender. It sounded more like a series of one-liners than two people talking.

Jesse scrubbed down the strings on his mandolin, stuffed the rag away under its neck, and closed his case—worn, green felt lining that hugged the strings and sides and fingerboard, and the snaps that went down stiffly like canning lids, one, two, three—watching Red and trying to get his eye one last time. He wasn't sure what he wanted or what he needed to say to him. Something. But Red wasn't looking back.

He slid on his jacket and went out through the empty dark bar room to the door, bumping his case against tables and chairs as he went, glancing over his shoulder, still trying to think of what he wanted to say. The last time he played here was with a local string band, the Hardhat Quartet, and they had practically cheered for him all the way out the door, calling their compliments and promises of future gigs after him.

"Hey," he said from the door, "thanks again for letting me sit in."

Red turned on his stool, not quite facing him. He raised his glass. "Great picking with you, kid!" he said, and drank.

Outside it was misty and warm for April. A faint rain hissed up off the pavement, reflecting the streetlights and the lights of passing cars like buried suns. He walked the two blocks through town to his truck. "*Contest material,*" he said under his breath. "What's the matter with me?" He got in and started up. He wasn't seriously displeased with himself; he knew he'd played all right and made a good impression. He just hated how he sounded whenever he tried to talk about music. Like he was at pains to conceal an outrageous vanity. Why? While the engine warmed he pulled out his wallet and slid Red's business card from between the few bills there. The print on it was raised black on a gray background, a drawing of a guitar on its side and Red's name written across that, his phone and address underneath. On the back were some dates, handwritten—when he'd be in town, when he was leaving again—and his wife's name, Nellie, in case she was the one around when he called. Red's handwriting was steep and jagged, clawlike, with no personality beyond the effort to be legible.

He turned the card around a few more times and slid it back into his wallet, took it out again, sniffed it, tucked it away, and put the truck in gear. Already he'd begun memorizing the sequence of numbers. 6-1-5, it began. Nashville. Same as Genny. His father.

Daylight glows in the sides of his tent, and for a moment as he rolls onto his back and off something hard that's been pressing into his hip the last few hours, bits of what he was dreaming surface and vanish—Michelle, the woman from the tent he'd seen undressing, a parade in the rain, Genny leading him through an official-seeming building with open ceilings and making him sign things. There's a good feeling left from the dreams, but nothing more specific he can recall. Two spiders sit upside-down on the dome roof of his tent. The seams in the fabric stand out like bones, each one dimpled and smeared over with seam sealant. Wind comes against the side of the tent, and he waits for sleep to sift through him again with its sound. But now he's too awake and thinking he should get on the road if he wants to make it the rest of the way before dark.

He pulls on shorts and steps out into the cold grass, still barefoot. It's later than he'd thought, the sky already marbled pink and blue. He stands by his truck pissing and watches the sun stream through some low serrated clouds. No one in sight. The woman he watched undressing the night before is gone already. Smoke and the barely perceptible waver of heat through cooler air and rising damp come from the ashes in her barbecue grate. He hears music in his head and feels the ache in his fingers to play, but now isn't the time for it. He ducks back into the tent to dress and pack. He's never been as far from home in his life.

(a)–V

Hours later, heading into the heat and haze, light dull on overgrown waxy-leaved trees he doesn't recognize, he begins thinking maybe his mother was right: he's a fool for doing this. He tries singing a while to clear his head, but it's no help. The radio's no good, either—DJs, advertisers, and singers all with the South in their voices, dipping and swaggering, nothing of comfort. He switches it off, frightened, and stares straight ahead. Everywhere he looks feels like a rebuke—hills he can't name, light that's too liquid and hot, clouds piling up dense as cities on the horizon, signs for towns and rivers and counties he never knew existed.

"What do you think, anyway. You're not headed anywhere—you're nothing," he says aloud. It's one of the last things his mother said to him two nights ago, drunk again and railing at him. He didn't believe it at the time—knew she was mainly insulting him to keep herself from feeling anything about his leaving. Now he wonders. There will be nothing for him in Nashville. Only Genny, some part-time work at her shop, and the phone numbers of people there he's met or played with over the last few years. Just over two thousand dollars saved from gigs and work the last several months. "You're too alone," he says. His mother hadn't said this (aloneness isn't something she'll talk about directly), but he knows it's true. And as soon as he hears himself saying it, he remembers he'll be there tonight, with Genny, not alone. "You stay as long as you want," she'd said on the phone a few days ago. "Stay as long as it takes you. You won't go hungry here."

There's a pleasing weight to the heat too, he decides—a way it soaks into you, forcing surrender. He could get used to that.

Now he's in West Virginia, past the welcome signs and speed warnings, afternoon sun slanting through the mist of a recent rain—the ceaseless snapping-grinding of crickets and cicadas audible even over the highway noise. Four or five more hours now, he thinks. Maybe she won't be home when he gets there. In a way he'd prefer that. He can sit on her porch, if she has one, and play. He tries to imagine how that might feel—how he'll swing his shoulder into the notes and find them there, hundreds of miles from home and all the same. Here is where the music originated, so it's only natural he should want to come too. He squeezes his fingers into the grooves of the steering wheel and tries to keep his mind on that.

Before she moved, Genny's shop had been at the foot of their mountain, set back from the road about a mile or two and up a tree-lined drive of silver thick-waisted maples. He'd seen the sign at the end of her drive for as long as he could remember—the piece of wood cut in the shape of a violin next to the mailbox and her name in yellow letters on the box. He'd never gone there or had anything to do with her until the day a few weeks after his first violin broke. It was cold then, early spring, and the surrounding fields were gray with mist. Her driveway, paved only in patches, was slashed with puddles and iced tire tracks and mud that sucked the soles of his sneakers, and he had to stop several times to catch his breath. Then he'd look back and see his progress and hear the wind in the trees above.

The house sat on a hump of bare hill like a forehead. The sides were tan and the shutters black. At the front door he noticed a business card taped to one of the side windows, sun-blanched at the edges, tape blistering from the glass—Genevieve Freed, violin maker, sales, repairs, estimates. There was no other sign, and he wondered if she was here still. He shifted his violin case to the other hand. "Anybody home?" he called and raised his fist to strike a third time.

She was short—maybe a foot taller than he was then—straight copper-yellow hair cut so it fell around her jaw line. Her lips were chapped and pink-rimmed, and her ears stood out through her hair, also pink. Wide cheeks and forehead. There was a rigidity about her features, hawklike, as if fixed by the force of some extra perceptivity or kindness. Her eyes were an amber-brown almost the same color as her hair. She wore a denim work apron. He watched her thick fingers coming in and out of the apron as she rubbed them clean; the backs of her hands looked swollen, skin bulging around the knuckles as if it were too big or belonged on an older woman's hands. She must be younger than his mother, he thought, though maybe not by much. A gust of wind came from behind him then, lifting her hair around her face and sweeping something to the floor inside, and there was the faint almond smell of violins and polish and fresh-cut wood. He didn't know yet what it was, only that he liked it.

"You must be the one who called before," she said. She waited a second for him to say something. "Sam, right? You're early."

He shook his head, thinking for a moment maybe he should lie. It could make things easier if she thought he was someone smart enough to call ahead. "I'm Jesse Alison. From up the road," he said. "Back up on the mountain there." He turned and pointed. It was covered in sheets and swirls of fog, barely visible.

"Ah," she said. "One of those people that actually lives up there. Why don't you come on in and tell me what I can do for you." She stood to one side and smiled politely in a way he thought was perhaps mocking of him, though he wasn't sure.

Careful to wipe his feet, he crossed over the sill and into the front hall.

Later, he couldn't remember if she asked him first or if he just fell to his knees before her with the violin case open. "I got this fiddle," he was saying. "My father found it in the attic when we moved in, and it don't play right anymore." There was a green couch whose back and sides were a single curled piece like a long arm, and an orange cat up on the marble end table next to that licking its shoulder. The floor was blue slate. "Really, it don't play at all. You can see, this part here came off."

She squatted next to him and traced a finger along the face of the violin, pressed down lightly once on the edge of the wood inside one of its front holes, and then picked up the broken part, turning it over. "You call this the tailpiece," she said. "And this is a busted tail-gut. Simplest thing in the world to fix." She paused. "Why don't you come on back in the shop where I can see better and set you up right. Looks like you need some strings." She tilted the violin to peer in through one of the holes. "And maybe a few other little things. Come on." She looked curiously at him a second, then lifted the violin in its open case and headed off toward where he heard music playing.

From behind she was almost like a boy his age, he thought, that thin and short, and he had to remind himself of the wrinkles in her hands and the adult way she had of addressing him so he didn't forget or become too comfortable and say the wrong things. Still, it was disconcerting. She went quickly ahead of him, gliding through bright square rooms with hardly any furniture and uncurtained windows that went almost to the floor.

"Are you moving?" he asked.

She laughed. "Not that I know of."

They went out through the kitchen and an enclosed breezeway, down a step and back up, and she pulled on a sliding wood door like a hay barn door, already half-open. "Lucky for you I was listening. I would have never heard you," she said, and went ahead of him into an open room with a concrete floor and a curving brick wall to one side. Two workbenches, long flat tables, stood in the middle of the room, and machines and bits of wood were everywhere—violins and cellos and basses in pieces and whole on racks above them and on the floor, and shelves of different colored liquids in labelless jars, and pegboards hanging with tools. Open crates of books and other objects were stashed under the workbenches.

"Used to be the carriage barn," she said. "Now it's my workshop."

She took his violin from the case and pulled back on the tailpiece so the remaining strings spun free from the tuning pegs. Then she tapped on the front and back of the violin and went around the sides tapping and squinting, turning the violin one way and another under a brilliant, metal-fixtured light protruding from the side of the bench on a jointed extension, like a heron's leg. She found the bridge in the case, looked it over a moment and put it aside with the pegs and then held the violin face down, shaking until what had been rattling inside fell out through one of the holes. A thin rod of plain wood. "We'll see if this sound post still fits OK," she said.

He nodded, as if this meant anything to him. "Sound post," he said.

"Your old man didn't find this in the attic, did he?" she said, not looking at him.

The warm air seemed saturated with that wood and polish

smell, so much he hardly noticed anymore. He felt drawn out of himself and half-asleep, imagining he would be all right telling her whatever he wanted. "No," he said. "He didn't."

"You must've got it new from one of those ninety-nine dollar special mail order outfits or downtown at Woods Music. That, or a pawn shop." She glanced once at him and blew dust from under the fingerboard, then slid a cloth in underneath and rubbed it back and forth. "Pay for it yourself?"

He shook his head. "My father," he said and looked at the ground. He'd always figured it was nothing special, the way it smelled and sounded; yet he had hoped.

She grunted. "Could have done a lot better for his money. Tell him, a couple hundred dollars more, he could have had you a real instrument." He looked up to watch her as she continued this, holding the violin at arm's length now. "Top's coming away from the side here a little, but just a little, and the nut's cut too steep and epoxy glued so I can't fix it, really, and the fingerboard is a mess, but it's fake ebonized, so I can't plane it for you. That's just always going to be a problem." She paused. "You ought to have a new bridge cut, too, eventually, though you can get away with this one a while. I'm sure I can make it fit a little better. And of course you need the new tail-gut. And strings." There was a sameness to each of her words, as if she were annoyed or bored with what she said and couldn't wait to be done saying it. "You wanted me just to set it up so you can play it."

"Yes, ma'am."

She sighed. "Well, I feel in a funny position, now." She put the violin down and crossed her arms, studying him. "Did your father send you here today?"

"No."

"Come closer."

He had been standing off to the side of the workbench so their exchange was like a series of one-way remarks, not much looking at each other or showing signs of listening. Just words. Now he came up before her into the streaming light from the work lamp. He could see everything here—the ripples in the texture of the varnish on his violin and the lines in her finger-nails and the sore-looking skin around each of her knuckles, the separate colors in her eyes and two strands of darker hair caught in some dry skin on her cheek.

"Look at me," she said, and he looked into her eyes. He liked her eyebrows, how dark and curved they were over her eyes, almost joining at the bridge of her nose—how one moved up while the other stayed level. "Why did your father send you?" she asked. "Does he not have money to pay? I mean, frankly, this is a little weird. How old are you anyway?"

"Nine." In his head he heard the song of his father's that had been on the radio—the way it ended with the pedal steel swelling up out of the mix and the bass thumping and the drums shuffling to the last beats. He kept hearing that ending and the last words of the song—slipping the lyrics around into other combinations until they came out, "I won't be the-ere anymo-oo-ore." The real words he couldn't remember just now.

"I was lying when I said that," he said. He heard himself

speaking but didn't feel his voice in his throat. "I don't have a father. Nobody knows him—I mean, where he is or anything anymore. I said that before because I didn't want to have to tell you."

She nodded. She didn't pull him to her or brush the hair from his forehead as his mother might have. Her eyes didn't tear up, and she didn't look longingly at him or say something desperate with emotion to make him lose track of everything he had been feeling. "Well, you want to know what I think?" she asked. She scratched her head. Now there was the prickle of warmth and good feeling across his shoulders and down the middle of his back he got when he heard some music he liked or when he knew what someone was going to say before they said it.

They became friends. When his mother was at her worst, he stayed with Genny—not often enough that the displacement of his trouble into her life became an intrusion. Every second or third month, when his mother was awake, filling the house with muffled sounds of her moving furniture, breaking things, crying—such sadness even alcohol didn't touch it except to rip it wider—those nights he stayed away, if he could. He escaped out the back and onto his bike, down the road to Genny's house. If the weather was bad and he couldn't leave, he buried his head in the blankets, swearing *tomorrow, tomorrow, I won't be here anymore.* He pictured it. How he'd sit with Genny in the half-circular room where she worked, the radio up loud and the

bright light making her skin so white it seemed almost translucent. He'd solve some math problems and watch her, waiting for
her to ask if he needed to stay. Or, he'd take one of the violins
she wasn't working on and head upstairs with it or into the
bathroom no one used, next to her shop, and play. He'd pretend
not to notice when she turned the radio down to hear him. And
if she began telling him about the tools she was using—how a
certain repair was done, which clamp to use when, where to file
or carve, tricks and shortcuts—he'd try to seem interested and
keep in mind a few of the things she'd told him before. He loved
seeing violins in pieces, their necks out and their backs and bel-
lies pulled apart, the different color of the wood inside and the
secret cryptic things sometimes carved or written there in pen-
cil, but he had no fascination for how it was done. "Am I being
a help or a pain?" he'd ask occasionally when he was working
with her, not because he was concerned really, but because he
was so bored and didn't know how to tell her. She'd lift her eyebrows and say, "You're never a pain, honey. You know that." He
learned that her skin was worst in dry weather and the only
lotion to help her was from Germany, a black, pine-smelling
concoction she rubbed into her elbows and forearms and
around some of her finger joints, leaving temporary shiny red
spots like something had been scraped from her.

Nights he couldn't escape, when his mother eventually
reached his bedroom door, he was always surprised at first by
the cheerful, detached tone of voice she used. "Hi there," she
might say. "Can't sleep. Mind if I bother you a few minutes?"

He'd roll onto his side to make room and wait, hearing her feet hit softly across the floor—her effort to keep quiet now making him feel they were both liars, considering the noise she'd made downstairs that he was now pretending not to have noticed.

At first it might seem everything was going to be all right. Her breaths would even out, deepen, and maybe she'd doze. But then suddenly her voice was pulling him up from his dreams and trailing him back down. "Can't think of a single thing in the world that's good," she'd say. "Help, Jesse—tell me anything that's good. I'm thirty-one years old and nothing in the world has worked out right for me. Do you understand that? You're the only thing." Sometimes there was the sound of skin hitting skin and the mattress quaking as she turned over and over. Always the smell he hated, the onion and metal smell of her breath from not sleeping, and the anxiety that made her sweat.

He waited for dawn and the return of color, the cold morning air seeping in from the window by his bed, which sometimes calmed her long enough she would finally sleep. He didn't say, "Take it easy, Mama. It's all right. It's always OK. Remember?" He'd long ago given up saying these things. Occasionally still, because he couldn't stop himself, he'd ask her what she wanted from him. But she didn't answer, and he understood from the silence it was worse having asked than not speaking at all. He comforted himself with picturing the room at Genny's. The bare room upstairs with the pale blue carpet and the one window too low in the wall so it looked like a mistake or made the floor like a mistake, like a badly made doll's house. He pictured himself going there right now, letting himself in with the spare key in the gutter and tiptoeing up to the room. Falling onto the bed that smelled of laundry soap and dust. He pictured himself in it and the stillness that let him slip out of himself with such intensity some nights he didn't remember he was there when he awoke.

Two verses and a chorus into "The Pretty Fair Maid in the Garden," he stops short. The wind booms through his open truck windows, and he doesn't know what stops him, only that the silence afterward is the same as the silence before he was singing, and this is oddly exhilarating. He clears his throat thinking to try again and doesn't.

Rounding a corner, sunlight spears in sharply from the right, turning the pavement ahead orange with black dots. His hands become dim shadow-outlines on the wheel, and he can't make out any of the gauges on his dashboard. A gray-blue Lincoln draws alongside him, and for a while they ride together like that, side-by-side, sun-blinded, the Lincoln gradually pulling ahead. The windows there are down too, and in the shadow thrown by his own truck Jesse sees a man's thick forearms and hands beating the wheel in time to music. For all he knows it could be his father. A white plastic Jesus bumps a yellow clover-shaped air freshener, and a magazine open on the seat flutters soundlessly, exposing naked women—bare legs and breasts, arms, heads thrown back. For a moment he even catches a distorted hooting-shouting sound like singing, then it's gone, the noise of tires and engines and the wind caught flapping between them gone as well. Through the blur of his windshield he can barely make out the trunk and back bumper and the turn signal blinking as the Lincoln jerks in in front of him. Tennessee plates. He presses harder on the accelerator, though it's already flat to the floor.

South of Springfield he pulls off for gas and something to eat—best not to show up at Genny's this late and unfed, he thinks. The pumps are like any modern convenience-store pumps with a sheet metal cover overhanging the filling area, layering it in shadow while the rest of the lot is bright with reflected early evening sunlight. The store looks like something from another century—bare clapboard siding and a gallery porch leaning off it like a pier. Inside there's the mildew smell of old refrigerant. A bearded man stands at the counter speaking gravely to a teenage girl up next to the register between jars of pickles and candy and jerked meat strips, her bare legs crossed at the ankles, a cigarette in her fingers.

Jesse walks to the cooler, picks a soda and sandwich, then goes up to the register to pay. Neither the girl nor the man gives him any attention until they finish what they're saying to each other. He can't get the gist of it or even turn half their speech back into words, their voices are that garbled to him.

Finally the man glances at him and starts ringing him up.

"Oh—plus ten dollars in gas, please," Jesse says.

"Sixteen sixty-five," the man says. Blue tattoos encircle both of his wrists like bracelets, and one hand is ridged with scars across the back. He shuts the register and snaps out a receipt, already talking to the girl again, just as seriously as before, pausing once to say something nearly comprehensible about the gas pump.

"Pardon?" Jesse says.

"I say, that pump's broke—don't shut itself off—so you be sure and stop it yourself when you get to ten." He smiles and moves his tongue in his mouth. His teeth are stumpy, yellow, the surfaces complicated by toffee-colored striations of decay.

Back in the fading sunlight, gasoline pouring into his tank, Jesse dips up the window cleaner from its bucket of black water and runs it across his windshield, amazed at the quantity of insects on the glass and stuck to his hood and headlights and radiator grill. By now, he supposes, his mother will be settling in for another night without him. She'll have figured out what he's up to, may even have called Genny to see if he's there yet. No— she'd save her pride. She'll be in the living room by the window, watching the last rays of sun vanish over the mountain, half-listening for the sound of his truck on the road up, because until he calls she'll never completely give up hoping. He doesn't wish he were there, but he can't stop himself from seeing everything and knowing what she's doing as she does it—feeling all her longing for him as if it were his own.

He finishes pumping and goes back inside for more food— something sweet for later on and gum to stay alert. Neither the man nor the girl so much as glance at him. They aren't speaking anymore and seem locked in a silent estimation of something that also involves pretending not to have noticed him.

"How far to Nashville?" he asks as the man rings him up the second time.

"'Pends where exactly—how fast you go. About forty-fifty minutes."

The girl kicks her legs. "Forty minutes if you drive like *him*." Her eyes are narrow and blue, brightened with mean curiosity that makes them almost pretty.

The man counts Jesse's change. "On your way to make your fame and fortune, or you got some other business down here?" he asks. Jesse hadn't considered that he is as conspicuously out of place to them as they are strange-seeming to him, though now he realizes of course he must be. "You 'ratter?" the man asks.

"Pardon?"

"I say, you 'rat *songs*?"

The girl uncrosses her legs and leans to one side for her cigarettes and taps one out. Her ankles and shins are dirt-stained, and the tops of her bare feet have brown squares burned in them where the sun's come through her sandal straps.

He shakes his head.

"Got ba-millions of *thim* coming every day," the girl says.

"I don't write any music, but I play," he says.

"Gui*tar* picker?" the man says. This seems to amuse him.

Jesse shrugs. "Some, yeah. Guitar, fiddle, bass, mandolin . . ."

The girl lights up and reluctantly passes her cigarette to the man, who drags on it and sucks smoke through a gap in his teeth up his nose. "Bluegrass?" he asks. He passes the cigarette back to the girl. Coughs bronchitically.

Jesse nods again, says he guesses so.

The girl ashes onto the floor and in response to a look from the man shakes her head angrily. "Get your own! Damn I'm sick of you always bumming off me."

The man hacks again, drawing himself up. "Well—bet you don't find nobody down there in bluegrass-land too happy today or the next day." He shakes his head. "It's too bad."

"What's too bad?" Jesse asks.

"Ain't you heard?"

The girl says, "Been on the radio a couple times already today how Bill Monroe had him a heart attack."

"What?"

She nods.

The man says, "He ain't dead, but ain't exactly a-rarin' to go either. They say." A crease deepens in the center of his forehead, and his tongue flicks through his lips again. "They was at the Grand Ole Opry backstage when it happened, I believe. Good old WSM . . ."

Jesse pictures Monroe in his blue suit jacket, the mandolin hooked over his shoulder, sagging to one side and going down. The floor is shiny linoleum, and he falls into his own reflection, the mandolin clattering beside him. *The good must fall,* he thinks. *This is how we know them*—his mother's words, though he knows it's not the kind of thing she had in mind when she said it.

"No," Jesse says. "You sure?"

The man shrugs. "See for yourself."

"Hillbilly music," the girl says. She stares straight ahead and kicks her feet.

He looks at the man, and the man looks at the girl, grinning crookedly.

"You're joking, right?" he asks. "It didn't really happen."

"You wish I was," the man says.

His fiddle teacher had been like the fiddle player in his father's band—smooth-fingered, with clothes that smelled sweetly of cigarettes and cologne. "If you can get a good tone on the violin, it'll be the hardest thing you ever did in your life," Dix said, the first day he was at their house for a lesson. He nodded seriously and lifted his spiky eyebrows as if this were a surprise for him as well. He was in a chair by the kitchen window, his violin under his arm, a cigarette going in the ashtray beside him. He leaned back and crossed one leg over the other and began playing again. When he stopped he seemed to want something in return. Then he seemed annoyed or embarrassed, maybe ashamed of himself for wanting it. He flicked a finger at one of his strings. "You can do it if you practice. Only if you practice." He nodded again. "Here's an old one," he said and played some more. Jesse watched. Already he loved Dix's thick black hair and his mustache hanging over his lip like a feather. How his collarbone moved in his shirt collar and his left fingers worked, fitting the notes together up and down the neck of the violin so perfectly and easily he seemed like he was asleep, his dull brown eyes turned liquid and sadly inward.

When it was his turn to play, Jesse tried to remember what he could of the physical things Dix had told him—this finger here, that one there, pinky curved, bow angled this way, chin pointed like that. Mostly he wanted to feel the way Dix had looked to him, playing. He remembered the song Dix was playing and bore down on the strings.

"Jesus! Ain't that something," Dix said when Jesse finally quit. "You just picked up that melody like that?"

He nodded. Shrugged. "You played it first," he said.

Dix laughed. "Yeah," he said. "Hot damn."

Then his mother was in the doorway, and he knew what a distraction this was going to be, always a distraction. He could almost imagine her as Dix would see her—because he'd heard boys talking at school and he was learning by then—her thin bare feet in the frayed hems of her jeans, belly showing almost to the hips and the shadows at her waistline as she stretched upward with her hands on the top molding of the doorway. She was always showing off her body that way, and he didn't understand what she hoped to get from it.

"Is he going to be any good, or should we buy him a kazoo?" she asked. Now she hooked her thumbs in her belt loops and sagged to the doorjamb.

Dix took a breath and shrugged. He looked frozen in place a moment. "He has a gift. What he does with it's anyone's guess. You want me to give him lessons, I'll be happy to try. You never know, with kids." He tapped the tip of his bow in his palm and twisted the thumbscrew once, winking at her as he continued, "You're going to be the one has to keep after him about practicing."

"Hear that, Jesse?" She gazed at him in the fond, overly protective way she used sometimes if people were visiting or they were out together and she wanted to be sure it was clear to anyone looking that she was his mother. "He says you're talented. What a surprise . . ."

"Ma," he cut her off.

"It's OK, honey. Dix and your father were acquainted. He knows all about our situation." Then, looking back at the fiddle player, she said, "We're supposed to not talk about it, you know, his father being gone and all. It still upsets him . . ."

"Does not."

Dix cleared his throat quietly.

She smiled and lifted a hand behind her head to tousle her hair. It was newly streaked with frost and still a pleasure for her to touch and point out to him and admire passing by mirrors and window reflections. "Practice," she said, turning from them and heading back into the other room. "*There's* a word I haven't missed hearing at all for a while!"

For three-and-a-half years Dix came to their house, and always it was more or less the same. First he listened to whatever he'd assigned Jesse for the week—the different tunes and variations and ornaments. He'd nod and smile, finger his silver cigarette case, turning it over in his hands and snapping its lid open and shut while Jesse played. Sometimes he played along to correct something or he chucked chords on the fiddle or guitar for accompaniment. Next he would play a while, searching his memory for a new tune to teach. He'd play and stop short, look up quizzically, shake his head. "No. Too complicated just yet," he might say. Or he'd tell a story about the fiddle player who'd written the tune and when or how it had first been recorded, by whom. Then he'd think a while more until something else struck him—Scottish, Cajun, Irish, Shaker, Canadian Maritime, Shetland—rolling together melodies from whatever style he felt like. There was no method to his selecting a tune and no apparent end to the store of them in his head.

"Here's one," he'd say, and now it seemed he must have known all along what he was going to teach that afternoon. The rest of it, the playing and stopping and talking, was a kind of showing off—a way of making Jesse see what went into this music. How little Jesse understood and how it was not good enough just being able to play a tune—you had to know them all and their histories and the families they were from and the men who'd recorded them. He'd start slowly, saying a few things first about what was unusual in this one and how its parts went together, building speed until they were playing full out together. "Good," he'd call, and, "Right!" the light flashing in his spectacles and turning the room over inside its reflections. And then suddenly he was laying a harmony on top of Jesse's part or coming in from underneath, and the sound between them was so wiry and loud it was hard to imagine anything outside it.

"Yeah!" he'd yell. "One more time!" When they were done he'd light up or drag on the cigarette going in the ashtray, smoke swirling around his face. "Now how about that old 'Rufty Tufty'?" he'd ask—it was his favorite to harmonize—and right away they started in, fresh rosin dotting the faces of their violins and coating the strings, smells of rosin dust and wood polish and the man's sweat in his shirt mixed with smoke and cologne transporting him to exactly where they'd been the week before, and week after week, making him feel nothing else in the world mattered, and they were never going to stop.

The last time Jesse saw him was five years ago at the fiddle contest in Roxbury. Lessons had been getting shorter and shorter by then, and there were days Dix never showed at all. Sometimes he kept his coat on and sat forward in his chair the whole time, ready to go, never taking out his fiddle or even lighting a cigarette, refusing to be impressed or to show any emotion. He listened to what Jesse was working on that week and then what he had taught himself from records—mainly Kenny Baker's recordings, since it was what Jesse liked then. "Walking in My Sleep," "First Day in Town," "Lazy Liz," "The Ducks on the Millpond," "Lost Indian." He was learning mandolin then, too, but he didn't say anything about that to Dix. He knew Dix would disapprove and thought Jesse was already getting ahead of himself, leaving out too much and ignoring too many other players and styles. "What about Vassar and Scotty?" Dix might ask. "Or Richard Greene? Or Dale Potter? He's the one, you know. He really started all the way-out shit in bluegrass." Always, Dix named experimental players, as far from Kenny Baker as possible. Or, he went outside bluegrass altogether and started naming jazz players—Stuff Smith, Svend Asmussen, Eddie South.

"I like Vassar OK," Jesse might reply. "But that Scotty Stoneman—he's *possessed*. I just don't get it." Stoneman had played with the Kentucky Colonels for some of their best years before drinking himself to death on a bottle of hair tonic in his motel room. He'd run out of whisky, and there were no stores close enough. So the story went. His playing was tortured and jubilantly egotistical—triple-stops and inconceivable dissonances and downward-rupturing chromatic smears. He wasn't satisfied just playing a fiddle, it seemed—he wanted some kind of violence in his music.

"A drunk. Half of them are," Dix would say, shrugging. "Hazard of the trade."

The week of the fiddle contest in Roxbury, he'd already stood Jesse up for a lesson twice—Tuesday and then the rescheduled day, Thursday—and had failed to come by the house, as planned, to take him to the contest. They didn't speak at all about that and didn't say anything to each other until after their final rounds, leaning against the rail fence at the side of the stage. By then it was clear one of them would probably win but not clear who it would be. Jesse became aware of Dix's smell first, his cigarette and bay rum smell coming up from behind. He was comforted at first, then a little sickened, knowing they would probably not play together anymore and wondering what he'd done wrong or what he might have done differently to keep that from happening.

"Hey," Jesse said, glancing once at Dix. Dix nodded and leaned next to him, hands in his pockets. Even on a day like this—hot and overcast and windless—Dix dressed as if he were on his way to a party. Pleated corduroy trousers and a silk long-sleeve shirt with a bolo tie.

"You played so fucking great today," Dix said. There was the hiss of him lighting up, then the match-burning sulfur smell and sweet first exhalation of cigarette smoke. "If you don't beat me, it's criminal." He cleared his throat. "Where'd you get that high shit on 'Roxanna's Waltz,' anyway? That was incredible." Dix shook his head. "Gave me a fucking bone. Almost." They laughed until Dix broke off coughing hard enough to shake the fence behind them, hawked once, and spat. "Those judges don't have ears if they give it to anyone but you," he concluded.

They'd never competed against each other. Most contests had a sixteen-and-under division Jesse entered on his own, and he'd never really considered that he might win today. It still didn't seem possible. He couldn't hear Dix's playing the way he heard other fiddlers'—didn't notice flaws or weaknesses, didn't even hear a violin half the time, and consequently couldn't compare himself with it.

"You're crazy," Jesse said. "You nailed that 'Wild Fiddler's Rag.'"

Dix drew on his cigarette. He nodded and for a moment appeared willing to accept the compliment. Then he was scowling and shaking his head, talking the smoke out. "I nailed it, same as I've been *nailing* it for the last fifteen years. Same old shit all the time. I'm so sick of that." He flicked the end of his cigarette and drew again on it, a muscle at the back of his neck twitching.

Jesse felt sweat release and run down his side. If this was true then what was the point in talking about it? He looked at the side of Dix's face, those familiar hurt and repellent eyes, thick eyebrows and mustache, and tobacco stained underlip, and he wished there were some way to impart his feelings to him. But he felt stopped. If he said anything the emotions would outstrip the words. "You're the best fiddle player in the state," he said. "You know that. You have *years* on me."

"Years. Big fucking deal. Bet you lunch you'll win."

They shook hands and leaned back against the fence, waiting.

Later, onstage playing together at the MC's request, after the winners had been announced, Jesse couldn't imagine anything more entwined—not wind through leaves or light and shadow. They met eyes just after the first section of the tune, and he felt the skin along his arms and shoulders tighten with pleasure. He moved in closer to the mic and bore down on the notes—those familiar strings of sixteenths in harmony and the low-down chugging third section of the tune in unison. His cheeks were cold and his eyes burned and he knew it was a long time since he'd remembered to blink. He shut his eyes. Inhaled. Opened his eyes again and watched Dix's bow on the strings. He couldn't hear their differences or even exactly where the sounds converged. "One more!" Dix yelled, and finally they were at the end, roaring down the scale and back up for the final chords. He could barely see, he was so elated by the volume and energy of the playing and the applause—laughing out loud because he knew how good they were together and because it felt like the best thing in the world, being inside that music.

They went down the shaky plank steps and onto the grass backstage. Dix touched him on the shoulder as he passed. There was the too-sweet smell of his cologne and sweat, then it was gone. "Owe you lunch," he said coolly. Jesse watched him bent over and packing up his fiddle, and he knew they would not play together like that again.

Back on the road he tries getting some news of Bill Monroe's heart attack on the radio, but no one's talking about it. To the west a storm builds, dividing the evening sky—lightning-threaded purple and gray clouds. He watches and can't tell if the storm is heading toward him or not. The radio doesn't say. He flips it off and sings the first verses of "I Am a Pilgrim," and then, because he has nothing else to do, begins thinking up some guitar riffs for the instrumental break in his head. It makes him sleepy and restive doing this, but once he's going he can't stop. He pulls the lag between the first and second phrases wider and comes into the third phrase striking the bass notes so hard they wobble into each other, buzzing comically. Then up to the middle of the neck to finish the phrase more serenely, with another nod to Clarence White. He feels the notes in his fingers and in his right elbow where the tone would originate. Then the song's climax—"That yonder city, good lord."

Ahead of him the sky is pale orange and yellow. More and more signs advertise gas and food, places he's never heard of—Shoney's, Stuckey's, Cracker Barrel, Huddle House. Each exit is a jumble of neon and streetlights spreading up the stumpy hills. He keeps looking for mountains lifting into the darkness beyond them, but there are none. To his right an airplane comes down, landing lights blinking at the ends of its wings, the numbers on its tail just visible. He's never seen one that close and watches half-amazed as it floats farther out of sight. "Holy mo," he says. And then the city is straight ahead. When he was younger his father sent them postcards—now he remembers it—this same city skyline at night and at sunset with "Nashville" printed underneath, flanked by guitars and musical notes. He never understood then why the pictures mattered or what his mother wanted, turning them over and over like she was looking for a way inside, sighing and laughing softly to herself about whatever he'd written. Now he's heading into that city. He wonders if he came for the music after all or if he's here to find his father.

(b)–I

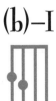

Three days he hasn't touched an instrument, and as always his longing for it has begun feeling like hunger. He pictures the neck of his violin—the fingerboard and finger-smoothed tuning pegs and the scroll carved in the shape of an old man's head, wavy hair and red-painted eyes and tongue; the crazed, golden finish of his guitar and ropy thickness of the low E under his fingers and the upper bouts pressing into his ribs. And when no one's looking he drums his fingers on his knees or the tabletop to heat the muscles and release some excess energy. The longest he ever went without playing is two weeks, finishing schoolwork for the year, and his feeling then was like this but worse. He was numb, half-asleep, and couldn't always keep in mind what he was going to say once he started speaking. He knew it was from not playing, but then he wasn't sure. The feeling was too big to pierce it with understanding. Now at least he's familiar enough with it to know what's bothering him.

His father is not listed in any phone book. The old number Jesse has for him is answered by a landscaping company. Most likely he lives out of town—Franklin or farther south, or maybe north around Goodlettsville—and keeps his number out of the book. Songwriters with money often do this, Genny tells him. He's still never said anything to her about his father, and he doesn't mention him now. "A guy my mother used to know," he says. "Wrote a couple of songs that did OK for Emmylou Harris. Ma hasn't heard from him in years, but there's no harm trying."

"Well, generally they like to stay out of town—you know, so they can be *inspired*. Then, whenever they come to town for a drink or a meeting with their song publisher or whatever, or to guest at one of those songwriters' round-robin things, they can run into their old buddies and congratulate each other on still existing." She rolls her eyes. "That's the way to find him, probably. If you really feel like it. Just keep showing up at those songwriter nights, and eventually you'll meet him—or somebody who knows somebody who knows him."

So far he hasn't been to any such events or met anyone who might know his father.

Afternoons they drive around town on errands, Genny pointing out neighborhoods where he might want to live—he likes the artsy ramshackle West End she lives in best—and taking him to the usual attractions: downtown, the Ryman, Country Music Hall of Fame. Nothing that sticks with him. They'll round a corner, come over the top of a hill, exit the freeway, pass a billboard, and Genny will look expectantly at him, eyebrows raised. "Know where we are now?" she'll ask, or "This one getting familiar yet?" Always he has to shake his head and laugh at his slowness. He can't see how to make the differences in these city streets and buildings stand out.

At night they go to the Station Inn for bluegrass. He couldn't find his way by himself yet, but he knows most of the street names and half-recognizes the surrounding neighborhood—the car lot and brick-sided warehouses and the men's club down closer to the freeway. Outside, it's more like a stone hut or shack than a bar, white-washed, with a lit-up sign like an old gas station sign by itself out front: Station Inn, live acoustic music. The walls inside are papered with posters from bluegrass events and concerts the world over, pictures of Monroe going back to the beginning, and candid shots of every great musician who's played here.

One step up are the back tables on a platform like a porch, so submerged in shadows you can't be sure you're any higher until you look back at the stage and see out over the rest of the audience. He and Genny sit sharing a beer at one of these tables near the sound booth, and she points out people for him, leaning toward him and speaking conspiratorially without raising her eyes to the person she's talking about. "That guy there," she indicates with her chin—a flabby, young-looking man with black hair stuck to his temples and a goatee, checkered shirt almost the same as the table cloths—"he's the new fiddle player in Jimmy Martin's band. Poor bastard. Ed something, up from Florida. There's a gig you don't want." As she says this the man smiles and rears back, laughing, one hand out to touch the shoulder of the person he's talking to. Jesse pictures Jimmy

Martin younger, pop-eyed, and choirboy sincere, next to Monroe at the microphone. There's a shot just like this by the busted piano. Why poor, he wonders? But he knows the answer, although he resists understanding. Booze, bad temper, uneven work. She's told him before.

"Not much of a fiddle player," she continues, "but he's OK on mandolin. And he can actually get a tenor to old Jimmy, God knows how." She laughs. "Tight underwear." She's closer now, beer-sour breath touching his cheek. Her smell is the same as ever to him—pine and soap and some dully bitter fragrance under that. Always the same feeling from the smell, too—something in it that repulses him yet holds him there, contented and assured, without much to add to the conversation. She's not unlike his mother this way, always silencing him with her facts and opinions and guidance, though in this case it's all information he needs. "They played here a couple weeks ago. I missed it. I think they're supposed to be on the Opry again sometime too—Pulaski, that's it. Ed Pulaski. I cut him a new bridge back when he first got to town and fixed a tailpiece crack he didn't know about." She pauses. "Piece of shit fiddle. He thinks it's French. Ha! What I wouldn't give to just quit repairs and build full-time." Here she lifts her hand and waves with the tips of her fingers. "Not like I need the money, really, only the connections—see if he remembers *my* name."

Always her introductions for him are the same, with variations. "I'd like you to meet my friend Jesse. He's new in town. Great picker." Or, "This here's Jesse. He's down from Vermont a while, see how he likes the scene. Monster player." Her voice becomes obliging and singsong, almost Southern. "Have a seat," she'll say and lean into the table, all concern and attention. He thinks, aside from the music, most people come to the Station just for this—the moment of greeting and being recognized, shaking hands with people and feeling the rush of blood into their faces as they say flattering things back and forth.

"This little gal," they'll say, one hand on Genny's shoulder or her arm, "she could fix *inny*thing. I bet you some old boy brought his wheelbarrow and a couple busted chairs around, you'd send him away with a damn fiddle!" Big wink. "But seriously, I ain't never heard my fiddle sound so good, ain't never *played* it so good since that work you done . . ." No one is lying, either. Any night of the week the Station is packed with hotshot players and music people, enough to make Jesse's head spin. Still, the compliment paying seems to him as much a matter of preening and territory establishing as anything else. He believes about half of it and only half-accepts any kindness in their eyes hearing what his name is. He remembers the note scrawled on the men's room wall by the urinal, the spastic handwriting and barely decipherable message—"Yanks are like hemroidls wen They com down an go bakc is Anoying wen they comFor good is a rel pain in the ass!" under which someone else has written "MORON." He wonders which, if any of them, might have written it.

"Well, thanks," Genny says. She nods and blushes. Says whatever she can to deflect attention, smiling archly and folding her hands. He's forgotten this thing about her, like her smell—the nervous Spartan thing in her that craves and hates attention. They're alike in this way, though she's less tongue-tied and better at it. "How's that new recording project coming?" she'll say, leaning a cheek in one hand, or, "How's things on the Patty Loveless showboat these days?"

It's too much to keep track of, but he absorbs what he can and tries to seem interested long after he's stopped being able to follow, nodding attentively as they tell him about the auditions and magazine listings and unadvertised openings in road bands and how to stay on top of all this—which emerging country artists are any good to work for, and so on. He wants only one thing. He wants to know when Bill Monroe will be out of the hospital. How soon before a spot in his band will come open? How can he find out about that, and how does he get an audition? He doesn't ask; he waits for the conversation to go that way, hardly aware he is doing so.

Afterward, in the loft-bed by the desk in Genny's den, he's unable to sleep. The air is warm and too still to erase the smoke smell from his skin, and the mattress, six inches of new foam rubber, keeps curling up from the loft floor, sliding with him every way he moves. People from the Station Inn invade his partial dreaming. They come at him with their hands extended and faces animated, bits of songs repeating meaninglessly. Men with gelled hair raked back from their foreheads and that look in their eyes—meanness and curiosity just behind the courtesy.

He sits up and beats his palms on his temples to make it stop, but it's no use. For a minute or two he's better, but as soon as he lies back, eyes shut, there it all is again—the bar distorting in his brain and the anxious feeling he's being measured but not according to anything he understands. He rolls over and over, twisting the sheets around him and waiting for it to stop. "Consciousness overload," Genny calls it. He thinks that's probably true, though knowing isn't much help. "Your brain's spitting back what it can't take. I wouldn't sweat it. You'll adjust." They don't mention his mother and the nights he used to slip away to Genny's house because of *her* sleeplessness.

He swings his legs over the side of the loft and after a moment drops down.

By Genny's desk are framed prints of Stradivari plates and scrolls. He's seen them so many times he doesn't register seeing them anymore, only the glass in the frames reflecting shadows and faint light from the streetlight outside the hall window, his own face, scattered through alethea bushes. He presses his fingertips to her desktop and moves around some loose papers—bills and notes and invoices—nothing he hasn't already picked up and looked over idly and put back down the previous night or the night before that.

He turns and walks naked out of the room, down the blue hall.

In some of the smaller rooms previous owners have painted over the floors in brilliant colors and drizzled the surfaces with shiny white and red droplets. The bathroom is sun yellow with white flecks, and the walls are paneled with navy wain-scoting. Each room is colored differently, too—tan, green, white, dull brick. "I've gotten to like it," she told him, his first day there, showing him around. They were in the kitchen then—green cabinets and yellow walls with white trim. "At first I thought it'd make me crazy, see-sick (get it?), and I'd definite-ly have to repaint the minute I had some free time, but it grows on you. Like, every room is a different mood or something." She scratched her head. "I like that. This one's so *cheerful.* Like a car-nival."

He sits on the edge of the toilet with the lights off, listening to water drip in the tub and staring down at the floor, so lus-trously shiny in the shadows it seems to lift the bathmat beside the tub like a cloud in a reflection. *Who am I?* he wants to ask. *What am I doing here?* But the questions evaporate the instant they surface. He can't wonder like that out loud. Too much like his mother. Also wrong, because, for now anyway, he knows what he wants and why. He leans forward and sees the moon up in the top left quarter of the window over the tub—and he thinks of home: grass and wheat fields ticking with bugs, and pines releasing their scent in the early summer heat. He sees his mother on the porch alone. Her hair is longer, the way he pic-tures it, like when he was growing up, and for the first time he wonders if his absence will really cause her grief or if she won't just go about her business as usual—work and home and nights out drinking. She might even prefer her solitude, not feeling forced into it as the escape from him and his constant music playing and wanting to be somewhere else. Maybe it's a relief having him gone. "Let her be OK," he whispers. "Let her understand." He pictures her waking up on the porch, the sun in the gauze netting, the smell of sun on the floorboards. "Please," he thinks, seeing the walkway down from the porch to the garden, the wood chips and roses, trees mixing the light with shadow.

Now he hears music in his head—Kenny Baker's "Hollow Poplar." The first music all night not related to what he heard earlier in the bar, so he knows this must be the thing troubling him after all, not just "consciousness overload" as Genny says, but plain disorientation and guilt and missing home.

The notes keep coming, and he heads down the hall to the kitchen for a glass of milk, then back again to the den, humming, and up the ladder. "OK," he says, and lies back, pulling the sheets around his stomach. "All right." He closes his eyes and continues moving the melody through his mind, punching in chords underneath and feeling the notes in his fingertips, rolling in the banjo backup. Much better, he thinks. Music I want to hear. He drifts. He's onstage now, loose and angular as Baker himself, the notes falling around him and winding into the chords again, and his hands don't feel like dead things from not playing. Then the tune vanishes, and he's suspended over a patch of silty grass-spiked earth—*home,* he thinks—watching it slowly flood with water. He turns and a man from the bar looms at him, hand outstretched. "Howdy, howdy, howdy," the man says, teeth flashing, "Good to meet ya," and that's it. He's wide awake again, heart pounding. "God damn!" he hisses. He taps his fingers on the mattress, watches them bump up and down. "Hollow Poplar" continues in his head, but there's no satisfaction anymore, and he is again staring at the ceiling tiles, waiting for light. He has to play, that's all. He has to spend hours and hours tomorrow getting back into the music to fix this.

Often, when he was growing up, his mother would remind him of the time his father had taken them to the recording studio in Montpelier; he was about four then, and the sound of the tape rewinding and his father's disembodied voice coming over the speakers had scared him so badly he wouldn't go near the record player for months. She told him about it until he almost remembered it like one of his own memories. And sometimes he thought maybe he *did* remember—that shriek as the tape ran backward, warbling and whining like some nightmare wind. For a time he was convinced they weren't taped voices or musical instruments he was hearing on the record player, but real men flattened in the speaker cabinets, standing in a half-circle around the drummer like the men in his father's band, eternally plugged in and singing. Any music, then, even the happiest, was tinged with this fear, and turning on the stereo made him not just lonely for his father but ashamed he was trapping the musicians again and forcing them to play.

And somewhere in all of this is an afternoon he does remember clearly—one soon after a visit from his father that he spent looking at pictures and listening to records his father had

left for them, new music by a band his father had said he was
sure they'd love, with chiming banjos and a slide guitar groaning like a doorbell and men singing as high as women, though
in a hard, unadorned way Jesse assumed even then was for men
alone. Like the wind dragging through a tree, he thought. Like
the high branches of that treetop turning inside out with the
wind. The pictures were new publicity shots and in every one,
Jesse thought, his father was like a different man. The face
stayed the same: high sharp cheekbones, swept-back brown
hair, upper lip puffed out or lifted so it seemed waxed in place—
so the man seemed aristocratic and carelessly sexy, brooding
even, though he was none of these things. The wrinkles in his
forehead stood out and were darkened with makeup and his
eyes twinkled falsely. *Glad to know you,* they said. *Good to make
your acquaintance.* Things his father often said in real life. But
who did he want to know and why? The expressions were so
changeable, Jesse couldn't be sure. Put next to his other pictures
from earlier sessions—ones where he had a beard or a mustache
or a different hairstyle, ones in full rodeo getup, cowboy hat and
elaborately piped and fringed western shirts with breast pockets
cut slantwise, ones in string ties and satin suit jackets—Jesse
could make no sense of it: who his father wanted to be or why
he was always changing. All afternoon he looked those pictures
over, the full shots and the sheets of little ones printed together.
And he kept lifting the needle back and back again to hear the
snarling hard-voiced mountain men his father had said were

the best, *simply the best.* He wanted to understand why and to keep the men trapped with him in the music a while so he wasn't alone.

The next day he is asleep past noon again. A note on the kitchen table tells him to help himself to muffins in the bag by the toaster and find her in the shop when he's ready. Ready, he wonders. And he remembers: today they're visiting a studio on Music Row, where her engineer friend, Max, is mixing a new project for an up and coming country artist from Texas. Dawn something. "A real go-for-the-gut singer," Genny had said. "Not your usual Big-Hair, All-Air. You know? Real country. You'll like her. Her voice, I mean; I don't think she'll actually *be* there herself."

He hardly remembers a time in his life Genny wasn't attached to all his musical opinions, telling him what to like and giving him words for it. Even by himself, listening, he'll think of her. He'll rewind breaks and bits of instrumental fill, places where one line falls into another perfectly, playing them for her in his imagination and anticipating her response. "Did you hear that?" he'll ask, or, "How perfect was that?" waiting to see if she's as impressed. Or, shaking his head, "Haven't heard *that* in a while, huh. Get an idea!" These are among her favorite things to say—*Get an idea* and *Did you hear that?* Watching and imagining her, he knows when a player's emotions have gotten beyond his technique and when he's just phoning it in, piling licks on licks without meaning any of it. "Don't think too much," she always says. "This isn't thinking music, it's feeling music." She points to her heart and her forehead. "Right? But you can't be stupid. Here and here. It's connected. Can't have one without the other." He nods like he knows this already, and for the most part he does; he just doesn't always have the words for it without her.

Outside, the air is heavy and hot, hot even in the shade. He goes up and across the yard to her shop, past the cat asleep in the monkey grass, the flagstones in the walkway from the drive to her shop door burning his bare feet. Cicadas saw and ratchet. Hard to believe anything can be alive in this heat, yet everywhere he looks appears to be teeming with life. He taps once, waves, and pulls the sliding glass door to the side and slips in.

She's bent between boxes, green Styrofoam nuts and bubble-packed items on the floor next to her—tailpieces, finetuners, bridges, a fingerboard, other things he doesn't recognize. There are four of the boxes, two big ones, open, and two smaller ones. Though she's worked here almost a year now, the place still seems to him only half-finished—ceiling open to the rafters and most of the window fixtures untrimmed with insulation popping around them. There's a story behind this, one he doesn't completely follow, about a carpenter indebted to a friend who's indebted to her. The floor is dark cement, and the air smells of sawdust and plaster as much as violins.

"Hey," he says. "UPS?"

"Finally. Supposed to been here last week. No, two weeks ago." She shakes her head and looks up smiling. "Welcome to the South." Except for the wrinkles around her throat, her face is so smooth and tan it's easy to forget her age. Thirty-six in August. "Sleep any last night?"

He shakes his head. "Sometime around dawn."

"Thought I heard you wandering around." She slices back, yanking up the folds of a box. "I wouldn't sweat it—you're still adjusting is all."

From this angle he sees down the neck of her shirt to her freckled chest and faded bra straps and the sunless white of her stomach—nothing he hasn't seen before or badly wants to see again, though he can't help staring either. Even if he hadn't known her most of his life, he supposes he'd feel the same: something about her that's so sexually overt it's almost repellent, and yet impossible to ignore. The other night, hearing that a musician she knew was newly in love, she had exclaimed, "Sex? You mean people out there are really sucking and fucking still?"—and he had laughed, returning her gaze as if it didn't embarrass him, the way she said this. Later the same night, when he mentioned Michelle—how he wondered what she was doing and if she'd ever contact him—she'd said, "God gave you two hands. What do you need that hole for?" Again he was stuck trying not to picture it or let any confusion and embarrassment show in his face. As long as he's known her she's been this way, and as long as he's known her she hasn't had a steady lover. She's talked about it—a Ukrainian poet-soldier with a political past who broke her heart just after college, the woman she moved to Vermont to be with and who'd shared her house off and on for years.

She stands, puffs once so her bangs fly from her cheeks and forehead, and tugs at the front of her shirt. Gestures with her chin to her work table, cluttered with parts and tools, a dirty silver carpet remnant pushed to one side with a fiddle on it. "Try that out—tell me what you think."

He crosses to it and lifts the fiddle, turning it around in his hands. Sniffs the front—dull smoke and wood smell—and plucks the strings. "Sounds good. What is it?"

"Try it, I'll tell you after."

She rips into the last box, and he lifts the fiddle under his chin, tapping his fingers up and down the fingerboard. The finish is thicker, like a sugar coating, and brighter red than any of hers—almost vermilion—so he knows it's nothing she built. The grain on the front plate is so coarse he can feel the ridges of it under his fingers. He holds it at arm's length, looking: fat, dented scroll and f-holes cut comically at a slant, like shrunken cello f-holes.

"Bows are right next to you there," she says. "In that case on the lower shelf."

"Aren't you even going to give me a hint?" He picks a silver-mounted, toffee-colored stick and tightens the thumbscrew, tapping the tip once at his wrist, and before she can answer he starts in playing—open strings, arpeggios, the beginning of "Monroe's Hornpipe." "Damn," he says, and keeps playing. She's sideways to him, listening, one wrist on her forehead momentarily. She grins and faces him, seeming to laugh and say something, though he can't quite hear it over the fiddle.

"What? What aren't you telling me?"

"Just play," she says. "So good to hear you."

He turns from her and digs in. His right shoulder burns and clenches against the bow strokes, and his fingers are stiff, but these pains only make him hungrier to play. The fiddle has a reedy, broken-open sound. Ordinarily he'd want to stop and figure it out, what's making the tone that open and which registers are warmest, maybe find a corner of the room where he can hear better. But playing feels too good—he's relieved to know he can do it still—and the fiddle is so easy-playing. There's an evenness that seems to keep lifting and opening out, every note, like the instrument is waking up. She's explained this to him before—how a long-unplayed violin will sleep under its mesh of varnish until someone comes along to work it, shake and loosen the wood molecules with sound vibrations.

He sticks with the standards, Baker and Monroe classics she's heard from him a million times. Tunes in A—"Big Mon," "Frost on the Pumpkin," "Stony Lonesome." "Baker does it like this," he says, because he sees how she's watching and listening. He drones the high E with his third finger, carrying the melody with his second and first fingers on the string above. "Took me the longest damn time to figure it out, but I think that's how he does it. Really makes the tune work, don't you think?" He turns from her and plays the same thing a few other ways, then into some B-flat numbers he's fairly sure she's never heard from him—"President Garfield's Hornpipe" and a showy version of "Georgiana Moon" going up to fourth position for double-stops the last time around. Then on back to A—"Road to Columbus," "Gray Eagle." He can't stop. Worse than showing off, he realizes, what he wants is to hurt her—shock and stun her and make her feel he's become unknown. The red fiddle helps; he barely recognizes himself, playing it.

"Won't win any beauty contests, that's for sure, but what a screamer," he says. "I give up. Where's it from?"

Her mouth twists to one side, and she goes back to picking over items previously packed in the boxes, pulling apart bubble pack. "Well," she says, "don't tell anyone. But that's one of the first fiddles I ever built. One of my first solo efforts, I should say, must've been . . . too long ago to tell you. I didn't even put my name in it, I thought it was such junk." She glances once at him, checks the packing order and folds it twice before tucking it into her pocket. "But now, after hearing you play it . . ." She scratches the back of her neck and flicks something from her finger tip, studying him, and doesn't finish her thought. "I don't know. The person who found it—you know what they paid?"

He shrugs, waits. "What?"

"A hundred bucks at a flea market. Makes me so crazy every time I think about it. Jeez."

He looks again at the fiddle as if it might help him to understand. It's not the first time he's been baffled by her need to figure out a particular instrument; this is what she does. Old sweat, dirt, and rosin have candied onto the varnish around the left shoulder and under the strings; and the fingerboard is notched with finger grooves in the lowest playing positions, so peering down it from scroll to bridge, the neck looks faintly segmented to him, as if bearing the fossilized imprint of some creature. "What do you get for one now?" he asks. In all the years they've known each other he's never asked.

"I have a two-year waiting list. You know that. It's two thousand dollars just to get *on* the list." She pauses. "I haven't sent a finished instrument out of the shop for under ten grand in years. Twelve, starting this fall. Most people get thirty-, forty-plus for what I put into an instrument, but my reputation's not to that level. If I wrote that one up and put in a label," she pauses, thinking, "you could get a couple thousand for it easy. At least. That'd be the honorable thing to do, right? That's what it's worth." He feels shut out by the pitch of her voice and the flush streaks in her neck and face. "But I can't. Not without trying to save it first, at least a little. I mean, look at that hack job. An apprentice could carve you a better scroll."

"He doesn't know?"

She shakes her head. "She. Just dumb luck she brought it here."

"Who is this person?"

She waves a hand, dismissing the question.

"So, don't tell her."

She scowls. "I can't do that."

"Why? Tell her five hundred dollars, I'll take it off her hands, as is. That's fair."

"No, it's not, and besides you can't afford it."

"Sure I can."

She looks just past him, sighs once, and crosses her arms. "She wanted me to fix the varnish and maybe put on a new fingerboard. That one's shot."

"So?"

"So, she's a new customer with some interesting connections, and I have to be careful how I handle things." She shakes her head. "You just go on back to the house and get ready. I should've never had you play it in the first place. You make it sound *way* too good." She tilts her head, smiling.

"No."

"Let's forget about it for now. OK?"

He sets the fiddle on the silver carpet remnant, bow loosened and lying beside it. "Forgotten," he says.

He and Genny did not share a tent, though until he was old enough to drive he never attended a bluegrass festival without her. Side by side, in the midst of her friends if possible and beneath pine trees for the softer needle-smelling ground, they would set up camp. Her tent was green canvas and almost tall enough to stand in. When the wind blew, its sides would billow like a sail, and its poles clinked and clanked. They dug ruts around each tent in case of rain, trailing the circles together in a crooked figure-eight, and strung her tarp between tree trunks for a kitchen, unfolding table and chairs. Always the bits of dried dirt, bark, and needles from last year's festival patterning the bottom of his tent or the insides of her cooler, the smells of wood smoke and mildew trapped in nylon or plastic, would remind him of the year before and the year before that—how little he'd known then and how much more he might know in another year. It was like standing aside from time and being forced to recognize how time was passing, both at once: here he was setting up camp, and everything outside the festival campground had once again ceased to exist. He'd spread his ground cloth beside hers and fit together poles, stretch the nylon and mesh, and pound in his stakes.

He came to recognize some of the bluegrass families that camped near them, their faces and even some names, but he did not get to know them. He saw how they watched him too, year by year—the curiosity and admiration. Children in those families always seemed to him to be under their parents' hands or dragging along behind them by invisible strings, up the steps of their Winnebagos and under the awnings of big family tents, always together. Sometimes he'd look up from playing and see one there—a bluegrass father with his face pinched and eyes gone blackly opaque, hand engulfing the shoulder of his daughter or son, or a mother, smiling and pushing the kid in front of her, saying, "Ask him—go ask, he won't bite!" He felt certain whatever they asked he would not know how to answer. *I have no idea,* he'd think. *I don't know how I learned this.* He'd look up through the trees, the straight trunks and needles outlined with silver, wind rocking through them, and he'd think, *It's just something I could do.*

One summer there was a group of younger men he admired and enjoyed playing with for hours—all night it had seemed, until the campfire was red-black ember light illuminating fingers and faces. Jesse felt then as if he were no longer himself, as if they'd all gone inside somewhere together or fallen asleep and begun playing from the same dream. He heard his fiddle switching around the edges of notes and melting through voices and instruments, but he couldn't say for sure anymore that it was him playing.

The next summer he found the same men at their campsite, hung over in the hot noon light; anxious to show them everything he'd worked up that year, he unpacked his mandolin. He stood to the side, outside their circle, chording and trying to break in with his solos and tremolo fills—waiting for an entrance, but they kept shifting to exclude him, moving subtly so their backs or hips or the necks of their instruments blocked his way. Anything he said, they ignored, eyes fixed on one another, and when he started up tunes he knew they had enjoyed playing just the year before, they spat on the ground and did not follow his lead. Finally, one of them, the one he'd liked most the year before—the guitarist, a velvet-bearded man with gray eyes and thin red lips, green dungarees, the pockets ripped out—turned from the circle to face him. Zeke, Jesse suddenly remembered, that was his name. "You must think you git paid by the note," the man said. The muscles in his arms and neck hardened, but his eyes were drained and there was a hole at the base of his neck when he sucked a breath. Jesse remem-

bered the year before, how easily their voices had flown together. "Ain't a contest," the man said, "—got nothing to do with
bluegrass if you flash it around like that. You wanna be a hotshot, go do it somewhere else, hear?"

Jesse watched and listened a while more, half-heartedly
chopping chords. Leaving now would be as conspicuous as staying or forcing his way into the group, and he couldn't see what
else he might do. The men laughed and joked with each other
and eventually closed their cases on their instruments. A light
rain had started, and when he stepped from under the trees he
felt it blow up, misting into his eyes. Then for a while he was
lost, wandering the little roads between campsites and up and
down hills, looking for anything by which to orient himself.
There were bands playing under RV awnings and voices echoing to him from distant jams, basses thumping and banjos
blanging. At some sites a man or a woman sat alone, tuned into
the stage show on a radio or strumming a guitar. No one would
meet eyes with him, and he thought they must all recognize his
failure, though at the same time he knew that wasn't possible.
Even when he finally spotted their two tents, side by side, circled
in trenches, Genny's red tarp stretching from the opened back
hatch of her car to tree limbs overhead, he felt cut off and out
of place. Genny was nowhere in sight. No doubt she'd be at the
stage area. He could picture her there—sun hat tilted back and
umbrella propped against one shoulder. And in his tent, the
light disorientingly bright, the sound of rain tapping everywhere around him, he could imagine her beside him still, hum-

ming and talking to herself, her tent zippers whistling one way or another, sleeping bag zippers, pants, duffel bag, each with its separate tone and depth of pitch.

The rest of the afternoon, after playing the red fiddle, he can't stay awake. What evaded him the night before won't leave him alone now, and he has to fight to keep his eyes open, his head up. He sags into the couch cushions at Max's studio, drifting in and out of consciousness, a copy of *Mix* magazine open on his lap. There are no windows and hardly any lights. Max and Genny sit at the console, speaking cryptically back and forth, punching buttons and rewinding fragments of a song about love and the hills of home. They separate out the bass notes, eliminate a hiss, and flatten the midrange, then bring in the thuddy kick drum, the off-beat *tssst*'s of the high-hat. Then the vocal by itself—a sad, generic voice that edges into beauty on the highest notes. He nods off a good while as they go back and forth, rewinding, listening, changing levels. He wakes and watches their reflections in the sloping panel of glass above the console—their arms and shoulders and the tops of their heads. Beyond the console and the glass is a cavernous unlit space where he can barely make out the shapes of mic stands and amplifiers. Max is a big man with a short blond beard and startled-looking pale green eyes. He likes leaning back in his chair with his fingers knit over the hairless crown of his head, listening, then dropping forward in his chair and punching buttons on the console, kick-wheeling one way and another, then returning to the leaned back posture with his hands on his head. "Better, better," Genny says. Jesse can't tell if they're lovers (he assumes not) or ex-lovers, future lovers, or just friends, but he's pretty sure Max likes Genny better than she does him—he can tell by the way Max cuts his eyes from her and the way he's always sure to wheel his chair back as close as possible to her. Once, leaning forward together to change something, their shoulders bump and their faces seem inches apart in the reflection. When Jesse wakes again sometime later, they're listening through the whole song on tinny-sounding car speakers while she stands behind Max massaging his shoulders and neck.

He pushes up out of the squishy sofa and comes forward to join them, stretching. Everywhere there's the smoky metallic and plastic smell of new audio equipment, a little like fresh carpet, though he only occasionally notices now since he's been here half the afternoon.

"Look who's up," she says, continuing to massage Max.

Jesse nods.

"What do you think?" she asks. She stops rubbing and gives Max a little push away. He leans forward to slide the master level up. There's a crackle over the car speakers and the volume rises; then Max clicks in another button, and the woman's voice comes over midsize JBLs, clearer, louder.

At the third chorus Max and Genny freeze, squinting into the darkness on the other side of the glass, listening. "There it is again. Damn if I can tell what it is," Max says.

"Let's hear it again," she says.

Max is already punching buttons on the caddie, a smaller console bobbing next to the main one on a goose-neck extension. There's the rewind-shriek, then the chorus—*What if I were just the one*, the woman sings. Next, a bass walk-up and a mini drum-swell and the other vocals coming in around her. Jesse wonders if he's been working out the solution for these mismatched tonalities in his sleep all afternoon, like solving a puzzle, and for a moment the song is also a reconfiguration of everything else he was dreaming: something about eating cheeseburgers, Genny's face, and the heads of fiddlehead ferns uncurling in the woods behind his mother's house.

"Baritone's flat," Jesse says. "And she's flat to the high E there in the guitar backup. *Hea-art. In your hea-art.*" He falsetto-sings the note. "Plus maybe your bass player should retune his A. It's out."

No one seems to have heard him.

"I mean, not way way out . . ."

Max sucks his lips and holds up a finger. "Here. Right. Listen . . ." he moves his finger back and forth with the beat and then lets it fall, ". . . right there." He looks only at Genny. "Hear it? Dave again. Just like I said. Damn." He jabs at the caddie and the music stops, whines backward again. "Have to go out there myself and fix it."

Jesse wants to mimic Max's accent—*Lak A sayed . . . Goo out thare masel*f. He moves his lips over the words not saying anything. Why pick only one bad note and leave the others? Must be something Jesse doesn't understand.

Genny motions Jesse back to the couch, and he flops there, rifling through the copy of *Mix* again, looking for anything he's ever heard of before—a picture, an advertisement, a person.

"I'm going out," he says finally. "Get some air."

Genny nods. "Actually we should think about going." She mentions the band at the Station Inn that night and asks Max if he'll be there. He grunts. He seems put out by their leaving, jealous maybe, too busy or weary to be polite. "Well, if you're there, you're there," she says. She leans forward and pats the top of his head. "It's all good," she says, and they turn to go.

"Nice meeting you," Jesse says, and Max holds up a hand but doesn't turn to face them or reply.

All the way down the marble stairs and through the faux atrium, past the guard, Jesse has it on the tip of his tongue to say something. "What was his problem?" or, "Who put dog shit in his cereal?"

"Poor Max," she says, as they swing through the glass doors and back into the world of ordinary sound and light. The sky is gold-coral in the west, brown and gray above that. For the first time since coming to Nashville Jesse is pleased by the burnt-smelling city air—the heat and freeway noise, people's radios flaring and fading in the distance, mufflers racing.

"So, are you two, like . . . ," he begins. He's not sure how to say it without sounding naive. "You and Max, are you kind of involved or something?"

She's getting her keys out and beeping the car, crossing to it.

"Please. Max?" She shakes her head. "Even if I liked men, as a rule, which I don't, necessarily . . ."

"Just asking." He walks after her, waiting for her to elaborate. Inside the car he crouches forward, moving as little as possible, letting the automatic seatbelt wind around him. The vents blow hot air, and the song on the cassette that had been playing on their way over picks up where it left off. Ricky Skaggs. They meet eyes, and he watches her check for traffic, signal, and pull out, then begin fooling with the temperature controls. Again she glances at him, worried maybe, though it's hard to tell because of the heat, and for a moment—her eyes sliding from his—he's struck by how pretty she is: her red-blond eyelashes, darker eyebrows, and amber-brown eyes; the sweat-darkened hair at her temples.

"So, what'd you think?" She doesn't look at him. Her tone is one of forced joviality, and he wonders what she's not telling him. "Your big first time in a studio. What'd you make of it?"

"Not my first time, Gen."

"OK, second."

He's about to remind her of some of the sessions he's played—the record of cowboy songs, the children's songs, the drunken country western band, and all the other no-consequence singer-songwriter demos and vanity recordings—when he notices a man on a ladder up against a billboard, unfolding glue-soaked squares of a woman's face and draping them magically into place, covering over an advertisement for Billy Ray

Cyrus. "Hey, cool," he says and points. The man is in an empty lot in the adjacent street. "I never saw that before." The man unfolds the squares and places them, then works a wiper on a long handle, smoothing wrinkles and bubbles and seams. Each square meets the next so perfectly that as the wrinkles and seams are erased, Jesse can't see any edges—can hardly imagine the woman's face not assembled. By the time they've gotten to the end of the street, most of the top right half of her is done— hair, forehead, eyes, and nose.

"Emmylou Harris," Genny says. Then, glancing again at him, "What, isn't it?"

He's swung around for a last look, but it's too late, and he catches only a glimpse. He had not recognized her, hadn't even felt a pang. Now, of course, he sees it: that same thin horse-pretty face, same beckoning, doleful eyes. The one whose voice and face had meant betrayal for so long because of the song his father had written that she'd sung all over the world while his father suddenly became unavailable.

"She's different now," he says.

"Different?"

"Older."

"Ha." She jabs the visors down on both sides and raises a vent so air streams at her face and through her hair, making him smell her sweat and soap. "What'd you expect?"

Back at her house they heat leftovers and boil water for fresh corn. He tries to notice everything that needs doing—

counters straightened and dishes washed, dish drainer cleared; those empty soup tins put with the recycling and the trash taken out. He sees it all and as quickly forgets. On the back steps he shucks corn into a grocery bag and rubs each cob clean, picking loose a few kernels for her cat, who loves raw vegetables as much as fish or meat and mills anxiously around his legs, tail shuddering. "Here kitty, kitty," he says, mashing some of the kernels between his fingers. He sees that his wrists and the backs of his forearms are glazed with sweat, though he's hardly exerted himself, and for the first time it occurs to him this heat is not something to put up with for a day or two like at home—here, it's the regular way of things.

Inside, Genny's on the phone, turned away from him, and he thinks, *Mama. She's caught up with me.* She stands at the sink, water running, the phone antenna coming through her hair and the phone pushing down the collar of her shirt. "OK," she says. "OK." Something in her hurried flat tone—it's got to be his mother. "Sounds great." Now she faces him, wiping her hands in a towel, blinking her eyes that are inexplicably damp, so he's forced to reinterpret. She gestures for him to hand her the corn, and he watches her drop it into the boiling water cob by cob, the whole time sensing she's ready to burst out with something. Instead, in a measured, beseeching way she says, "Look, we're about to eat. Yes he's . . . Yes. Can I?" She beeps the phone off and sets it on the counter, groaning.

He watches her lean into the oven. Water splashes onto the burner, hissing.

"I thought for sure that was my mother," he says, hopping onto a counter. He waits for her to correct this, kicking his feet. "I don't know why—I walked in here and I thought, that's it. She called."

She blows on a forkful of casserole and bites it, staring at him, preoccupied and trying to seem as if she's not. "So what if she did, Jess?" She bangs the oven shut with a hip and spins the dials to Off, chewing and tossing the fork at the sink. "You don't have anything to feel bad for, do you? Call her yourself. You should. You know it's probably the real reason you don't sleep so hot anymore." She faces him. "Guilt." She turns away again, sliding drawers open and shut.

"Oh yeah, I figured that out. Kind of—last night, you know, staring at the wall, thinking." He watches to see if this will bring her close again, the fact he already knows how she might advise him.

"There's the phone," she says. He says nothing but nods a few times until she smiles knowingly at him over her shoulder. "Maybe tomorrow, huh? Give her long enough, she'll figure it out herself? No point calling her if she's not going to call you?"

"It's no big deal," he says.

"Oh, of course not."

He slips down off the counter and heads outside for the bag of corn husks.

After dinner, after cleaning up, he scoops the spare keys to her shop from the wooden bowl on the kitchen table and leans into the living room. "Gen?" he says. But her armchair with the lace squares on the armrests is empty. An ad for Budweiser flashes over the television screen, the sound low. Down the hall, creaking floorboards, he goes past the bathroom and her bedroom to the den. From the door he sees that most of his stuff has been pushed neatly into a pile by the loft-ladder—his jeans and shirts and the white canvas laundry sack he took from his mother's back hall closet. "Genny?" He taps once on the doorjamb, and she turns, desk chair creaking. She has on reading glasses, and through the reflections in the lenses he sees her eyes are damp, pink-rimmed, and shiny with the same odd intensity as when he interrupted her phone conversation earlier.

He glances to the pile of his clothes. "I was going to do that."

Her chin comes up, and she shrugs but says nothing.

"So, I thought maybe I'd go play that fiddle some more, if you don't mind."

"What?" She crosses her arms. Smirks. "No. You want to play that thing?"

"Sure. Break it in." Her desk light softens the room with its orange-yellow tones, and he realizes that lit this way and with her in it nothing seems as nightmarish as it will later if he's by himself and not able to sleep. It's like any other room, and there's something for him to understand in this, but he can't see what.

"I don't know." She scowls, smiles, flattered maybe, then shakes her head to cover that with puzzlement. "I guess it's all right. Keys are in the . . ."

He holds them up, jingling them.

"Right," she says. Laughs and drops forward again in her chair. "Now don't get attached. I spoke with the owner again, and she won't sell. Not yet anyway."

He kicks the toe of his sneaker at the floor. "Too bad. That thing's sure killer."

"*Killer.*" She shakes her head. "If you say. Leave about nine-thirty?" She's already turning away.

In her shop he dims the lights and pulls a floor mirror to the center of the room so he can watch himself. "Walking in My Sleep," "Cheyenne," "Daley's Reel," "First Day in Town." He stays with G and G-minor and B-flat tunes, loving the differences and similarities, key to key, the changes in finger spacings and the different muscles each key heats up. The fiddle plays even more easily than he remembers—pitches never fuzzing, and a surprising volume, though the action's too low and the fingerboard is rutted and worn thin. But it's been too many days and his concentration is off, his hands weak-feeling and stiff, and sometimes he has to force himself to go on.

He moves from the mirror to the sliding glass doors and watches himself in the blurry reflection there, then back to the mirror—his fingers working and his chin by the fine tuners. "Mr. Monroe," he thinks, and suddenly he's sweating. He tries it again, out loud. "Mr. *Mon*roe." Either because of the heart attack or because he's here now, in Nashville, closer than ever before, he can't make the fantasy work anymore. "I'm your new fiddler," he says. He plays a while more, thinking these words over and over and trying to make himself believe them—himself as a Bluegrass Boy, the white hat, tie, slacks, and smart blue suit-jacket. "I'm your guitar man and lead singer." He grins. All he sees is men from the Station Inn—men with mustaches and goatees and gel-slicked hair.

Then another fantasy—one he hasn't indulged in some time. His father, guitar in his lap. His right arm rests over the top ribs and one fingernail taps resonantly at the shoulder wood in time with Jesse's playing. Then he's stubbing out his cigarette and feeling for a pick in his pocket, a capo, asking, "Say you're in B-flat, son?" and screwing in his capo at the third fret. "Kick her off!" It's that first chord Jesse wonders about and wants so badly, the burst of sound that brings them together and drives them on. No way to hear it accurately, only the feeling that's always the same—his throat shutting hard and eyes flooding, as if his peripheral vision had suddenly lost its hold, though he's not conscious of crying, only of release.

Just before nine he quits. He slots the bow back in its case and sets the fiddle on the workbench. And as soon as he's put it down, he wants to pick it up again. Sniff it, play it, feel it vibrating his jawbone, and hear the notes that let him know he's alive. He looks back a last time and cuts the lights, slides the door shut, and heads up to the house, humming, the fiddle's afterimage burning in his mind with the red finish floating around it like a halo.

Late that night he wakes up sweating. At first he doesn't remember any of his recent trouble sleeping, only sleep itself.

He's groggy, drifting back off before he's even awake . . . a bus, a dirt road darkened with rain, cliffs running alongside in overcast light, and two people seated behind him, arguing breathlessly. Their voices keep swirling together with some irritation outside him—he can't place it—and soon he's awake again. His eyes burn and his joints are sore. He kicks his legs wide and stretches, muscles shuddering, then rolls face down again, one arm under his chest. And now suddenly he hears them as clearly as if they were in the same room with him. No words after all, and no mistaking what's going on or what woke him up: Genny is getting laid.

He rolls over onto his back again, fully awake. Dim light shows in the curtains and against the ceiling, so it must be close to five. He stares and stares. This is embarrassing. Worse. Doesn't she realize? One moan engulfs the next—"Unnhhh"— so loud at first he wants to laugh. If there are two voices crying out, he can't tell them apart. He looks desperately at the open door—there's no air-conditioning vent in this room, so he has to sleep with it cracked or swelter—and several times in his mind he gets up to shut it. Imagines slipping down quietly and across the room and then back to bed. The braided carpet under his feet, the satisfying click of the door latching into the frame, the rungs of the ladder going back up, the silence after.

There's a louder thump, something hitting the floor hard, followed by a cry so piercing it tightens the skin on his scalp with alarm. Then a woman's voice—"Unnhh, yes, yeaa-as!"

"Christ," he hisses and drops down, crosses the room, and

swings the door shut too hard—harder than he'd intended.

For some time the thumping-slapping sounds continue through floorboards and walls, but with less vocalizing. He lies face up, waiting, his eyes flicking open and shut as the light comes stronger against the window. Except in movies, he's never heard two people screwing—certainly never anything like this. Not that he didn't usually know when a man was staying with his mother, and not that he didn't understand the hours-long silence on mornings when his father was visiting. Sometimes, those mornings, he might imagine tremors in the beams over his bed or convince himself he'd felt some subtle dilation of the house's architecture to contain them. But he never heard a thing. Even during his mother's worst years, Jesse's middle-school years, when it had seemed there were always new men in her life: ones who came for a night and disappeared; ones who stayed a little longer, all their stuff piled in the back seat of a car; ones who made her laugh or filled the hall outside her room with their own laughter; ones with gifts and a way of looking after her, their eyes so lit up and doubled with affection he wondered what they saw; one, an electrician with a bent nose and a mustache the color of earwax who returned skulkingly, week after week, hardly speaking, his boot heels clicking room to room after her, though she kept saying she'd never marry him, he was better off taking his affection somewhere else—*leave now before it gets any worse for you,* she'd say, or, *I can't be the fixed point for your ideals;* another, a man with a scrawny neck and pinched little mouth, a surprisingly deep voice, and the same questions for Jesse whenever their paths crossed—was he staying out of trouble, and how was the little old gal anyway; once, his own math teacher from the previous year standing in snow up to his waist under Jesse's window, rattling a broken rose trellis against the house and calling up pleas meant for his mother.

There's a final rush of slapping and pounding, Genny's voice murmuring along with it, giving encouragement or directions, he can't tell, a lone floorboard squealing. Soon after, there's the front door. Next, a car door chunks shut and an engine comes to life, and he hears Genny slipping down the hall to the bathroom. The winter his mother was sick she'd wake him shivering and chattering in her sleep sometimes, and his feeling then was like this, but worse, finding her there beside him with her nightgown twisting around her. He still remembers her too-thin arms reaching for him—her stroking the back of his head for her own relief, threading her fingers into his hair, and the smell of her surrounding them. Everything in him resists, but he can't help remembering. There's the sound of the toilet seat bashing down and water running in the pipes above his head, running and running. Long before it stops, before he can sleep again, he knows he'll have to leave.

(c)–IV

Church bells beat in the insect-thick, muggy air. He's outside waiting for her to get up and waiting for the phone beside him to ring. The bells change timbre with each wind shift, fading, then pealing so close he can hear tones within tones, deep bronze inside each silver, flute-high stroke. Two of the numbers he has were out of service. The other, Red's, answered with a machine—a woman's voice surprisingly crisp and unaccented. *Red and Nellie can't get to the phone right now. Thanks for the message.* But he had no idea what to say and hung up. Half an hour later he tried again, this time blurting something shrill and Yankee-sounding (even to his own ears) over the whine of his blood and the bells: "Don't know if ya remember me, but we met back last spring in Winterhaven and played some. Jesse Alison. Play mandolin and some fiddle. Now I'm down here in Nashville a while, and I got a place to stay, but I don't know how long. So, I guess," here he tried to lift his voice some, "—give me a call if you're not doing nothing or if you feel like picking." And Genny's number at the end, slowly, leaving no chance for error.

There's still his mother. He turns the phone over in his hand and pushes the antenna in and out, noting the grime in the keypad and the shell-smooth wear around the ear. *The telephone is a lonely woman's best friend,* his mother had said sometimes, always with a kind of smile, as if to imply there were uses for a phone he might never imagine. When the bells stop, he thinks. But it's too early—nine-thirty—she'll be asleep still.

Behind him he hears the screen door open, spring singing tight.

"There you are," she says, and after a moment he turns to face her. She crosses one bare foot over the other, arms folded, the door open against her shoulder. "What are you doing . . . ," she presses a hand to her mouth, yawning, ". . . out here?"

"Phone calls. Didn't want to bother you." He lifts the phone for her to see. There's a silence. Where she's standing he can see right through her nightgown—her breasts and the points of her hipbones and the outline of her underwear. She raises her chin and clears her throat, flexing a foot so the bones pop.

"Sorry about that—last night, you know. Hope we didn't keep you up, I—"

"Oh, not at all."

"—I was . . . ," again she clears her throat, smiling with all her teeth and touching the neck of her nightgown, looking away so for a moment he's free to study her face. The skin around her mouth and under it is a little red and puffy. She pushes her fingers through her sleep-creased hair and looks at him again. "Been a while for me I guess."

"I already called some people whose numbers I have." He follows a car passing in the street to avoid looking at her. "Maybe I can find someplace else a while, give you a little privacy." The door snaps shut, and he glances back again in time to catch her coming toward him, the look on her face—concern or aggravation, he's not sure. Her arm goes around his shoulder, breast pressing into him, and he strains against himself not to feel it—not to smell her or register whatever's left on her from the lovemaking. But there's only her usual odors—shampoo, pine-scented lotion, the smell of her house—and he remembers the shower. The water running.

She shakes him slightly and withdraws her arm. "Hey, I'm sorry, OK? It was inconsiderate and stupid. I, ah—I've always had a little trouble" —from the corner of his eye he sees her gesturing—"knowing how much I'm throwing my voice when I orgasm."

His blood jumps and he continues staring between his feet. *Orgasm.* He's never heard the word used like that before. "Not a problem," he says. Her bare feet are beside his, the little toes bent in so far they never touch ground, the other nails all pertly curving, pink and creamy as petals. They lift and squeeze back down, bending into the step.

"What then? You're mad at me?"

He shakes his head.

"Feeling lonely?"

"Not really," he says.

"Jealous?"

He shrugs. "Weird." Her breath touches him on the neck, raising the hairs there, and he locks his hands between his knees, hunching farther from her.

"Sure." She sighs again, and there's another silence in which he realizes the bells have stopped ringing. "Fair enough." The wind comes up then, swirling some leaves in the driveway and dropping them. He hears her scratching herself again and feels her shoulder push against his as she stands. "I've got coffee going—come on and have some. We'll talk more about it. OK? It's too hot . . . ," she pauses to yawn again, ". . . I can't even think out here."

The phone begins ringing and he reaches for it, stopping himself just as he's about to answer and looking questioningly at her, into her eyes, finally, which are bloodshot and sleep-rimmed but otherwise unchanged.

"Better let me get that," she says.

The last news he had of his father was two years ago, at a recording session with an engineer who had some connections in Nashville. Jesse's friend Gale had gotten the call, and the two of them made the drive together to New Hampshire, an hour south, an hour east. It was only Jesse's second time playing in a recording studio, and all the way Gale was giving him advice. "Make sure you got the balance in your headset all right so you can hear yourself—that's what you'll be playing along with, you know. What you hear on the headphones." Gale pinched his own earlobe and moved closer, as if Jesse might not know what that meant. "Sometimes you gotta even take one ear off, just to hear yourself and stay in tune with the track. And don't be afraid to tell them guys you don't like the tones they're getting on your mandolin, neither—they're total rockers. They wicked don't know shit about acoustic instruments." For years he and Gale had been rivals at fiddle contests. Then Gale, who was a few years older, moved on to the older Open division, leaving the Junior winnings to Jesse, at which time they became friends. Still, there was an element of competition between them—to Jesse, everything Gale said seemed pointed toward reminding him he was younger, less experienced, less accomplished, naive. By the time they'd gotten to the studio, Jesse was so sick of him, his blond-fuzzed jaw and constant chatter, he wanted nothing more than to be left alone in the isolation booth, playing.

He sat hunched toward the microphone, strap looped over his shoulder and boot heels locked on the rungs of his stool not to make any foot-tapping noise, hammering out the notes— "Pike County," "Monroe's Hornpipe," "White Horse Break-down"—until his hands were good and loose and the annoy-ance had left him. Eventually a voice came over the headset: "Got you down, man. Ready to try one?" He assumed it was the same man, the engineer (he'd met them all in the control room earlier but didn't remember names)—the one in a striped tie and jeans, who'd come out a while ago to replace the micro-phone they'd been using on him with one shaped like the end of a golf club, suspended in a shock-mount of thin rubber bands. The man had screwed the new mic in place and popped in a cord, smiling quizzically at Jesse. "Hope this one'll do ya. Too much high end on the Sennhieser—ever have that problem before?" he'd asked. Jesse shrugged, said he didn't think so, and the man moved the mic in a little closer, then lower, aimed at his gut. "Figured. Try and not move around too much. This one'll pick up everything." Again the half-questioning smile, and he was gone.

Later, listening back in the control room and waiting for Gale to do his parts, he found out about his father from the man in the tie, who said sure he knew him—had seen him recently even, just this past spring at someone's party. "What the hell did he tell me then . . . ?" the man said. He leaned back in his chair, satisfied-seeming, arms folded. "Some new scheme to get rich and quit the music biz. Of course." His mouth compressed at the corners, not quite a smile. "What was it this time—something with buying and selling restoration-model tube amplifiers. Ha! You know that guy. Always a plan for something."

Jesse nodded.

"Why don't he just sit his ass down and write another God damn million-dollar song, if that's what he does best? He's got the talent and the connections, you know—why all the fiddle-fucking around with every other thing that comes along?"

"Sure," Jesse said.

"Guys like that . . ."

He tried to remember if he'd ever heard his father mention plans for anything outside music and decided he hadn't, though it wasn't surprising to learn this about him.

"How do you know Hank anyway? Worked with him?"

"No, no. Friend of the family." Jesse caught himself smiling back falsely at the engineer in the same half-amused way, as if it meant nothing to him. "Friend of my mother's actually," he went on, ignoring the pain between his eyes. "She'd want you to say 'hi' for her if you see him around, probably."

"Will do. What's her name?"

"Janelle. Bathroom's downstairs?" he asked, standing, and when the man told him where, Jesse went out of the room, down the hall.

He stayed away long enough to be sure there'd be no more questions when he returned and no chance for more conversation about his father. In the half-lit alcove-lobby at the ground level he stood a while at a pair of vending machines, looking for something to eat or drink. There were no brands he'd ever heard of, and he wondered how old any of the stuff was. "Ah, the good life," he said, feeling in his pocket for change. It was what Gale had said when they pulled into the lot, before realizing what the building was like inside—busted windows, lights gone, cobwebs, paint stripping from the walls, the studio itself a lone oasis of order up two steep flights and all the way at the back of the building. He wondered if his father might have stood under these same flickering lights, once—if he'd pulled that knob for a bag of stale chips, say, or punched that button for a cola. Nothing much would have changed in the ten years since he'd been close enough to have worked here. He'd be whistling maybe or muttering verses of the song they were recording, half his mind on the selections before him, the other half gone in the song still—ways to shift around the phrasing or change a word here and there.

Jesse dropped in two quarters, and they fell straight through to the change slot. He lifted them out, still warm from being in his pocket, and tried twice more before heading back upstairs to the studio, empty-handed. Not a whisper of sound in the building, only his own feet shuffling over the wet grit. He touched walls and kicked through piles of sawdust, nails, and leftover wood pieces, wondering about his father and feeling close to him, certain he'd been here too. "Dad," he said out loud, and then again. He didn't remember the last time he'd said it. Only a word. It could mean any one of billions of men in the world. In his head the two songs he'd put down parts for still looped around and around—bad piano, bass notes bumping against the beat, nasal-pitched male scratch-vocal fading in and out between tangles of pedal-steel clichés. *How can he ever believe in her, when she'll be leaving him?* A few hours from now he'd forget both songs completely. For now they were an accompaniment to his every thought. He slipped back into the control room, easing the door half-shut, got his mandolin, and went back out again, down the hall to find an empty room in which to play.

He's in the living room with his mandolin working through an old Jesse McReynolds recording on his portable tape player, stealing ideas, when he hears the front door slap shut and looks up in time to catch her waving through the side window as she goes by, across the lawn to the shop. Nudging the volume a little higher, he draws one foot under him and leans in to concentrate. Always something about McReynolds's playing he can't copy exactly—his too-bouncy attack or the way he switches his cross-picking patterns between chords. Whenever he hits *pause* to play back what he's just heard, he only hears how he's altering it, smoothing things and switching around the notes however he likes.

Eventually he gives up, slumping into the couch with the mandolin on his belly and listening, occasionally ghosting notes, hammering them with his fingers, but not picking. The music floats through him and takes a physical dimension in his mind—riffs bobbing into each other and sinking through the chords. "Today has been a lonesome day, today has been a lonesome day, tomorrow's a gonna be the same old way." With a yawn, he lowers his mandolin to the floor, stretching out fully, eyes already half-shut, and kicks off his sneakers. The springs push comfortably through the cushions into his shoulders and back. "Did you ever hear them church bells ring, did you ever hear them church bells ring . . ." Right here was where Genny had sex last night, or maybe it was on that white oak table— somewhere in the room. He tries to see it. A thick-necked man like Max on his back underneath her or kneeling over her, the bald top of his head crimson from his efforts. He remembers the crash, the floorboards squealing, and the final flurry of pounding, but nothing visibly out of place suggests how or where they did it. He turns on his side, leather rumbling against his skin. Probably they avoided this couch. Genny's so protective of it, she doesn't even like him resting a drink on the arm.

Just as he's dozing off the phone rings, and he clenches inwardly, eyes snapping open. He waits, letting the machine pick up in case it's for Genny. "Yeah, message for a Jesse Alison." Red's voice snarls hollowly over the phone's processors, compressing and decompressing, bright against the floor tiles, echoing through the living room to him. He sits up, thinking to get it, but doesn't move off the couch—convinced, irrationally, if he picks up now he'll interrupt whatever it is Red would tell him. "Thought you might wanna know about there's a jam down the Station Inn tonight, it's over there on Demonbreun—happens every Sunday night and, you know, it's a jam, but can be kinda fun. I don't know but I might not head on down myself some time. Check you later!" The machine beeps off and he waits a moment, nodding to himself, thinking, *Well, good—that's nice. An invitation.* He draws a breath, filling his chest, and leans for his sneakers. He has to tell Genny and make some plans. Maybe she'll let him take that red fiddle—give it a test run to see how it blends. On second thought, maybe he should erase that message and let the day run out keeping to himself, then slip into her shop for the fiddle just as he's leaving, if there's an opportunity; tell her about it afterward. Or don't tell her at all.

Late that afternoon she stops work for a swim at the Y. He follows her room to room, hoping it's not too obvious how anxious he is for her to leave. She comes out of the bathroom, hair slicked down with conditioner and darkened in streaks, shorts still unbuttoned, the shiny metallic green of her one-piece swimsuit showing. There's the guttering sound of the toilet behind her. "Sure you won't join me?" she asks. She passes close enough he can smell the pine and lavender emollients in her hair. In the kitchen she drinks water, pops energy pills from a foil package and swallows them, watching him over the rim of her glass. "What will you do?" she asks. "You wanna become a vegetable? You gotta get *out* at least every now and then." She splashes the remaining water into the sink and goes back through the living room, Jesse following and watching her punch pillows, straighten magazines on the coffee table. He must have knocked them out of their piles earlier with his tape player, practicing. "Wait," he says, "I'll do that." She rolls her shoulders, not facing him, and strides by, down the hall to the linen closet for a towel, into her bedroom, then back again to the living room, stopping for a magazine—an older issue of *Strings* she slips into her knapsack.

Finally she faces him. Scratches her forearm and pinches her nose once, looking just beyond him and seeming to scrutinize something at the other side of the room. "I'll be back around eight," she says. "Just after dinner—maybe later. Sure you'll be all right here?"

He nods. "I can eat those leftovers."

"I don't mean to criticize but, you know, Jesse, you're here. You're *in* Nashville. This isn't the dress rehearsal anymore. So, I mean I realize these things take time, but you gotta get out, be proactive. You can sit in your room and practice anywhere."

"I know that, Genny." He has it on the tip of his tongue to say something about Red and his plans for tonight, but resists, thinking of the red fiddle. "That's why I was calling people this morning."

She touches his shoulder and then draws him to her, squeezing; he feels her breath come and go and the light strangeness of her body against his. "I'm sorry. You're right. You're trying. I know you're trying. It's not easy making your way in this town." She sighs once, and her breath touches his neck, lips press him, and she stands back again. "OK. See you about eight?"

They go out the hot hallway to the front door, and he waves a last time through the screen, swinging the door shut. He waits for the whine of her car backing up the drive and a few more minutes to be sure, and as soon as he knows she won't return, he strips. He leaves his clothes in a pile on the kitchen floor and walks through the house—her bedroom, the living room, more or less retracing their steps, ending up in the bathroom. His skin feels different in the cool air, sweat-caked and burning with sweetness, and his hands on it are strange—coarser and more probing. He licks his lips and tastes sweat in the new stubble, also unfamiliar, and again he wonders about last night, tries to picture it. That word, *orgasm*—the way she used it, an action or condition out of control, not a thing. He imagines it's her hand on him down there, the pink knots and wrinkles in her skin, but there's nothing pleasing in that. Michelle always said, "The woman's in love with you, Jesse. Please, any fool can tell—you're her baby and her long lost youth all rolled into one." But Michelle was wrong about that; he knew it. The feeling between them was not so straightforward. Instead, he remembers Michelle coming, how her eyes would flatten into his, the heat pouring out of her—how it always ended like that, something embraced and expelled. He finishes, as he often does now, picturing one of their last nights together: on the couch in her parents' living room in the firelight, Michelle mostly clothed, a leg lifted and tipped to one side, hands moving inside the opened fly of her jeans as they kissed. His knees hurt from kneeling so long beside her and his bladder was achingly full, but he couldn't tear himself away and he wouldn't stop kissing her. Already they'd drawn somewhat apart, experimenting this way (it was her idea, showing him how it was without him) and testing the memory of being together even as they experienced it. She slid her fingers into his mouth alongside her tongue, kissed him harder for the taste of it, and again there was the trembling, the choked sounds at the back of her throat like sobbing as she came, the heat, her hips rocking emptily on the couch.

If he thought it was a good idea he'd call right now—find out what she's doing, what she's thinking about. But she won't be home from school yet—summer intersession—and the way she'd spoken to him last time he tried calling her at school had left him with a sense of her isolation from him that was finally better to accept than to pick away at or attempt to talk her out of. "It's nothing wrong with you," she'd said. "The problem's all me, I know that—but for now I can't be your girlfriend anymore." Better savoring these actual memories than going into that again—arguing, driving her farther away. He'd ended that call saying, "You look me up when you're ready—when you've got it figured out, you call," and she'd agreed to this so quickly he took it as the worst possible sign. Best now just to wait. At the most, write her. Send a postcard.

Afterward, after shaving, eating, dressing, he goes out through the heat and snapping bug noise, the mossy sulfuric smells of city air, herbicide and lawn fertilizers, to Genny's shop. He doesn't want to sweat up his clothes—the new summer shirt with palm trees and blue parrots and his only clean pair of jeans left. So he goes slowly, punching the alarm code in the keypad, barely breathing, then the thermostat, the lights, and back to the door again, sliding it shut. The lights flicker purple and white and come up fully, and there it is: the red fiddle, on her workbench, unpegged, fingerboard gone. Where the ebony had been now only the ridged glue-dirty wood of the neck shows—a little oblong of smoother wood high on the violin's belly where the fingerboard had overhung it like a drawbridge.

He crosses the room quickly for a better look. Picks it up to sniff the wood and feel its chalky finish, the weight of it. Who did it belong to anyway? "Damn," he says. He sets it back on the carpet remnant, shoving his hands into his pockets. Well, he'll take his mandolin. Play fiddle only if someone else hands him one to play. Tomorrow he'll talk to her again—see if there's really no way she can convince that person who owns it to sell.

At the jam he plays rhythm only, no fill, hitting the backbeat so hard he's afraid if one of his pick fingers grazes a string he might slice it open. When one of the circle of pickers looks at him for a lead he declines, or if they persist he steps up, smiling and plugging the notes until he can feel strings bending under the pick, almost breaking, everything tuneless and clanging, barely audible over the racket. One banjo player in particular he'd like to strangle—a nervous-looking man with too many teeth and greasy hair and oddly flat little ears; he rolls through everything, thumb-pick scraping the banjo head and jerking away from the beat. Then there's the guitar player beside Red, an oblivious heavyset man in a seed-cap with an elaborately inlaid new Martin, louder and brasher than Red's old D-18 herringbone. The man leans back and farther back on the beat, dragging every song to march tempo with his leaden, ringing strums. The bass player's eyes pop wide and the veins in his neck show, and Jesse guesses, the way his lips work, the man must be on the tenor part again, though Jesse can't make out a note of it over the gnashing spoons and the banjos and guitars. Saliva sprays up and no sound reaches Jesse.

This is when he decides it's time to stop. Go find a spot for himself at the bar, where the fiddle players keep retreating, and wait a while. Hope the crowd thins or an opportunity comes to duck off somewhere with fewer musicians.

"Lost our mandolin player," he hears someone comment as he latches down a button on his mandolin case, turning toward the bar.

"Ain't lost, just taking a break."

"You let us know if you hear any mistakes," someone else says, and Jesse wonders, because of the tone of the man's voice, just how obvious his irritation was. Red lifts the neck of his guitar and plays the first notes of the theme from *Deliverance,* deliberately botching the last one. The man in the seed-cap misfrets a chord for another musical joke, whanging on it out of time and laughing.

"There you go," Jesse says, but no one seems to hear him.

He sits at the farthest corner of the bar. Asks for a Coke and turns on his stool to face the musicians, as if reserving a place among them. In no time his glass holds only ice and he feels nervous. He wishes he smoked or had a newspaper, magazine, anything to make him look like a person absorbed in solitary activity—wishes Genny were here giving him her usual advice and commentary, telling him who's who and what to expect. He grabs a handful of corn nuts from the bowl on the bar top and signals the bartender. "Pop?" she asks and he blinks, nodding. Her eyes, that crease over her mouth when she smiles and the way her lips pull back showing her neat white little teeth, she's just like someone from home. He can't quite think who.

Pop, he remembers suddenly—that's what they call soda here.

Just then another group of players arrives, and as they're

getting out instruments, tuning, shaking hands, Red and one of the banjo players—a tall, mustached man in khaki shorts and Birkenstocks who's hardly played a note all night—exchange looks. Moments later they slip toward the back room beside the restrooms, instruments pushed over their shoulders like knapsacks. Jesse glances once at the bartender. She's handing change over the bar to a customer now. "Forget that pop," he says and doesn't wait to see if she heard. He gets his mandolin and goes after Red, striking an A chord and tuning one of his D's down and back up. Floorboards creak underfoot, and for a moment he can almost smell the wood and lemon-polish smell of his mandolin through the smoke and beer. Someone at the bar says, "He would if he could of, but he cain't and that ain't the worst of it." The phone rings, and one of the jammers starts singing "Montana Cowboy" and stops short; then seconds later begins again, the rest of them dragging and thumping after.

In the doorway Jesse stands a moment watching—bare forearms and elbows almost touching as they lean together tuning, the light shining through the thin hair at the top of Red's head. Jesse wonders why he didn't remember that about him or just how piggishly and appealingly clever his eyes are. The room is brightly lit and crooked-seeming, off-kilter somehow, as if the floor and walls weren't squared or the ceiling were too low. There's a metal desk in one corner and an air-conditioner in the window. Seeing him, Red motions with his chin, waiting just long enough that Jesse understands the invitation is probably conditional. "Man, *that's* a motherfucking guitar," Red says. He grins and punches his pick across the guitar strings, sound hole lifted at the banjo player's face. The sound is crisp and nose-stingingly bright even where Jesse stands. His adrenaline rushes.

"So, how's it goin', son?" Red asks, now facing him, whipping the pick into his lips, hand extended for a shake. "How ya been? Close that door would you." But the banjo player's already back there pushing it shut with a foot.

"Doing all right," Jesse says.

"How long you say you're down here for this time?"

He shrugs. He wonders if Red's forgotten who he is already. "Till whenever. No plan just yet."

"All right. Well all right." He gestures toward the banjo player. "This here's Steve Bryant. He's just learning the banjo tonight."

The banjo player snorts. "Right," he says. *Rahht.* He stops plucking chords up and down the banjo neck and spits in a Styrofoam cup, which he replaces on top of the air-conditioner. "Feels about like it tonight. Glad to meet you." Steve reaches for Jesse's hand, smiling. The picks latched around his right index and pointer fingers are like spear ends, old Nationals worn at the edges, and his thumb muscles and the ridges of muscle around his tendons are thick as tree roots. His hand engulfs Jesse's.

"Give me a G there," Jesse says, and as soon as they do he goes back to tuning. He bends closer to hear, the mandolin scroll pushing into his sternum while Red and Steve talk back and forth—a story about someone they know in common: "He didn't want to learn nothing, just thought he'd show up at the session and be Tony, you know? Haw haw. 'Here I am, roll tape.'" They laugh some more and Steve says, spitting again into his cup, "Didn't know what he was in for, did he." Now and then one of them glances Jesse's way as if to include him, but they never explain anything, and he's too preoccupied tuning to piece the story together.

"Yeah man," Red says finally. "Let's pick one." He clips his capo to the fourth fret and turns away a moment, tugging at one of his strings, then back again, his pudgy fingers flying over the fingerboard—a joke riff ending in a stream of smart lounge chords. Then staring hard at Steve, his neck stiff like this is something he means to say, Red launches into an easygoing, pretty tune in B. Jesse's never heard it before. "Oh yeah," says Steve, "Forgot all about her," and begins deftly rolling in the backup. Steve's so tall it looks as if he's straining to make out the frets of his banjo, and he keeps one leg bent, playing, his knee lifted, big toe flat to the floor. Like a grasshopper, Jesse thinks—a big floppy cricket. He moves a step closer to keep Steve's fingers in sight, following to catch the chords and then the melody; when it's Jesse's turn for a break, Red looks to him, an eyebrow raised, the light flashing over his glasses, and Jesse nods—sure, he'll try one. *Easy*, he tells himself, and *Don't think*, dropping his eyelids so things blur—the sweat-darkened ruts below the frets on Steve's fingerboard and the worn felt lining in his strap; Red's pudgy wrist cocked and rocking over the sound hole, pinky pointed up—and feeling in the intersection of his ribs just how he wants this one to go. He starts with double-stops, chunking and off-time, striking low under the strings for that bluesy mailed sound, and at the bridge section focuses back into the point of his pick, flashing up sixteenths, long phrases each running into the next. He ends with a classic Monroe turn-around, dragged triplets, pick back to the bridge saddle, hard in his grip. Now and then, playing, Jesse catches Steve nodding at him and smiling as if over a shield, and the skin across his shoulders prickles with good feelings. "Perfect," Steve says, or maybe "Purdy." He's not sure. Red kneads a funny two-note phrase over and over, bending a string and wobbling his head forward and back as if he might topple, so Jesse and Steve have to join the joke with off-beats of their own in the backup, until all at once things run smooth again. "Ha!" Steve says. But then a little way into his next break he falls off suddenly, cursing, letting Red take it. "Lemme," Steve says, "lemme just try that agin *with* a damn capo." He's already digging into his pocket for one, hastily spiking his fifth string, and when it's his turn again, he plays the tune straight through, rolling and bending out the notes.

A few more tunes, one after another, hardly any talking in between, and when Jesse looks up he sees they've been joined by one of the fiddle players from out in the bar—a kid about his own age but shorter, with a quivering shock of shiny black hair like a rooster's comb. Carson. Both Red and Steve seem intensely glad to see him, also ready for some agreed-on amusement at his expense. "What it is?" they say and, "Aww, man, you were so cross-eyed that night you didn't hardly see nothing *but* the truth," and other things Jesse can't decipher. The kid endures it, smiling and blushing, occasionally ducking his head as if this embarrasses him, though Jesse's pretty sure he enjoys the attention. The left side of Carson's neck and jaw is a welted pink callus, sloughing skin—signifying hours of hard practice, Jesse knows—and he seems anxious to try every last new thing he's learned on them. Riffs and smears from Benny Martin and Vassar Clements recordings, even some Scotty Stoneman hair-raisers. "Check this out," Carson says. "Got *it* off a old Dale Potter recording!" and, "Ain't that the coolest thing you ever heard?" The wood of Carson's bow grinds right to the strings, he's so wound up, and often he's too busy figuring out what he'll play on his next pass to listen to what anyone else is doing. When Red mentions this to him—says: *something, something . . . Dang, you been doing some* wood *shedding there, ain't ya*—the kid's eyes widen. "Damn straight," he says. "I'll get this thing down if she kills me!"

At Red's suggestion, Jesse and Carson trade for a tune. Carson's fiddle is black-brown with shredded-looking f-holes and high arching, set up with thin steel strings, a sink-plug of a bridge, and such stiff action Jesse can hardly see how he plays it at all. The oversized walnut chin rest pushes into his throat like a bone, and the fingerboard is damp with Carson's sweat. Jesse's wrists feel agonizingly stiff from playing mandolin all night, and he keeps snapping off the string with his third finger, hitting wolf-tones every time he crosses to the E.

A few times through "Billy in the Lowground" and he hands it back, wincing apologetically.

Carson won't quite meet eyes. His face is pale with spots of pink. "Sure can play that thing though, can't ya," he says quietly, running a finger under his nose. "Got a job in town yet?"

Jesse shakes his head, hooking the mandolin back over his shoulder and pressing down to feel the pinch of the strap at his collarbone. "Only been here like a week."

"You lookin' at all?"

"Not yet really. No." He considers saying something about Monroe, how he's waiting for him to recover, but either out of superstition or because of a sudden knowledge of just how wrong that would sound, he doesn't mention it. He strokes a B-minor chord, then an A and back again—the strings silky-feeling and hard under his first finger, giving him that ache through his wrist and the back of his hand that he loves. "Eventually."

"Shouldn't be too hard, playing like that."

Jesse frowns, shaking his head.

Red says, "He's staying out there on Sixteenth with that Genny Freed. Know her?"

"Sure, heck yeah—everybody knows her." Carson licks his lips and snickers, eyes bugging slightly, though it doesn't have to mean anything—he's always doing that. "Y'all in G there?" Carson asks, shoving the fiddle under his chin and lunging toward them. "Ready for a little 'Katy Hill'?" And before anyone can answer he's sawing in the first measures and popping his foot up and down on the floor. For the fun of it and to make things really cook, seeing Carson plays it exactly the way Kenny Baker recorded it, Jesse steps in doubling him note for note, pounding it out, each note of his stamped through one of Carson's. "Yeah!" Carson says. Sweat breaks on Jesse's forehead, and he falls back to rhythm, blood beating in his face now, pleasantly distorting his vision. But when it's his turn for a break, he shakes his head and looks to Carson. It's too good being in the rhythm, socking and driving the beat with Red. The kid's hair quivers silver in the light, his dull blue eyes wide, everything animated but his mouth, which stays set tight in a near lipless line.

"God dang!" Red says afterward, popping one of his strings for emphasis. "And we ain't even sung one yet!"

Later, on their way out of the bar together, Red introduces Jesse to everyone they pass—singers and players, the bartender, people from out of town, people with jobs and family histories in the music industry, even two or three men Jesse's met here before, nights with Genny. Now they hold his eyes and don't look away as quickly, voices less sing-song. They don't protest any of Red's compliments or his excitement about Jesse's playing, but smile and ask Jesse what he's doing here. "Looking for a *job* and a place to *live*," Red answers, before Jesse can speak. "Same is anyone."

He sits at the kitchen table eating what's left of a two-day-old Kroger cherry pie, crust limp with sugar, sticking to the bottom of the tin. Each bite turns acid in his throat and doesn't fill him, but he keeps eating. His ears tingle, and there's warmth left in his shoulders from playing. Where he sits he can see into the living room—the leather couch, her armchair, bookshelves, and the framed prints on either side of the hall doorway. A few steps farther, invisible from here, is her room, the door probably cracked open to keep air moving. Later, he'll pass by and imagine he smells her—her sleep and the dust-smelling blankets she likes piling on two or three deep regardless of the season. He'll lean against the wall, listening for the sound of her breath or just imagining it, and maybe he'll push the door open with a finger to see inside. Without thinking of it exactly, he remembers the last things they said to each other as she was leaving—the feeling of something still not right between them. He eyes his own note to her where he left it for her to find, at her place at the table: "Gen—went to the Station for the Sunday night jam thing with Red S. Hope it's ok. See you shouldn't worry I'm getting out after all. Don't wait up. Check you later. J."

He tosses his spoon into the sink and drops the pie tin into the trash with his note, heading for the refrigerator; lifts out milk, letting the door bump shut behind him, and raises the carton, guzzling. Cold falls all through him, almost to the pit of his stomach, pinching between his eyes, and he remembers: *Scary thing is, this kid's so good he don't even know how good he is!* Red had said this introducing him to one of the men they'd met on their way out of the bar together. Such nervous pleasure gripped him then, it was all he could do to keep from bursting out with laughter. He shakes his head, embarrassed now and hating himself for it. "What's the matter with me I care so much what *he* says?"

Then outside in the humid moonlit street, how they'd all stood awhile talking, semis shuddering through the underpasses on I-40 below and cars slapping over cement spacers, distant storm clouds flickering, and bugs swarming in the streetlight: *How come we ain't heard of you before?* they said, and, *Didn't know anybody up there even played bluegrass worth a shit!* Already he's forgetting the exact words. They leaned over their cases, sweating and saying things back and forth to flatter each other, trading news of famous friends—another, subtler self-flattery (he knows this, though looking right at it confounds him). And at the end they'd exchanged some phone numbers. Steve assured them he would call as soon as he's back in town. "We'll get something goin' for sure then," he said, and they waved to each other, heading off down the street to their cars.

But it was better than that, the music, not just puffing and preening. He hums quietly now, sings under his breath— "Sophronie from Kentucky." His break on that one was so raunchy with crooked rhythms, it was almost like shitting. He chuckles, remembering, and raises the milk carton for another swallow.

"So *that's* what happens to the milk."

He turns suddenly, splashing some down his chin.

"Startle you?"

He smiles, nods. Wipes his chin with the back of a wrist. "I didn't know you were up," he says. He's half-conscious of a change in his voice—a twang and shade of new cockiness like Red's.

"I didn't know it myself, until I heard you come in." Pillow creases mark her cheek, and her hair is flattened on one side. She has on a faded silk robe, red with a green and yellow floral print—a gift from a college friend of hers from New Jersey, he knows, yet he can't help always supposing it's something exotic signifying her age and sophistication. "So how was it?" she asks. Her eyes fix on him and move away, not seeming to have taken him in, and he wonders what happened while he was gone— why she's really up this late. "Have fun?" She pulls the lapels closer across her chest and reaches past him into the freezer.

He nods, names the men he met, and watches her eyebrows lift, her mouth tuck approvingly. "Tell me all about it," she says. "What'd you play?" And they move to the table together, Genny offering him a spoon and prying away the top of the ice cream container. Back and forth they push the ice cream, taking scoops and licking the backs of their fingers, talking. "Last one for me," she says, and after a few bites more, says it again. "OK, really this is it." But they don't stop until the container is empty and he's finished telling her everything he can think of worth repeating.

"Well," she says. She puts her hands on the table between them, thick fingers with the dirty tips spread and pink stains in the skin around the knuckles—the same stains etched up her wrists now, too. "Must be past two o'clock in the morning," she says. Something glaring in one of her eyes catches him then, hard and schistlike—a kind of envy or malice, he thinks, maybe a challenge, though he couldn't say to what. The other eye too, he sees, has the same thing, but farther down and sadder, lost the instant he thinks he's perceived it. He remembers the red fiddle then—how much less than itself it had seemed with its fingerboard pulled, the varnish on the right shoulder all bubbled and discolored and eaten through with sweat.

"What?" he asks.

"What what?"

He shrugs. "The way you were looking at me. I thought you were going to say something."

She shakes her head as if to clear it. "Nope," she says, and yawns suddenly and stands, pushing her chair back behind her. They are heavy chairs with vined wrought-iron backs and thick cushions in the seat, not easy to move in or out of, and as she leans over the table at him, nudging it farther behind her with a heel, her robe drops open on one side. He cringes involuntarily, looking and trying not to look at the same time, his teeth clipping together and a feeling in his gut as if he were about to fall. Her nipples are pale pink, only the slightest shade darker than the surrounding skin, snout-shaped, and the one most plainly in sight is pierced with a neon-blue circular pin. "Oops," she says, and stands quickly back, arms crossed, the robe folded around her, her mouth bunched to one side; then, in a mocking, coy tone, "Jesse. Trying to see down my shirt again?" She laughs and lifts an eyebrow, and before he can say anything she heads out of the room, pausing to kick a foot into one of his sneakers. He'd toed them off earlier beside the door and left them there. "Night night—don't let the kitty cat bite." She waves her fingers without turning and shuffle-clomps through the living room, still wearing his sneaker. He watches after her, the darkness surrounding the doorway to the living room and then the light thrown down the hall from her bedroom as her door opens and bangs shut behind her.

Later, he wakes with music so loud in his head at first he thinks it must be coming from somewhere outside him. His father's face, leftover from whatever he was dreaming, hangs in his memory—those pursed lips and falsely pleased eyes. For a moment he wishes he'd brought one of his pictures with him, even if it was just to be sure he remembered what the man looked like, so he'd recognize him when they met. And now something else is coming back as well—maybe part of the dream: his father at the kitchen table, playing. The jagged way of his bare foot slapping the floor, almost out of time. His straight-wristed style of strumming, the pick pinched awkwardly between his thumb and the flat of his forefinger, eyelids drooping half-shut and head swaying side to side as if he were in a secret, musical trance. No sound. Jesse sees it all so clearly, he wonders how he ever forgot, or if he had.

Hopping down from the platform, he gropes under his clothes for his mandolin case, pops it open, and hunches into Genny's desk chair. The mandolin smells like bar smoke heavily enough that for a confused moment, identifying it, he feels as if he wants a cigarette himself. He punches *record* on his tape player and leans over the microphone, first only hammering his fingers on the frets not to drown out the music in his head—not to force it into the habits of his playing, but let it cross over just as he heard it, asleep. The sun blisters in the window, and his stomach is viciously acid from too much ice cream and not sleeping. Only as he starts playing it for real does he hear what the tune is—something like "High Dad in the Morning," crossed with "Big Mon," minor chords dropped between the two opening phrases and an extra two beats at the end.

Done, he clicks *stop* on the tape player and stands, stretching until something cracks in his chest, and heads back up the ladder to sleep some more. But as soon as he's lying down again, the music shifts further into him—chords and phrases from the new tune repeating and rooting to other phrases, suggesting more tunes and ways of rearranging the new one. And before long he's back in Genny's desk chair, crouching over the tape player. The sun is high in the window, burning his shoulder, and both sides of the tape are full, by the time he stops. He clambers back up the ladder and flops in the heat, so happy he's here he almost doesn't care if he never sleeps again or if he doesn't find his father.

(d)–V

Days pass. At night storms come, ear-splitting thunder and gusts of wind that rattle rain through the gutters outside his window, but the heat never breaks. Within minutes of getting into his truck, his shirt is sweated through. He brings an extra and keeps a towel under the seat to mop himself as he drives. Afternoons he's either at Red's—a renovated Georgian in East Nashville, with towering ceilings and central air—or helping Genny in the shop. Red's wife works at the hospital so much Jesse's almost surprised when she comes in the door or when he discovers something of hers—pink socks in the downstairs hall, Slimfast shakes in the refrigerator, mascara left on the bathroom sink ledge. He knows the house is mainly hers (she's paying), and a complicated kind of shame attaches to this, but no one mentions it.

Musicians come and go—a beret-wearing bass player from up the street, home between road gigs with a famous contemporary bluegrass musician Jesse's never heard of; a mandolin player with such fluid attack and glowing tone you can hardly make out the edges of his notes, his pick hitting the strings (it's disconcerting, maddening even, nothing like what Jesse wants and is used to—nothing like Monroe); a woman with a voice as glowing as the mandolin player's tone and a swinging-hard style on fiddle; twin brothers from Washington, dobro and banjo. Singing, Jesse loves coming in under them with the lead on choruses, feeling the air tighten between them and vibrate harder with feeling.

He plays what's needed. When no one's on bass, he drags out Red's old sour-smelling Kay from behind the couch. He slaps and drives the beat until his fingers blacken, redden, and swell. Sometimes, for fun, he socks rhythm on the guitar, squaring off against Red with his Doc Watson- and Norman Blake-style breaks. Mostly, and always when the woman isn't there, he plays fiddle. He has a new idea: he wants the fiddle in everything, hanging suspensions under chords and ghosting other players' notes and rhythms. Make it sound like the fiddle is everywhere and nowhere particularly. It's his sound still, but lighter-sinewed, and parts of the fingerboard he'd never considered seem the most obvious places to fit notes now—half-position and second-position backup lines in B and B-flat, odd drones against the A string in F, swampy low thirds and sixths in C and E. He still pictures Kenny Baker, playing—that dour, laconic look and his straight line always to the heart of the melody. When it's Jesse's turn for a break, he leans up his right shoulder and squeezes his bow into the strings. He tries to hear away every discrepancy of pitch and rhythm, fit himself in closer and closer, imagining the five sounds as one, no part out of synch with another. And even though he doesn't love the style of that mandolin player, ringing out every note, chop-chords more plangent than percussive, he knows this is where the impulse starts. They can't help it. Wherever the mandolin goes, everything follows. If the music were one body the mandolin would be its head; the bass, its back; guitar, the midsection; banjo, legs; fiddle, everything else—heart, arms, throat, fingers, blood. Meanwhile his own joints ache sweetly, and his fingertips feel pounded beyond sensation. His muscles are always sore for more playing, and the skin at the left side of his neck and jaw hurts the moment he stops, lifts away the fiddle, and packs it up to go back to Genny's.

When people mention work, auditions for new bands, new openings in old ones—Jim and Jesse, the Osbornes, Larry Sparks—Jesse takes note, but he doesn't participate. He focuses on the neck of his old fiddle, the red eyes and tongue of the old man's head in the scroll or the cryptic and decorative carvings in the back and sides, and he thinks, *No, not yet—not for me.* The others don't know what he wants or is waiting for. He hasn't said, and he's beginning to feel a little unsure, a little strange, even, himself. Bill Monroe won't be playing until he recovers. No one knows when that will be, and no one knows of any openings there; no one talks about it; it isn't the best band in town or the best gig by far, and Jesse realizes that, though it isn't the point. The point is something else more obscure—something he can't put his finger on and would never say aloud, having to do with honor and with knowing himself and with believing in his heart he's destined to be a Bluegrass Boy, to wear that suit and hat, and something else more embarrassing relating to his father: *I'd like him to see me on the Opry,* he thinks. *That's how he's meant to find me—there on the stage with Monroe, playing my heart out.*

He pictures her on the porch with her feet on the railing, bare legs extended and toes pointed, occasionally running a hand over the stubble on her calves, her white-strapped sandals on the floor beside her, with her cigarettes and a glass of something leaving octagonal rings on the floorboards. It's her customary summer talking-on-the-phone position. Her voice is soft, and there's a lazy satisfaction in it from which he knows the night before must have been a good one—high times with a lot to drink and maybe someone she likes trying to flirt with her—though for the most part she sounds sober enough. For a second time now she's telling him about Michelle's parents, Tad and Margaret—something about running into them at the restaurant a few nights ago and the work Jesse did on their boat last summer, work he was supposed to have continued this summer.

"No hard feelings there, I suppose. At least, so it seemed to me." He hears her draw on her cigarette. "They expect Michelle any day now. Too bad, you two would have really had a summer here on the lake again."

He's beside one of the AC vents in the kitchen to stay cool, on the iron stepstool between two overgrown hanging plants, a cracked feeling in his forehead already from listening to her.

"No lakes down there worth a damn, if I remember. That's what I always said was the problem with the South. All the water's in the air." She laughs. "Well, you can have it." He pictures her leaning from her chair to rub out her cigarette. "You can have it—you can keep it. They still serve those godawful grits with everything you get down there? Jesus I just hated that."

"They're not so bad. Put enough butter and salt on anything it tastes OK."

"That's your father exactly. His very words."

He's silent a second. "I never heard him say it."

"He's your father, honey, and you might as well look him up while you're there. No sense letting all *my* trouble stand in your way." He pictures her tilting the glass for a swallow, stirring with a finger or splashing in a little more from the bottle to strengthen whatever feeling's caused her to say this. But there's no sound of her swallowing. Instead she drags again on her cigarette, and he wonders if she's already lit up a new one or if he's just getting it all wrong. "Hell, who knows, you might get lucky and he'll help find you some work or give you a little cash to tide you over. Would be the least he owes you. This may come as a surprise to you, honey, but you're going to need all the help you can get down in that town—lot more than your little lesbian friend can offer." She breaks off coughing. "Ain't Winterhaven."

The AC stops blowing then, and he stands, stretching, the phone held out in one hand, then crosses from the kitchen into the living room. The light here is cooler, more shadowed and tranquil, and there's not as much of a hum from the freeway. He veers from the couch and drops into Genny's armchair, legs out on the ottoman. The back and seat are worn comfortably to her shape so it feels almost like being held.

"I didn't know you'd ever set a foot down here, Ma," he says. "When was this?"

"A lot you don't know, honey." There's no sound behind her voice, and he can't picture where she's gone anymore or anything she might be doing. Instead he remembers his grandmother—her mother—the one time they visited her in a nursing home downstate, almost in Massachusetts, just before she died. How the burnt, stifling smell of that place stuck in his hair and seemed not to leave him for days afterward. She was a tall woman in a bed that bent up like a deckchair, one plastic tube under her nose and trailing up to the wall, another taped into her hand and attached to a bag of fluid. Wherever he moved in that room her eyes seemed to be following, boring into him with such might and curiosity it seemed to him almost like being scolded. Her fingers clasped together on the sheets made him think of the dead bird chicks he'd found in the back ditch at home a few days earlier—two months old with soft yellow beaks and pink mouths, already dead. She didn't say much, only stared, listening to what his mother said, one craterlike ear turned up, her eyes following him everywhere.

There's the distorted fluttering sound of her breath coming into the phone, as if she'd suddenly pushed her nostrils right into the mouthpiece, and something clangs noisily behind that. "You can just ask your father when you see him—get his version of things first, see how it agrees with you, then maybe I'll give you my side of the story."

"I don't know what story you're talking about."

"Course not. You wouldn't remember back that far."

A car rolls into the driveway, tires crunching over gravel, and Jesse goes to the window. He pulls aside the curtain to see who it might be. A woman in a shiny blue Geo. As far as he knew, Genny wasn't expecting anyone today, though maybe he's forgetting again—always forgetting something lately, like a part of his brain has come unsprung. The sun flashes white across her dark hair, and she stands out of the car, lifting her sunglasses back on her forehead like a visor. Her mouth is painted thickly red-purple, and she has on a white tank top, hair pulled back to show her neck and pointy, freckled shoulders. She ducks into the rear seat of her car and a moment later nudges the door shut with her foot, eyes skimming the window, not seeming to take him in. She goes up the walkway to the shop, fiddle case in hand, bumping one of her long bare legs.

"Gotta go," he says. "Someone just came into the shop, and I don't know if Genny's out there." He moves to another window to watch how Genny will greet the woman, but the woman's already gone inside, and he can't make out their shadows through the door. "I better see what they want."

"Well, I thought I should tell you, in case you wanted to know . . ."

"No," he cuts in. "No more. Whatever it is . . ."

". . . he's not *in* Nashville anymore, your father—as it turns out. I spoke with his wife. The one who used to be his wife anyway."

There's a silence. Her breath gushes into the phone line, mixing with the sound of his own, and a chill tightens the skin at the back of his neck. He rolls his weight and hears the floorboards move under him as sunlight jumps from one end of the room to the other with the sound of wind lifting outside. Tree shadows swirl at his feet and just as abruptly vanish. "Where is he?"

Under the light from Genny's work lamp the woman is older than he had thought, midforties at least, heavily made up, with ribbons of some chemical stain in her hair, which darken and seem to lift the hair in wisps and flyaway screws. She sits with one orange-brown leg hitched over the other, the red fiddle in her lap, now neckless and headless, her skinny fingers with their huge red nails over its stripped shoulder. Something has unnerved her in a stiff, possessive way—he senses this right off. But maybe she's always like that. One of those people. She's said his name twice now, once when Genny introduced him and again later when she said it was him who wanted to buy that fiddle. "Not mine to sell, Jesse-honey," she said then, looking nervously at Genny. Still he feels unrecognized by her, invisible almost.

Now Genny is explaining why she took out the neck.

Something to do with the angle of the fingerboard and wanting more string tension against the face. Jesse thinks, watching her, the truth is she just doesn't want to let that fiddle out of her shop yet, if ever; whatever the reason, she'll go on making fixes and improvements until it's transformed or destroyed. Next she'll probably want to take the top off—shave the bass-bar and reshape those f-holes. The woman shifts her grip on the fiddle, looking speculatively at one thing and another, poking a fingernail at the purfling and nodding as if she were impressed with what Genny's saying.

"Jesse here," Genny lifts her chin in his direction, "he's hoping for a shot to get with the Bluegrass Boys. Words of advice?"

The woman smiles. Puffs air through her nostrils. Swings one burnished, dented shin over the other. "Say you played banjo at all, son?"

He shakes his head. "Not much. A little, yeah."

"Give him five minutes, he can pick up anything." The way Genny says this—face still turned away from him, apparently more concerned with how the woman will register the compliment than anything good that might come of it for Jesse—all of a sudden he understands: this is Genny's lover, the one who woke him up the week before last and again every second or third night since, despite Genny's promises, and he wonders how he had been stupid enough not to realize it sooner. He blinks, feels the blood stinging into his face, and looks away to keep from revealing anything in his expression.

"They'll need a banjo player right soon, might could have

yourself a job if you got on to it," the woman says. She bats her eyes and squeezes glitter-painted toes into the soles of her sandals, looking from Genny to Jesse and back again. "He wasn't the picture of health last I saw him, but he'll mend. Got a show at the White House coming up, next month I believe it was, and I know he can't stand to let go of *it*." She pauses. "Not everyone can get on with that man though—I can tell you stories. Other people, people in the agency I work for—they'll tell you stories."

Genny leans over the workbench, picking at her fingertips. Her foot moves subtly in time with the music from the radio. "He's not as young as he looks," Genny says.

Half as young as you are desperate, he thinks. And just under that, the advice from his mother—*never place your ideals in another human being, it's the quickest path to destruction*. Not that she'd ever followed it. Though he wishes he could stop himself, he keeps picturing the blue pin in Genny's nipple, glancing now and then at the front of her shirt to see if there's any evidence of it through the material, and wondering if the other woman is similarly pierced.

"How old are you?"

"Twenty next month."

The woman's look on him narrows, her neck and the corners of her mouth tightening as if a wire were pulling inside her. "And what instrument did you say you played?"

He shrugs. "Fiddle, I guess. Mainly. Guitar, bass. Anything really."

"Sings too," Genny adds.

"Got any family? Wife—kids?"

He shakes his head, smirking a little at the suggestion. Glances to Genny to see if she's as amused, but she's not looking.

"Well it'd stand in your favor some, being young and free and nothing else to do. He *has* had more than one fiddle player in the band before, as you probably know, back in the day . . ."

"I know all about it."

"I'll bet you do!" She snickers. "That Robert Bowlin, now, you've heard him, I guess; he's as fine a fiddle player as they ever had in the Bluegrass Boys—got a real clear style. Far as I know, he ain't looking to quit at all, though you just never can say—Tater Tate, too, he plays a fine fiddle, when you give him a half a chance. I'd say between the two of 'em they got that job pretty well sewed up." She pauses a moment. "And Tom Ewing, now I don't believe he's looking for work anyplace else either. So you see how it is." Her eyelids pop open and shut a few times, and she fixes all of her attention back on Genny. "So what's this you're telling me about a auction up north—are we going or what?"

He stares at her fingernails on the face of the headless fiddle and can't move his attention from there—those red-lacquered nails like hooks and the wood showing between them, stripped to the white on the shoulder where it needs touching up. The rest of what they say to each other mostly slips by him—dates and times to meet, a dealer connection in Philadelphia, auction pieces to watch for, the woman protesting she won't accept any commission, if she does go. He's stuck outside the exchange, staring at those red fingernails, wondering: *How? How do I meet him? When?*

Finally the woman stands, holding out the fiddle for Genny to take, and when Genny doesn't move, she replaces it on the bench top—no head, no neck, no one to play it. "Best be going," she says; then, to Jesse, "Nice meeting you. You be sure and let me know whenever you're in town next."

She moves to the door.

"Wait. How do I get an audition?"

"Audition?" She purses her lips, puzzled. "What—with Monroe? That what you're dying for?"

He stares back at her. Forces a smile.

"Well, I don't know. Get him backstage some place and introduce yourself, I guess, if you want him to hear you."

"But when?"

"Any time at all. I don't see what the difference . . ." She fluffs her hair. Her fingernails disappear into her palms and show up again, glowing against her waist, tugging inside the hem of her skirt and again touching at her hair. "Tell you what—you really want to know. Here's what to do. When you're good and ready, you just go and knock on his dressing room door there at the Opry, or wherever you happen to cross paths with him, and you mention my name—say Verlinda sent you. Say we're friends or something and that you'd like for him to hear you. He won't mind. But you better be on your best behavior and look sharp, get yourself a haircut, and don't dare cuss in front of him." She laughs. "He can't stand for any type of foul language."

"That's OK."

"Well, I know it's *OK*, honey—I wasn't asking you if it was."

"I know. I mean thanks. Thanks for the information."

"You thank me later, once you met him, see if you still feel like it's anything to thank me for."

Genny catches his eye. Looks back to the woman and comes around in front of the workbench. Jesse can see the pulse in her neck and flush spots in Genny's cheeks, one mounting her chest just under the neckline. "I'll call you," she says.

They touch hands briefly before the woman lets herself out, wiggling her fingers a last time at them through the glass.

"Holy Christ."

"That's Verlinda."

"She's for real?"

"Real as it gets."

"That stuff about Monroe? Is she like—does she work for him?"

"The agency works for him. I'm not sure what her personal connection . . ."

"Hot damn. Just like that. Man—," he smacks his hands together. "I'm gonna do it. I'm gonna be a Bluegrass Boy!"

Genny laughs. "One thing at a time, Jesse. You heard what she said. She wasn't exactly . . ." she trails off, shaking her head. "Find out when he's playing in town next, if he is. See about getting backstage . . ."

"Man. I'm on it." He goes from one end of the room to the other on his toes, punching a fist in the air. "That is just too cool."

Genny laughs some more and hunches onto her stool, glasses down, light enveloping her. After a while Jesse follows her lead, picking up where he left off in his latest efforts to fit new wedges for a bow rehair. It's a struggle keeping his mind on it—besides being preoccupied, this is only his third or fourth time cutting plugs, and he knows no matter how many times he tries, there will be the inevitable gap or wood hanging outside the groove; Genny will praise him despite this and set things right in seconds. The knife blade feels oversized in his hand, and sweat tickles along his hairline. Such smooth, obscure wood he can hardly feel or see where its grain is. There's the usual fizz of exhaustion through his temples, the boredom and that grim, halted feeling in his throat like something shutting down inside him. *Monroe, Monroe,* he thinks. *I'm gonna be a Bluegrass Boy.* Today especially, he just can't stand this work. *Ten more minutes,* he tells himself. *Three more tries. I'm out of here. God I hate this.* On the radio a woman is laughing unmelodically while a man complains over the phone to her.

"Sure would be nice though," Genny says, swinging out of her seat for a different file and resuming work, blowing once to clear wood dust. "If things worked out perfect like that for you."

He's never understood how she can do that—how her mind and fingers work so independently. The way she bears down on a piece of wood, he thinks it's almost more biological than mental—an itch, a hunger satisfied, nothing in it to occupy her mind.

"But you know, if it doesn't . . . ," she continues. A drawer clatters open and shut and he looks up again waiting, watching her bend and drop back onto the stool, legs open, elbows in. "There's other bands, other folks to play with. In fact . . . I mean, I know he's your idol and everything, but in a lot of ways Bill Monroe's best days are probably behind him. I mean—well, you know that."

"Of course." He's heard it. He knows it. He refuses to believe it.

Here her eyes draw up to meet his a moment, and her fingers almost stop moving. It's some effort not letting any disagreement show in his face. "Did you—what'd you think of her? Aside from that. You liked her?"

He shrugs. "What's not to like?"

"I know. She can be a bit much at times." She resumes work, and he knows, from the way she's said it, she's not as certain of this assessment as she would have him believe. "Anyway, I don't know exactly what it means yet, but we have been sleeping together on occasion."

"I figured."

"Yes, well—but I wanted to be sure. That you knew. It's the challenge, I think, being with someone as . . . different from me. Like it's a conquest. She uses feminine hygiene spray, for Christ's sake. What am I thinking . . . ?"

"Genny! Please." He mimes covering his ears. "Way more information than I wanted."

She doesn't reply. Vern Gosdin croons on the airwaves. Their work settles closer to its usual rhythm of sounds and

movements as concentric and interwoven as the grain of the
wood they're working.

As always, pulling up at Red's, Jesse checks the cars parked
in the street and backed up in his driveway to guess who's
here—what's in store for the day's picking. There's the usual
rush of nervousness and anxiety that comes with this: his
attachment here is new enough that any shift in the mix of
musicians may as easily as not leave him out of the loop, alien-
ated again as during his first days in Nashville. It hasn't happened yet, but it may. Mainly, the anxiety pushes him on with
an excited, eager feeling like he can't wait to get in there and see
what's what. He'll do well. He knows it. He always does well.

Today there's a silver Honda, like Genny's, with Tennessee
plates, he hasn't seen before. Shelby County. *Who?* he wonders,
and heads up the glistening walkway to the front door. Knocks
once and pushes the door in, already listening. He has two of his
instruments—fiddle and mandolin—the guitar is home at
Genny's.

Standing with his back to him is a kid Jesse doesn't recognize, about his own age, maybe a few years older, in an orange T-
shirt, hair just past his collar, playing fiddle. A mandolin player
Jesse doesn't recognize either, five or ten years older, with a rat-
tail braid, overalls, and a hand-rolled cigarette burning in the
corner of his mouth, frayed and duck-billed baseball cap low
over his eyes, sits across from the fiddler on the ottoman. What

Jesse catches as he comes through the door, the last section of a mandolin solo, is so exactly like mid-'50s Bill Monroe it's like someone's gone inside Jesse's head, taken the notes he might have dreamt to play, and brought them out perfectly. *Wow,* he thinks, *damn,* and *wow* again as the man starts chopping, raking out the chords. Red and some of the other players Jesse recognizes are positioned variously around these two new musicians, and as Jesse pushes the door shut behind him, attention fixes back on the fiddle player. His bow arm swoops out and back fluidly, thumb on the outside of the frog, just above the slide— w*rong,* Jesse thinks. But his tone is not affected; it's as powerful as anything Jesse's heard: bright and cutting as metal on the one hand—reedy, nasal, crying—and meltingly lush on the other. The effect is heartbreaking. *Jesus,* Jesse thinks, part of him instantly set back to a kind of spectator's idiot awe and envy he hasn't felt for years. *How in the heck?* he thinks. He lowers both cases. Stands there. The tune is one he almost recognizes—Dix had wanted him to learn it at one time, but he'd never cared to— a Scotty Stoneman favorite. "The New Lee Highway Blues," that was it. Leaving his instruments, he steps around closer and to one side to watch the fiddler's left hand, see how it's done, but it's no help. Jesse knows those notes. He's played them before—he has four fingers, four strings on his fiddle too. He can get around the fingerboard. He just would never have thought of doing it like *that.* The fiddler's inside the melody and pushing through it at the same time, bending and rearranging it, in and out of second and third position, floating up an octave then dropping back down, conjuring dissonances and spiraling rhythmic syncopations that make Jesse want to laugh. The notes hardly sound like notes, they're so connected and expressive. For a few measures he's exactly like Kenny Baker, then like Eck Roberts, then he's morphed into a horn player, then back again—something like Vassar or Scotty. Something like Benny Martin, Byron Berline. Every change is seamless, driven by a single line of thought, and evident only if you know what to listen for.

"Yeah, man!" Red says when the song's done. "Sounding good, buddy!"

Everyone breathes and shifts instruments, sips drinks. The fiddler coughs into his hand and plucks out a melody on his fiddle strings a moment, humming under his breath. He doesn't face Jesse. The yellowish spot under his jaw where the fiddle connects is like Jesse's, but different; the fingers, the hands, the veins in the backs of his hands, all are exactly like his own. Only the wrists are different—denser, with poor muscular definition, and patchy red-blond hair.

Red glances briefly at Jesse and Jesse nods hello. "Look who it is—have y'all met before?" Red asks. He leans again for his drink, vodka and lime, Jesse knows, in a purple Plexiglas cup shaped like a cable insulator.

Jesse shakes his head.

"This here's Jesse Alison."

The fiddler faces him, and Jesse feels exposed—stared through, dismissed; also, a kind of spontaneous liking and kinship. He is close enough to Jesse in features and demeanor that seeing him is almost like looking into a mirror.

"Duncan Haines," the fiddler says. "I've been hearing about you." He clears his throat, coughs again, and holds out a hand. "Red's talking you up all over the place. Glad to see you."

It occurs to Jesse, as they shake, that judging from his puffy eyes, limp hand pressure, and that cough, he's probably stoned. Jesse peers around the room for telltale signs. Nothing. Sounds of conversation and laughter reach him from the kitchen— women's voices mostly. Instruments being tuned. The cigarette smoke is too overpowering for him to tell if there's been a joint smoked.

"Ha," Jesse says. "All lies, I'm sure."

Before they can play, Duncan has to make a full inspection of Jesse's fiddle. He's got ideas for changing the setup—drop the action, flatten the bridge and fingerboard, carve out the bridge some more, move the sound post, different strings. "Kind of a hobby for me—tinkering with fiddles. Don't listen to a word I say though, if you don't want to. It's your fiddle," he concludes, handing the instrument back, and for a moment, for the first time in recent memory, Jesse feels no connection with it. *My fiddle*, he thinks, *piece of crap*—and shoves it in under his chin. Tightens the hair on his bow and draws a few notes. "Yeah," Duncan's saying, as Jesse continues to tune. "See you could probably get rid of that nasally sound, make it a little more like you *want* to hear if we fooled with it. Lemme just—lemme see something for a second . . ."

Jesse hands the fiddle back over.

"Hey. Y'all wanna play or you just gonna stand around talking fiddles?" Red asks.

Duncan and Jesse meet eyes. Laugh.

"What's it gonna be?" Red asks.

There's no time to think. Twin. What does he know a twin part to? He can't think.

"How's about . . ." Duncan says, and before Jesse can say yes or no, starts into a tune Jesse only knows from having heard it. "Tallahassee." They double on the melody for a few measures until Jesse's sure he remembers; then Duncan jumps over him, harmonizing—sixths and thirds and fifths—doing the nearest mirror-perfect imitation of Jesse's own style and phrasing. It's like seeing himself Xeroxed or partially erased, and with more than a hint of mockery—an ostentatious squareness in the bow changes and rhythm Jesse instantly interprets as criticism or a prompt to fix his own playing, which he does, breathing in once sharply and out, and deeply in again, watching Duncan's bow on the strings and easing his grip on the rhythm so the notes blur and float, melt, one fiddle into the other. "Yeah!" he hears Red calling from across the room. People have come out of the kitchen to hear; they stand with their backs against walls and doorjambs, listening, swirling drinks, smoking, talking quietly. Jesse looks again to Duncan—they're coming up on the top of the form, then playing it through a second time—and he sees he's being prompted again to change, move just ahead of the beat and focus his tone in the tip of his bow. *OK,* he thinks. *I can do this.* But again, as soon as he's sure of it, he hears some new mockery in Duncan's mirroring of him, some shortcoming, and again he does his best to adjust—shift out of range.

Next up, the mandolin player has his turn, and Jesse's too busy recouping, chopping the backbeat with Duncan, to really listen. He's not surprised at what he does catch—a kind of trapeze act in work boots, a rhythmic reconfiguring of the melody that allows the man to hang at the top end of the fingerboard, suspending and droning notes, slapping two and three sets of strings at once. Next up is Red.

Duncan leans to Jesse, breath warm in his ear, a mossy fungal smell like earth under a blown down tree. "Dumb fucking tune," Duncan says, "why'd you pick it? I hate this fucking tune." They both laugh. "Let's mess it up," he says. "Trade fours." Jesse realizes the smell has nothing to do with his breath—it's his fiddle or maybe his armpits. Then after a pause, "No, trade eights and fours." Jesse tries to act as if he knows what this means. Smiles. "What—?" Jesse begins. "Follow me," Duncan says. "I'll cut you in." And before Jesse can think any more about it, they're trading. First Duncan for eight beats, then Jesse. Then four beats, then two and two and back to fours, and from there it's a blur. There's no more mockery in Duncan's playing—at least none Jesse can detect—now it's straight competition. It's all Jesse can do to keep up, counting beats, trying to remember the chords, the structure of the tune, and sustain some basic outline of the melody in his head, at the same time trying to make what he plays overlap Duncan in the way Duncan's note choices keep overlapping and outdoing his own so perfectly. "Together," Duncan says when they're back at the top of the form, and they play it through again, harmonizing, but differently. It's as if the air's been sucked out of him, Jesse's focusing so hard on what he plays and hears—as if they were splitting notes into fragments and smaller fragments.

"Hey, that was fun," Jesse says when it's done, but no one's listening. Before he can catch a breath, Red's launching into another number—punching the rhythm and getting ready to sing. "Hold What You Got," in A. Jesse rests his fiddle back in its case, latches the lid shut. He points with his chin to the bass in the corner behind Red's couch, indicating that's what he'll do now, play bass, but Duncan seems unconcerned. He's hardly looking. No one's looking. Jesse crosses the room quickly and gets the bass. Presses his head to its side a moment to hear if he's in tune and jumps in. *Defeated,* he thinks, though for the moment, anyway, he's also happy to hear what the bass adds; the rest of them seem pleased too, nodding in his direction. Boom-chuck, boom-chuck. *Loser, loser,* he thinks, in rhythm with the song. *The first time in God knows how long. But at least I know when I'm outdone. At least I know when to say* give.

The rest of the afternoon he keeps his mouth shut. Stays on bass, underneath and thickening the rhythm, soaking up everything. He watches Duncan like it's a sickness. When the joint comes Jesse's way, as it eventually does, he draws smoke. Holds it down. Draws again. But the shift in perspective doesn't help much—or maybe it does. He's getting used to this and almost starting to hear flaws and imperfections in Duncan's playing—like watching a stunt skier, he thinks. Eventually you get to take it for granted, judging things you'd never pull off yourself, one against the other—flips and triple flips and splits and bunny hops and tip-stands. *Wow, wow, wow,* but what does it all mean? No, he thinks, I wouldn't do it like that. That's unnecessary. I'd stay with the melody there. I *like* the melody. He pictures Monroe with his mandolin hooked over one shoulder and raised to the microphone. The stubborn line of his jaw. Remembers something he once read the man had said, his voice so clear in Jesse's head it's like he's channeling it: *Sometimes you get a feller wants to play a lick a little flashier than the rest of the boys, and naturally everyone else is gonna try and copy it, or do a little better. Bluegrass is a competitive music. That's a part of it, a part of the music, and bluegrass is as fine a music as you'll ever hear. But you've got to find your own way of playing and your own style, and once you've done that, ain't nobody can beat you.* The problem, Jesse thinks, is not how good Duncan is, the problem . . . But he loses the thought, hearing Genny's voice now instead: *Learn, baby, learn. That's what you're here for. Pain and heart and practice—there's no other way. We're wood until we know better.* Also, the words from his mother: *The good will fall. This is how we know them.* And without understanding why, exactly, he's picturing his father, feeling sorry for him. This, or something like it, must have happened to him once. Maybe it's even why he quit the business. *Family of quitters,* he thinks. *I'm from a family line of quitters.* He plugs the notes a little harder, trying to let himself go—let this feeling out through his arms and hands and sore fingers, into the music.

There's no break in the playing until food arrives, several cheese and pepperoni pizzas in octagonal boxes from Domino's; then the room goes as quiet with the muffled sounds of chewing and digestion, slurped drinks, as it had been raucous with music moments earlier. Jesse wonders what they put in the pizza to make it taste so good—like milk and sugar with a hint of something else crisp and bright—mint?—but more satisfying. He can hardly swallow fast enough to get to the next bite. He tries analyzing the sensation start to finish—how it goes from a scent to a burning sweetness at the center of his tongue to a plugged, tasteless back-of-the-throat fullness, the opposite of retching, to a yearning for more.

"Sounding pretty good there."

It's Duncan. Jesse licks grease from his fingertips and bunches the food to one side of his mouth, chewing and speaking at once. "Man, I don't even want to touch the fiddle again after hearing you. Serious!"

Duncan expels a breath and squints. Says nothing. His hair falls over his eyes. He folds his slice in half and has a bite.

Jesse tries again. "I mean you're just playing the shit out of that thing. That 'Sally Goodin,' man . . . you wicked kicked its ass all over the place." The words fall so short of what he means it's pointless. Insulting even. Fawning and foolish. Or maybe it's only the way Duncan receives him. Jesse doesn't know. "Shit," he finishes. "You're good."

"Got a job yet?" Duncan asks.

"No. I don't know." He folds his slice in half to be like Duncan. "I'm waiting. Red and I were talking about getting something going, yeah. Tell you the truth though, what I'd really like is a gig with Monroe."

"Bill or James?"

He shakes his head. "Bill. I didn't know James . . ."

"Son. Oh, you don't even want to go there." Duncan bites into his slice. Chews thoughtfully. "I mean you could, if you wanted to. Probably hire you in a flash, got a nice tour bus and a bunch of festival bookings, but fuck that's some scary shit." He swallows. "Bill—now that'd be a job for you." Here he lapses into an imitation of Monroe: "The father of bluegrass music has always said he loved the sound of the twin fiddles above anything else, except maybe sixteen-year-old pussy, and you and Robert Bowlin now that would make a powerful match, for sure." He chuckles. Nods his head. Drops the imitation. "You wouldn't get much out of that, though. You play as good as Bowlin already. Anyway those guys, man, the band, they're carrying the whole show lately. Monroe can't hardly sing or play a note—but don't tell anyone I said that. Here." He reaches into his back pocket, draws out a card with his name on it, and hands it to Jesse. "Make sure you jot down your number for me too before you go, and I'll keep you posted if I hear anything. In fact," he pauses, again lowering his slice onto his plate, "there's a band out of West Virginia I've been filling in with when I'm free lately. They're looking for someone permanent. Fucking great singer, I tell you what, they're on the way up, and they got a full calendar. Just . . . yeah, give me your number. I'll keep an ear out for you."

Jesse nods. "Thanks." Has another bite. "I'm staying out with Genny Freed—over on Sixteenth. You know her?"

Duncan shrugs dramatically, shakes his head. "There's so many people in this town. Doesn't ring a bell."

"She builds violins, does repair work—"

"Hey—I know what, tell her to build you a fiddle you can fucking play then." He lifts an eyebrow, gives Jesse a half-stricken look. "Excuse *me* a moment," he says, and turns and ducks up the stairs for the bathroom.

After dinner, she realizes they're out of ice cream and sends him around the corner for more. "While you're there, would you mind . . . ?" she asks, slipping a list from under the magnet on the refrigerator. She goes back to the sink, piling in dishes.

"I'll do those," he says. "You cooked."

She waves him off, not turning, and he goes out, past his truck at the edge of the lawn. Rust-eaten gutters and bed, black-trimmed doors, windows half-down despite her constant warnings about security, that familiar burned oil and rubber smell— it makes him want to get in and drive. Be on his way, feel the road vibrating up through the steering wheel and into his arms and shoulders. When he gets back, maybe then he'll tell her about his new plans. They'll be in the living room with their feet on the coffee table, colors from the television flickering across her face—her expression shifting in response to whatever they're watching, almost as if wishing she were pleased more than she actually is. He won't mention his father by name. "That friend of my mother's," he'll say. "Turns out he's not in Nashville after all. Somewhere out near Memphis, in the Mississippi Delta or something." He'll watch her nod, eyebrows angling to show her concern for him, her skepticism. He can tell her about the afternoon at Red's, too, maybe—what he learned about himself playing with Duncan, and his decision, for now, to let things ride. Think and wait.

Up the drive and into the street he continues walking, past the rows of little houses and kudzu-draped trees, the baseball diamond and picnic area, where a single family sits at a table near the parking lot. Smoke leaks from the barbecue hood at the end of their table; they don't look up or glance his way as he passes, though he's openly staring at them. He wonders if this isn't another North-South difference—people from the North are always looking at each other, and if you get caught it doesn't have to mean or invite anything. But down here, if you meet someone's eye you're obligated to a conversation or at least an overblown greeting. *Howdy, hey, hi, how y'all doin' tonight?* he runs the options in his mind, almost to the point of saying one as he passes. And just after he's gone by, he hears, "Ain't a question what you think he done to . . . *something something something* . . . things don't change around here he won't live another day to regret it." It's the man speaking, an accent less drawling than what Jesse's grown half-accustomed to, but still thick on all the vowels—maybe from somewhere else in Tennessee. Jesse scuffs his feet in the dirt to cover whatever follows, picking up his pace, the store only two blocks ahead. Upwind of the barbecue now he can almost smell the tar roofs and dank bitter sides of each house he passes, each trampled front yard loosing its heat in the windless evening air. And inside each house he pictures Duncan: Duncan in a playpen, two parents cooing over him; Duncan practicing fiddle; Duncan with his own wife and baby; Duncan looking out the window with his hair falling over his eyes, scowling; Duncan shooting hoops with his dad and teenage friends; Duncan on a tire swing in his backyard. Jesse knows Duncan isn't from here—he's from south of San Francisco someplace and as much of a transplant as Jesse is—but he can't stop himself from picturing it otherwise. *How is it . . . ?* he asks himself—a question Genny might put to him—*How does it feel knowing there's someone in the world who's so much better . . . ? No, the question is* why? *Why does it feel so . . . ?* But he doesn't have words for it.

Back home again, the kitchen is gleaming, dishes lined up in the rack, and a cake on the table with two plates and forks beside it. It's a small cake, more like an oversized muffin. No sound of television comes from the other room, and once he's put away groceries he goes to find her. "Gen," he calls, and she yells back from the bedroom. He slouches into the couch and picks up a magazine, the page he opens to coming in and out of focus—musical notes written out, "Jenny's Welcome to Charlie," with an Irish fiddler pictured at the top of the page and his explanations for the tune in italics running alongside: *Fiddle players of County Dingle know this tune by another name not fit for print. . . . The triplets can be fingered or shaken in at the frog with the right hand. . . .*

"Want cake?" she asks, and he nods, sure. "Then I'm off for the evening," she says. She twitches aside hair. Again he nods. She's in a white skirt and sleeveless blouse he's never seen, blue with marbleized nublike patterns in the cloth and tiny buttons up the front. Following, he watches her bare heels come in and out of sight and the quiver of tension in her calves, her shoulders glowing pink with sunset light as she passes in front of the window, and for a moment he can almost imagine wanting unbearably to touch her—feel the weight and shape of her against his palms, her heat, and the way her muscles overlie bone. Down the step into the kitchen he follows, punches up lights and spins them dimmer, then sits across from her.

"Sure you'll be all right on your own?" she asks. She cuts in and licks frosting from a finger.

He laughs. "You always ask me that."

One day he was on his way up the road to her house, dragging his denim coat on the wet ground behind him and singing at the top of his lungs. Sunlight flew through clouds lifting the shadows around him so sharply he felt as if he were continually falling from one world into another. Just beyond the sound of his singing and the wind through bare trees and the birds, another noise was distinguishing itself—a mechanical vibration like the distant drone of an airplane engine. And almost before he could identify it, jumping up to the bank for safety, a woman in a blue VW tore past. Her angular features were all focused forward, and her ginger red hair was swept to one side from the wind, eyes glistening and streaked black. He didn't think she'd noticed him, and although she was not exactly like in the pictures, he knew who it was. *Sister,* Genny had called her sometimes—*Girlfriend*—though he knew they were neither related nor even exactly friends. He watched after her—the way she took the ruts and corners, so fast at times the car bounced out of the tracks and once sank hard enough he could hear its muffler and rear bumper ring against the center hump. At the turnout before the final stretch of elms, she veered from the drive altogether, straight out over the grass, leaving two flat-printed tracks until she went out of sight. Moments later at the sound of her engine chirping higher, he turned again to watch. But he didn't see her down there climbing the incline to the highway. Only after, once she'd made it safely up and there was the sound of her winding hard into each gear, did he catch a last · glimpse of her through the fields on the main road, going west, fast.

At the top of the hill Genny stood in the circular patch of grass-spiked silty earth where people usually parked. The garage doors were flung wide, which he'd never seen, and there was a cart of gardening utensils on its side, Genny next to it with her head cocked stiffly, a look on her face he couldn't read.

He dropped his coat and went to her.

"I'm so glad you're here," she said. She turned one shoulder to him, carefully fingering aside some of her hair so the white of her neck showed. "Can you look—I'm pretty sure I've got a wasp or bee or something stuck in my hair."

He had to control himself and almost jumped at the sight of it, purple-black, one armor-crusted leg reaching, then the other. "Yes," he said, pointing. "It's all tangled up." Genny was allergic to wasps and bees; he knew this, and yet it wasn't quite registering with him.

"Great. Can you find me a stick or something?" She leaned farther, still watching him from the corners of her eyes. She pointed. "Should be something in the yard there. You could use it to brush him away. Gently." The rocks at his feet looked wrapped in the pale earth. No sticks here. More than being afraid, he felt stopped; something in him resisted understanding how to go along with her. *No,* he wanted to say. *Get it yourself.* Her cat jumped down from the roof of the garage, gurgling in its throat, and sauntered drunkenly toward them, eyes squeezing open and shut.

"Jesse?" she asked with more alarm. "Can you?"

There were shattered pieces of tree limbs and bark everywhere in the yard, under the apple trees. He found one with twig-ends coming out in a few directions like a rake. When he returned he saw she'd managed to shake the wasp out from the underlayers of her hair—there it was though, still knotted and moving its wings. "Lean more," he said, and as she swung lower, a half-moon of her belly showing, he slipped the stick in. He brushed once, then again more firmly, and with a motorized droning like the woman's car invisible at the end of the drive-way, the wasp went awkwardly up, right at him and then in a circle around them, heavy with rage and bombing in closer until it was caught in a breeze and blown off.

She shook her head, scratching her fingers in her hair. "God," she said, then took his wrist firmly in her cold, chapped hand, the skin tough against his. "Thanks. I owe you." Her eyes were pink at the edges too, glazed and worn-looking, wider than usual, and he knew without her saying that it was for the same reason the other woman's had been, speeding away. They'd fin-ished with each other again—were always finishing with each other one way or another. She'd told him before. He didn't ask about it or mention he'd seen the woman on her way down. Together they replaced what had spilled from the overturned gardening cart and went with it around to the other side of the house, where he sat against a stone and she scratched lime and fertilizer through the soil and dug in seeds. And when he'd been there too long to know how to bring it up anymore without its seeming wrong or too awkward, she glanced once at him and smiled. She didn't stop what she was doing. "If you felt like stay-ing tonight, I'd be happy for the company," she said.

He nodded. "I don't got any homework."

"Have." Still squatting she moved a few steps to his right, Keds grating in the dirt. "*Have* any homework." She pointed.

"Can you . . . ?" she asked, and before she could finish, he was handing her the thing she needed.

Many times, he's heard how she fell in love with building and fixing violins. It was her father's interest as well—hack tinkerer and old-time Ohio fiddler; he owned several fiddles ("Gourds, all of them," she says)—and together, each summer, they'd mix a batch of new varnish: pine tar, spirits, floor paint or urethane, bull's blood, lemon juice, sometimes their own urine. They'd strip the fiddles and slop them over, coat upon coat, and hang them in the yard to dry. Each fiddle was rigged with a red thread leashed to its sound post, too, so her father could easily make adjustments for tone as seasons changed and wood shifted or shrank. "That was my favorite part," she always says. "I'd be on one side of the room and he'd be on the other, and then he'd tug a little on that red thread, like he was fishing, and play some more and ask me to describe what I heard—whether I liked it better or worse. To me it was just like magic, how you could do that." Once she and her father soaked a violin overnight in a mixture of beer and salt and another time baked one in the oven at a low heat for a day. And inside most of his fiddles were charms and trinkets of some kind—rattlesnake rattles, Genny's baby teeth, dried parts of chickens and lizards. All of this she'll recount, different bits and pieces, when she's signing a new customer and wants to emphasize the essential mystery of violin-making and her own lifelong connection with the magic of them.

The night she finishes work on the red fiddle, two days after Verlinda's visit, Jesse slips into her shop to play it and see how any of the changes she's made will affect its sound. He knows the varnish on the touched-up shoulder will need another day or two to fully cure, though this shouldn't make a difference. On its back, in the cone of light from her work lamp and fully assembled, it's still not the prettiest violin he's seen—blunt, fat-cheeked scroll and clumsy f-holes, the neck protruding stark white from its red-painted heel button. He strokes a finger up from the f-hole to the refinished wood to feel if there's any shift in texture to correspond with the patch of new finish, but there's none. Genny has matched it exactly, sugary-coarse and overlaying the thick grain of the wood like a second skin. He lifts and sniffs it and puts his mouth over the f-hole, blowing once into the wood, then slips the instrument under his chin. The chin rest warms instantly to the temperature of his skin, tail-gut sticking slightly, catching against his stubble. He taps his fingers up and down the new fingerboard, a wave of feeling like love or lust, like what he used to feel touching Michelle, mounting in his chest (again the radiant sound of his fingers knocking on the strings), and he remembers what Genny's always told him about violins having a gender: "Every violin is a sex," she's said. "And the best violins, the best of *all* violins, are both sexes at once—male and female, one in the other. Equally balanced. You can hear it." He never understood, though until now he'd always considered that was probably because of something lacking in him—some way he was not smart enough or a good enough player or well enough experienced. Now he sees she is plain wrong. A violin is a violin, each one assembled and shaped more or less imperfectly to mirror and contain any player's soul. And this violin—he feels it in his wrist and throat and collarbone, as if the understanding were coming through the fiddle and no part of his own will or imagination—this violin is *his*. It's meant for him to play. He's never felt as strongly about an instrument before.

He crosses from the workbench to Genny's safe for a bow, noticing as he passes the peeling fake-leather case he saw Verlinda carrying up the walkway, now stored on the floor under Genny's other workbench. He bends and draws it out and squats to open it, thinking at first he's only doing this to find out more about her. Inside the case is purple-lined, with a snap-down strip of heavy velour to cover the violin's neck and strings and anchor it in the bottom of the case; there are twin bow slots in the top, the ribbon backing for each sagging and dusty with old rosin. Under the ill-fitting lid of the storage compartment is a grooved rosin cake and a silver tuning fork, a bridge, and some shattered bits of rosin like melted glass stuck to the velour. He carries it back to the workbench and slips the fiddle in to see how well it will fit—snaps the halves of the covering cloth together and shuts the case. Perfect. The metal in the handle has begun wearing through the fake leather and cardboard of its grip, so, carrying it, his hand slips toward the butt of the case, its front end bumping his knee. He circles the room once, looking out through the windows to see if anyone is watching. *My fiddle,* he thinks. *This is my fiddle. It's my time now to have it.*

On his way out he pauses to set the thermostat and the alarm, kill the overhead lights, and lock up. The violin in one hand and damp night air welling around him, he crosses the yard to his truck. *I could turn around and put it back now,* he thinks; *she'd never know.* But he can't, or won't. He leans in through the passenger's side window and wedges the violin down behind the seat, atop his tools and the spare extension cords and two flashlights that no longer work.

The heat wave breaks, and for the first time since his arrival, it's cool enough to sleep without air-conditioning; every window in the house has been left open—crickets, cicadas, freeway noise blowing through the rooms. He falls in and out of sleep, dreams that are mostly shallow or hazy reconfigurations of his waking thoughts; the seven hundred dollars from his savings, banded in a wad with his note to Genny paper clipped to it (*Please give this to Verlinda + tell her I am sorry*), pressing lightly through his front T-shirt pocket and reminding him. Toward dawn he dreams he's pulling a sled with a woman's head on it over hills at home, through stands of snowy trees and yellow grass. The head keeps talking to him, scolding him and giving advice. The blue skin in her eye sockets and the hair wrapped at the torn root of her neck are too distracting, and he can never focus on what she's saying. He's lucid enough to wonder why it's perfectly natural for her to be speaking to him like this, without the rest of her body, but it doesn't stop the dreaming.

Just before light he wakes and moves his stuff to the middle of the living room floor; the money and note for her he leaves in the cup full of pens on her desk. She'll find it later today, maybe tomorrow. *Time now,* he thinks and goes back to her bedroom, pushing open the door with a finger and entering. Her window shades scrape in with the breeze and back out, and he drops to one knee beside her, leaning through her heat and the smell of her hair and sleep.

"I was going to just leave a note," he says, "but I thought— better not. Better say something too."

She shifts, shrinking into the bed, then turns on her side facing him, an arm up to support her head. "You're going?"

As his eyes adjust he sees more and more of her—light from the hallway on her neck and bare chest. Her chin. Her eyes flashing open and shut. "Only a few days—a week, maybe . . ."

"Just like that? You can't say where?"

He draws another breath, the smell of her settling in his throat now so it's hard to think about anything else. "Sure. It's somewhere like almost to Jackson. Mississippi."

"That friend of your mother's."

"Right."

He drops his other knee, and at the same time she rolls back, arms lifted. "Hug?" she asks, and before he can answer there's the pressure of her hands, one on his shoulder, the other at the back of his neck, and he falls forward, her forehead cool against his cheek a moment and hair catching in his eyelashes. "Don't say too much," she says. "Remember that. Mention your

mother as little as possible, and don't ask for favors unless you
have to." She sighs. "And don't tell anyone when they're playing
out of tune, even if they ask—all right?—you've got ears, but no
one loves a show-off. It's unappealing. Just keep your mouth
shut and play." She breathes once under him, and he exhales
with it, the muscles along his spine relaxing. "You'll be all right,"
she says, and then for a moment he's almost not sure what's
happening—if it's her mouth or the velvet heat of her breath
enveloping his ear. There's a noise like water moving, like being
underwater, and then he's sure; her tongue pushes into him,
sensation flooding his neck with it and beating into his groin as
she nuzzles in behind his ear almost to the welted skin at his jaw
line, sucking; then the stinging soundless pressure of her teeth
on him. He feels turned over and floating outside himself,
sparkle patterns through his eyelids and an extra heart in the
soles of his feet. "Mmm," she says, "this isn't a dream, is it? It's
really you," and the magnified sound of her voice echoes in his
head. Another swish and air rushes over him cold until her
hands cup him, one on each ear, and she draws him down again
kissing his chin and throat now, sawing into his neck in the fold
where the fiddle connects. He opens a hand on her stomach and
lowers it until his fingertips brush the soft skin at her waistline.
"No," she whispers. She's shaking her head too, he can feel it, but
he wants the points of her hips—has to have them under his
palm and between his fingers now. "No," she says again, "Jesse,
stop it. That's not—I wasn't inviting you to do that." Her voice
sounds higher—pressed out of her from his weight, sing-songy

and almost childlike. He lifts himself and comes back down again, through her arms, which push and thrash halfheartedly at him. The heel of her hand butts up against his chin, and he moves one way, then another to avoid it, then down again on top of her—the whole of him flat on her finally. "Jesse, no." She writhes a moment, laughs once—"Get *off* already"—and again her mouth closes on him, this time her teeth dragging harder against him, through the skin almost, and he jerks back.

There's a silence, and he gets to his feet, rubbing his wet ear with the sleeve of his shirt and thumping once at the side of his head to clear it. There are the crisp sounds of the world again, his feet on the floorboards, and the shades sucking in and out of the windows. He breathes the sweet early daylight air and lifts his arms slightly until he can feel it on his belly, the wetness in his shorts too, burning as it touches and attaches against his skin.

"I realize that wasn't entirely your fault, but you know . . . You fucked up kid. You know how wrong that was? Never ever ever ever ever force yourself on a woman. Jeez." He hears her scratching a finger in her hair, and there's a thump as she straightens one leg against the mattress. "Do you understand?" She hunches toward him, rocking, a foot in her palm and light from the hall on her legs and shoulders, on the white sheets and blankets around her. "It can't happen again."

"No," he says. "It won't." He starts obediently for the door.

"Wait just a minute." Behind him he hears sheets whipping back and bedsprings bouncing, a zipper, her shoes dropping to the floor. "I'll see you outside—get you some coffee for the road. You'll need coffee." She snaps up one shade, and dawn light fills the room.

"Thanks. Think I'd rather just go."

"Let me at least see you outside."

The dew-wet grass and mist hanging low, all the smells in the cooler wet air are like home—early summer with apple and pear blossoms and thin pale grass. They slide his guitar and clothing under the orange tarp in the truck bed, weighting it with rope and a bucket of nails. The other instruments he'll carry with him in front. "You're still welcome here any time at all, Jesse, in spite of that, whatever you want to call it . . . what just happened," she says. "I hope you know," and he nods with her, leaning against the side of the truck. "In a way, I suppose it's unusual it didn't happen sooner, right?—but, that said, I think we both can agree a sexual relationship just is not in our future. You're too young, I'm way too demanding, our kids would be freaks, your mother would kill me—should I keep going?"

He laughs, shakes his head, and kicks his sneaker toe into the ground to prevent her coming any nearer or seeing into the cab of the truck.

"All right then. No hard feelings?"

Together they go around to the driver's side and he climbs in, clangs the door shut, and starts up. As the engine warms he cranks down his window, and for a moment they hang together, both her arms around one of his shoulders and his hand in the textureless warmth of her hair. Then he leans back and gears into reverse, still watching her. The windshield is streaked with condensation, and the air in the cab is stale, warmer than he'd anticipated, vinyl stiff and cold against him, fast food wrappers on the floor, lifting their smells through the oil and road dust and gasoline.

He taps once on the horn, waves, and backs toward the street. When he looks again she's still there at the end of the drive, arms crossed, one lifted now and waving. Then she ducks her head and walks a few steps up the drive, stooping for the paper. Puzzlingly, all his feelings for her seem intact and unchanged: a muddle of likes and dislikes, confused longing. The front door slaps shut behind her, he can almost hear it, and he swings onto the road and up the hill to Broadway and past the Shoney's, to I-40 west. He has all the lanes to himself, the sun low behind him on the horizon at first, then bloating up gold and red in his rearview mirror. In a while there are hills but still no real mountains. Sandy rivers and knots of deciduous trees and stubby softwoods he doesn't know the names for, bare humps of marble and granite gleaming between them in the shadows. The highway rises and falls, cutting away steeply at times and curving for the tops of passes. The air is sweetly charged with the higher elevation. A whole new world, he thinks, dropping a hand behind his seat and leaning up until he touches the shoulder of the red fiddle's case—like home, but not.

(e)–II

A child's wagon, tricycle, and other toys lie scattered up the walk, too small to distinguish from where Jesse's stopped, the house itself half-hidden under broad-leafed trees and weedy brush growing almost as high as the windows. On the porch is a bowed boxlike couch and two lawn chairs, torn seat webbing moving in the breeze. Tarpaper, made to look like brick or stone siding, pulls from the walls. There's no movement behind any of the windows and nothing visible through the front screen door, which hangs crookedly outside its frame. He eases the clutch up, inching forward, still trying to see inside. Around the other corner of the house is a shed with front-closing doors and a rutted track leading through weeds to it. From the oil stains burned into the grass, he guesses it's more for parking than access. There's no vehicle in sight.

Sweat trickles into the corner of one eye. He stops, pulls the truck out of gear, and clamps the emergency brake set; wipes his forehead and eyes with the sleeve of his shirt, then wipes again and sticks an arm out, instantly withdrawing it at the touch of burning door metal. Again he checks the numbers on his slip of paper against the numbers nailed to the front porch post. He looks up and down the road at the houses like this one, each on its overgrown, weed-choked lot. A dog barks, and somewhere in the distance a car moves toward him, subsonic bass noise wavering in the stillness and hollowing back again. Wind rattles in the trees and grass and blows hot through the windows of his truck, bringing a smell of burned meat and kerosene, laundry, and something else blandly rotten. Inside the front door now he sees a face—the outlines of a man's nose and cheeks, eyes like his own looking out. Next there's a flash of movement, white behind the screen, and the door begins falling forward and out to one side. Jesse lurches from the shoulder, still watching in his rearview mirror until he sees him again: definitely him, out in the middle of the road with one hand over his eyes, the other at his hip like a cowboy ready to draw. His legs and midsection ripple wide with the mirage, white T-shirt, head, and bare arms.

All the way to the frontage road he's jittery, thinking he'll see him again back there. He catches his own reflection in the rearview mirror too—eyes cut thin and mouth flat. Sweat films his forehead and pearls around his lips. He looks away and back again, wondering. Ahead of him the freeway splits out its on-ramps. *North*, he thinks, and draws the map closer on the seat beside him. He watches the signs and flips his turn signal, accelerating, thinking only *north* and *Highway Fifty-five*, every nerve in his body alert. Only later it hits him: twelve years, finally he knows where the man is. He slaps his hand once on the wheel and leans into the bright heat through the glass.

Later that afternoon he's at the counter of a Huddle House restaurant. The men seated beside him—one in gray polyester slacks and two in jumpsuits off a work-crew, one of whom breathes through a plug in his throat—smoke while they eat; the smoke burns in Jesse's eyes, though he's glad enough to be in air-conditioning he hardly notices. He takes his time eating—shriveled wedges of French toast that flatten to nothing under his fork and a pool of grits with salty bacon. He alternates between sips of coffee and sour ice water, watching the cook at work—how he ladles in the grease and cracks eggs into steel cups, one-handed, unpacking meat patties from wax paper wrappers right onto the griddle, occasionally pausing to poke back his glasses on the bridge of his nose or twist together a few brown fingers in the egg-stained rag hanging from his back pocket. *There's a job for you,* he thinks, the way Genny might say it, disdain inlaid with concern and sympathy. Sunlight burns in the dirty window glass by the two empty booths nearest the doorway, and he thinks of summer at home—his mother, the lake, the boat, Michelle. It's all impossibly far away, and he tries eavesdropping on some of the conversation going on next to him to distract himself from this—to imagine how each of these men has a life here, but there's nothing familiar in what they say or how they say it. The man in gray slacks nods, returning Jesse's look. Jesse nods back. Next, the man says something with exaggerated irony, ending on the word *thank* and then laughs as if the two of them were in on something. "Yeah, man," Jesse says and goes back to eating.

In the Kroger across the lot Jesse pushes a cart aimlessly around the aisles, sweat freezing under his arms and in his hair. He takes items from shelves and replaces them again—Genny's conditioners and shampoo, her brand of frozen chicken breasts, ears of corn, bags of puffed cheese, his mother's favorite kind of boxed cruller. He feels better and worse doing this, connected with them and reminded how far away they are, and annoyed with himself for caring. *Alone, alone, alone . . .* he thinks in time with his footsteps up and down the aisles. And then, almost as if the force of his thinking had caused him to materialize, there in the aisle for Bread/Cookies/Baked Goods is a man just like his father in faded jeans and a blue dress shirt. The man tips up one snakeskin boot on its heel, leg out straight as if on display. His hair is mashed in places as if he'd recently gotten out of bed. Wrong lips, Jesse thinks, before he realizes what he's doing—who he's comparing the man with. Also the way his nose pinches to one side. Closer now, their eyes meet, and the man lets his glasses fall on a string going around his neck. They are the same as his father's eyes, though—smoke-gray, dreamy, and always that questioning affection in them: *Don't you like me? Don't you like me? Well, too bad.* The man puts a loaf of bread in his cart and turns. His boot heels hit confidently against the linoleum.

Jesse watches after him and wonders if it will be the last time he makes this mistake.

That evening Jesse returns. The toys and wagon have shifted from the walk up onto the porch, and the tricycle is nowhere in sight. He leans at the mailbox, scratching a foot in the dirt. He's certain no one's home. More than the cumulative detail— the silence and darkened windows, no car at the side of the house—he feels it like the imprint of something under his skin: no one's here. Light drops lower under the horizon, and he chews the inside of his mouth, wiping sweat from his face with the corners of his T-shirt. Headlights swing toward him and away again, the sound of tires following, magnified in the stillness.

Up the walk the smells intensify—wet earth, weeds and grass, cooling house smells. The porch floorboards boom and shiver under his feet, and he slips in behind the couch, leaning to the window to see inside, both hands up for shade. But the sun is too strong behind him still, and he can hardly make out a thing through his own dust-raked reflection. He turns again with a hand on the back of the couch.

Everything here is part of his father's life: the peeling porch posts and porch floorboards humped toward the middle; the walkway surprisingly white and unsplit running out through weeds and grass to the road; the sagging lawn chairs and two milk crates of toys by the doorway, one pink, one white—plastic action dolls with faces rubbed bare, a tiny glove, and a card-board citadel, two cloth Raggedy Anns, a stuffed duck, a rabbit, swimming goggles, other things he can't identify. *Whose?* he wonders.

He gazes past the porch posts to the adjacent lot, the under-growth there broken through in places by machinery—tire tracks in red-brown dirt. *His house,* he thinks. *Dad's house.* He tries picturing it that way—himself as his father, looking out, a drink or an ashtray on his leg and a guitar beside him, its neck wedged in the cushions; in his head, electric guitar distortion and horns and a voice singing out of time—something like what he's been hearing lately on the country radio stations. He has no idea what his father might want to listen to or play any-more.

Again, he presses to the window, both hands up for shade, and this time he sees in: green carpet, white-topped metal kitchen table, woodstove disconnected and missing one leg, braided rag rug on the linoleum hearth. Beside the table is a blond Hondo guitar, a mini practice amp, and a cutaway, arch-top Gretsch. A poster of a man wrestling a snake hangs above the table—he can't make out the caption. His breath bounces back in his face, steaming the glass, and he keeps moving aside to see better. He's not sure why he's doing this or what he expects to find here, but there's something he wants badly and would like to destroy—maybe the wanting itself.

Around the side of the house he swims through bushes that whip his neck and bare arms. Leaves stick to him, and branches poke at him painfully. He's surprised to discover the house sits on a foundation, not concrete pilings, unlike most houses he's seen down here. The cement is damp and flaking and bears a faint odor of decay. There's even a cellar, he sees, its hatchway lashed shut with an iron cord like a bicycle lock, ends attached through a combination padlock. He steps up and bounces once lightly to be sure, and then bends to force his way under some low-hanging tree limbs and across. Before he can take his next step there's a crunch of wood splitting, and he's thrown down, half falling, half stumbling against the plank steps, grabbing out to catch himself, one wrist hitting broken boards. Another moment and he's on his ass, looking up at the patch of sky and branches where he fell through. He can't get a breath and something's fallen across his legs—the worn grip of a rake or hoe, he realizes, thrusting it away. There's the musty, rank smell of unfinished cellar and a pipe dripping somewhere in the silence behind him.

He gets up on his knees, squeezing his wrist to feel how badly it's hurt, then lifts himself to a standing position and shuffles in a few steps farther. The darkness lifts a notch as his eyes adjust, and he makes out the shapes of some things—a stack of windows against one wall, a holding tank or furnace, and high shelves loaded with junk. "Dad," he says. He limps in a circle, feeling walls for a light switch, kicking over objects, and blinking hard against the darkness that seeps up from the floor, enclosing him on all sides. The sun must have gone fully under the ridge now, or is about to, and not much daylight will remain. If he turns away from the hatchway, he can't make out anything. He flaps a hand in front of his face and rolls his eyes into his sockets until he sees the familiar white flash of his nerves and colors inside his eyelids again—black-flecked amber and rose. Then it occurs to him: no one will know he's here. His truck's parked far enough away—no one will suspect it. He's not in any danger. He can wait, listen, and watch, observe things unknown, once his father returns. When the moon rises, maybe he'll see better.

He makes his way back to the hatchway, settles on the lowest step, legs outstretched, and after a while eases down off that, lying back into the dark of the cellar, an arm upcurled to support his head, waiting. Warm air comes in gusts down the stairwell and over his legs. The sink drips. Bats whip in and out of the darkness—he sees them through the tangle of tree limbs and undergrowth above.

There must be something he can go back through, beginning to end—something good to think about that will take him out of the darkness, pass the time, and maybe let him sleep. *Sleep,* he thinks, and warmth tingles in his neck. He remembers Genny's mouth on him—the enveloping softness and how it had made him feel as if he were no longer himself, only an ear, a heart beating, her breath blowing in and out. And suddenly there's music in his head, too—an old-time tune he can't place right off. Something Dix must have shown him years ago that he hasn't played much since. There's the familiar knot of high notes repeating at the close of the first section—how good those notes always felt in the tendons of his first and second fingers, hard and bright over the quick four chord, their quirky logic and the way the rest of the tune seemed to ravel out of it; then the second part of the form, all double-stops in D and A and the final dissonances leading home again to G. "Fiddler's Dream," that was it. Another name had come with it, older and Irish, and there were different versions he'd liked—Benny Martin's, Lyman Enloe's, somebody else's.

The music vanishes, and he's back where he was—pipe dripping, musty cellar smell. He tries picturing Bill Monroe at the microphone, chopping a G chord, and thinks back to the first time he ever saw the man play, live. It was at the New Hampshire State Fair, and he was about twelve years old, with Genny. Monroe never said a word to the men he played with, yet they always seemed to know what he wanted, when to move in to the mic and sing or play a run of notes. At times it was so clear, Jesse could make out the hiss of Baker's bow on the strings and his fingers bumping the fingerboard; Wayne Lewis's picks bouncing against the strings, banjo notes drifting around everything like shiny cut jewels. Monroe would turn stiffly one way or another, smiling, and always they'd give him what he wanted. It was the most spontaneous and measured interplay among men Jesse had ever seen. When Monroe raised the neck of his mandolin to chop out the last chords of a song, they all went with him, driving down to the last beats of the measure.

Afterward, Jesse remembers, there was a rainstorm. He and Genny had gone to stand outside the tape marking the back-

stage area where Monroe's bus was parked, sharing an umbrella and waiting to catch a glimpse of him, maybe even to ask for
an autograph, and for the first time Jesse had thought of his
father—the signed pictures of him his mother still kept around
the house in spite of herself, and the way his father had always
drawn loopy circles to dot his *i*'s, sometimes big enough the circle was like a whole separate letter. Phrases he'd written her:
Your always in my heart and *Best baby in the world* and *All my
dreams in you, all my dreams come true . . .* He'd felt a pang of
longing and loneliness then—an ache in his gut like he wished
to speak about this with Genny, though he was pretty sure he
shouldn't. Then there was a knocking sound, the bus door
opening, and Bill Monroe stepped down into the mud. Even in
the dull rainy air he seemed somehow lit from within. A deep
lungful of air and he bent to address a child in a yellow slicker
who'd slipped the tape and run up to him. "Go," Genny kept
whispering. "Go talk to him!" But Jesse couldn't move. The rain
fell, splashing up mud and dotting Monroe's blue suit jacket
and running in a stripe like a string of beads from his hat brim.
Impossible to read the dim-sighted expression behind those
glasses when his gaze finally swept their way a moment; then his
almost prissy way of handling a pen, tapping it against the
record jacket the girl in the slicker had given him to sign, and
signing it.

     With some defiance now Jesse thinks of his mother's
advice—not the words for it, but the stricken, adamant look on
her face as she said them, and the anger beneath, always point-

ing the words through themselves to other meanings: *Don't place your ideals in another human being. It's the worst and most pitiful mistake.* Even then he'd known she was mostly lying. Pick someone better, is what she'd really meant: pick someone worthy, more righteous or reliable.

Again, he pictures Monroe at the microphone, chopping the G chord. He says something quick and muttered about their next number, and Kenny Baker swings to the mic, his right wrist flicking out and back: "Can't You Hear Me Calling?" The bass notes plunk and slap, holding down the tonic against the dissonant suspensions in Monroe's vocal at the chorus. Jesse's skin prickles with it, and then the applause. And as soon as that one finishes, there's another, and another—he remembers almost the entire set—"It's Mighty Dark to Travel," "Close By," "Columbus Stockade Blues," "Monroe's Blues." His breaths slow and steady, and he slips into sleep.

Later, he doesn't know how long, a thud somewhere overhead brings him to—pipes clanging, water rushing, and a water meter clicking. Next, voices surprisingly near, a man's, then a woman's, and light prongs into the cellar, accompanied by sounds of something falling—laundry piling through a chute, more like a hole in the ceiling, and onto the battered top of a washing machine. Moments later the light flashes again, quicker this time and closer than he'd figured. More laundry. There's the snap of a door shutting and blackness. In the afterburn, images settle against his retina: shelf here, furnace there, ancient ragged recliner. There's light enough to maneuver by, coming through the hatchway behind him. He stands and goes slowly back through the darkness toward the recliner, hands extended; a step, another step, and his shins bump it—the chair rocks, squawking—and he lowers himself into its prickling, mildew-smelling shape.

They had not always lived on the mountain. There was another house he used to remember and against which he must have measured his perceptions for a time. He feels this in the back of his mind without seeing or assigning words yet, know-ing only that it's always been there—always this thing floating just outside whatever else he remembers from childhood. He pictures his bed at home, tree shadows swaying over the walls and the feeling something had been lost.

Floorboards squeeze and there's a rapid clattering noise—a woman speaking. More footsteps approach. Floorboards buck-le and bounce alarmingly, right over him, the sound of tired, prolonged laughter beyond that. Dimly, too, he can make out music—banjo or piano and someone singing. Again the clatter-ing noise bowling over him and a woman's voice exclaiming, "Oh!" and then "Joey! Joey!" The music continues, and floor-boards cry out. Someone's foot taps half-rhythmically. Without music to understand it, the sound is weirdly insistent, a pushy scratching noise like something caged. There's a crash, and the floorboards continue bouncing, and suddenly he under-stands—can almost see it right through the blackness above him: they're dancing. His father and some woman like his mother. He stares up, trying to feel the sounds on his skin, through his breath and face bones so he can anticipate—know what's coming next. But the details won't coalesce as with sight.

Now he remembers the room they'd all three lain in together: the pale carpet that prickled his skin and the sounds blowing through open porch doors on air that was familiarly wet and left a leafy, mildew smell over everything. His father's lips were beaked and frail pink despite their coarseness on him—always swooping in huge and tickling, covering his belly and shaping sounds he knew he was meant to feel something for but only heard. He remembers their reflections in the window at night too—his mother younger, in a white skirt and vest and calf-high boots and his father on the couch. The object his father has in his lap keeps driving her out of the room, its threads and points of sound pushing her from him. But he loves it, and Jesse loves his fingers for the way they move on it, their square ends and blue veins and the muscles in the backs of his hands and forearms. Now she returns, standing close beside his father and resting a hand on his shoulder, a different sound coming from her throat—one not meant to communicate with either of them, he supposes, because of the way it moves without their looking at each other or at him. But this is less clear, and he thinks he might be making it up: the bored tilt of her hips, one leg crossed behind the other, and the way her mouth makes the sounds without recognizing what they are or caring how they fit. She's angry because she wants the man to herself. She sings with him only as another way of having him. And at the end, when she reaches to tousle his hair and he leans from her, almost quick enough, almost far enough to escape the touch, Jesse feels that too. His father wants her not so near.

Meanwhile his father goes on playing. Eventually she comes back to stand before him, a hand at her waist, swaying with the music. She lowers herself over him and tugs him to his feet and walks with him to the next room. All this Jesse can envision, though he's no longer sure if he's remembering or making it up. Only his father's rhapsodic attention there on the couch, play-ing—his half-sleeping eyes, head falling forward and back, mumbling and feeling for the notes, the words, fingers stirring over the sound hole, and strings sticking under his skin with a sound like words—that much he's sure of.

Next comes another memory, not from the last time he saw his father, though often enough he's thought of it like that: his father in his mother's bedroom, packing to leave, again. Instead of his usual Stetson, he wears a new felt hat like a gangster hat, low-brimmed, black, and crushed back from his forehead. He moves quickly around the room, gathering what's his, clothing from the floor, the closet, things out of drawers. He sniffs shirts and socks and crumples them into the duffel bag on the bed, humming under his breath. His eyes narrow as he scans the room for whatever's left, too absorbed to notice Jesse just out-side the doorway, shivering in his pajamas. Occasionally, catch-ing his own reflection in the dresser mirror, his father will pause to examine himself from different angles in the new hat. He never smiles, and his eyes don't linger long enough to suggest real pleasure, Jesse thinks, only a kind of relief, as if he'd been unsure, in the moments between looking, if he still existed. He crams and rearranges the things in his duffel, turns from the mirror a final time, and begins tugging together the zippers. Jesse watches. His father's shirt rides up from under his belt, showing the muscles and slim white hollow of his back, his spine, his wallet pressing into its faded square outline in the back pocket of his jeans.

The music is louder overhead, floorboards scraping and popping, the man shouting to be heard. Something's changed in whatever is happening up there, and it's time now for him to leave. His scalp prickles with the knowledge of this, and the skin along his shoulders and neck. He stumbles upright, goes quickly to the hatchway. One side of its covering still hangs in place, leaning precariously inward; the other is fully broken through. He goes carefully past this and up, moving aside broken boards. Hot night air blows over him again with the sounds of insects, voices, and wind in the trees. Fireflies stitch light in and out of the darkness. He picks his way back through the underbrush and out.

No one is dancing. A heavyset, light-skinned black woman leans in the kitchen doorway with her arms crossed, a bottle of beer hanging between her fingers. She appears to be pacing in place, lifting her weight foot to foot in time with the music and singing. From the way her eyes move against her eyelids, throat muscles tensing, Jesse knows it's her voice on the recording as well—she feels the notes too closely for it not to be. "Praising, praising, praising," she sings. A tight knit shirt shows the folds of her stomach and flattens her breasts to her ribcage. At the table two men sit, one with a waxed black mustache, wearing T-shirt and jeans, the other similarly dressed but red-haired, with freckles covering his face and forearms. The red-haired man shuffles a deck of cards hand to hand and pops one foot up and down with the music. He's wearing old white sneakers. The man with the mustache seems midargument with someone, although no one is countering him or demanding an explanation for most of what he says—his voice rises and falls, winding to its points, accompanied by hand gestures. The woman occasionally drops her eyes at him, nodding, then retreats to singing.

From somewhere deeper in the house, Jesse hears a child shrieking—pleasure or terror, he can't say—and suddenly the kid runs out, hard-soled red shoes skittering over the floor. She lands between the woman's legs, an arm around each thigh, and the woman drops a hand to touch her between the shoulder blades, not looking, still singing. The way the hand hangs there, crooked and immobile, Jesse guesses despite her singing the woman doesn't play an instrument. The girl is not crying or laughing; her eyes are pure reckless excitement and something else—something not exactly right. Opening his arms to her suddenly, the red-haired man exclaims, "Joey, Joey!" and she runs at him, shrieking as he lifts her and swings her around and drops her to her feet again.

At the other side of the room, now a man stands, one hand

in the small of his back, the other up to support his neck, fingers tugging at a mess of silver-black curls. Even before he turns so Jesse can be sure, he knows it's him—knows from the shape of his arms and shoulders and that way of standing, everything about him. His waist is huge now and his gut swollen under his T-shirt in a way Jesse would never have imagined. He turns to catch the girl and carry her out of the room, and Jesse glimpses him full on—same hooded gray eyes and narrow pocked chin. It's as if the extra fat had skipped his head, stranding his face in time and out of proportion with the rest of him. The girl's legs go around him, and he's absorbed, talking and gesturing to her as he carries her back out of the room, never looking in Jesse's direction. And as soon as he's gone, Jesse heads down the walk and through the adjacent lot to his truck. Here he leans with a hand in the door window, a hand on his knee, vomiting every last mouthful of Huddle House grits and bacon and French toast and water, the dirty hot sunlight in the restaurant window, too, streaming through him, up his throat, and into the underbrush.

It's too hot to sleep, and all night there's noise from a neighboring campsite—hooting laughter and bottles clinking. The air is so dense he can hardly feel where his body is in it. His legs ache up to the small of his back. Blood squeezes in his wrist like a weight. *This isn't real,* he thinks, *not the real world.* He lunges upright and after a moment lies back again, still as he can, covered in sweat, arms outspread, sticking to the floor of his tent.

He remembers (can't get it out of his head) the trees off to the side of the highway coming back here from his father's; how strange they'd seemed to him, growing right up out of the swamp on roots like stilts, the black water in them reflecting his headlights. He flips over and over, and every time he's drifting off there they are again—those trees with the water in them and the roots clinging down, bonelike, not floating. *What am I doing here?* he thinks. *Why?* and tries to calm himself, picturing his truck and the highway back to Genny's. He can leave whenever he wants. He's not stuck here.

Outside his tent he stands a while, glaring through the darkness where the noise comes from. It's no cooler here than inside his tent; now he's out of it, though, he can't imagine getting back in. He'll never sleep, never feel good there; what's the point?

Back to the shower house for another cold soak and another refill on his water bottle. But within moments of stepping out of the shower he's sweaty again, hating the mildew, Pine-Sol, and backed up sewage smell of the shower house. Moths batter the windows or just rest there, wings unfolded against the screens. He hurries out without drying, towel around his neck, sneakers clopping against his bare heels. Heads for the telephones at the far side of the building and picks the one closest to the path with the most light. Here he crouches on a metal and plastic folding chair, leaning up slightly so the phone cord will reach.

A good sign. She picks up on the third ring. So he hasn't

woken her; she may not be too drunk. She accepts the charges—he hears the interchange between her and the operator; anticipates, with some wonder, the ways her voice will change as soon as the operator is gone.

"Jesse?" she says. She's out of breath, maybe on the verge of tears. Half in the bag. "Jesse, it's really you?"

"Yes, Mama."

"Tell me you know how much your old ma misses you. Tell me that's what you're calling for."

"Yeah. I wanted to make sure you're all right. You're all right?"

"Oh, Jesse. You know how much I miss you?"

Heat clenches in his underarms, and sweat tickles along his scalp. His father would have felt something like this—would have called her and heard these words and not known how to respond. Briefly, he remembers: *It's your daddy on the phone. Tell him how much we miss him. Say he should come home soon and see us.*

"Of course. But I'm not dead, Ma. I'm right here. I haven't *gone* anywhere."

"You don't miss me?"

"I'm homesick to death half the time. You know that. But I couldn't just sit around forever, right? I had to come to Nashville and find out—you know, play with some people."

"I thought you'd . . . I thought you were off in that hell-hole, the swamps of the Mississippi Delta."

"How'd you hear about that?"

"Oh, Genny—I called and she said you'd gone, but she didn't know where to exactly. We put two and two together, her and I. Sort of figured it out. You should have heard. All this time—she thought you were in Nashville to make money and get famous and didn't realize it was all about your father. Why didn't you tell her? It's just beyond me how you can . . ."

"Mama, I *am* there for the music. And it's none of her business what I do." He wonders whatever possessed him to make this call. Longing for clarity, maybe. Loneliness. But he should know by now that asking his mother for clarification is like sticking a flashlight in a lunatic's hands. You might get random flashes of something useful, no saying what or when or how. You might not see anything at all.

"Don't worry, honey. She's not upset. Not in the least. She said you might have had some kind of a misunderstanding. None of my business, I figured. It couldn't be the sex though—not between her and her so-called lesbianism and you never caring half as much for anyone as that damn music. But all's forgiven. Those were her words. All's forgiven, and you should call her as soon as you're able . . ."

"I will." He leans an elbow into the shelf under the phone, switches hands, and tips his chin up a little higher, winding the phone cord around a finger and releasing it. Sighs. Flips the coin release lever down a few times and dips his fingers into the slot.

"Is everything all right, Jesse?"

"It's fine. I just . . . I was calling because I wanted to ask you—you know you said, before, I could have your version of the story after I got Dad's, but I didn't . . . I mean, I guess I'd like to hear that now. Your side of the story."

"You don't like what he's telling you?"

"I haven't spoken to him yet."

"Why ever not?"

"I only just got here. It's like an eight-hour drive from Nashville. I went by the house once, and no one was home."

"He's a *saved* man now, dear, so I'm told. Did you know that? He won't tell you a lie anymore. Insofar as he's able to tell the truth—his truth, anyway—he will be truthful. Has he tried selling you on the Lord much yet?"

"I just told you. I haven't spoken to him."

"Who's to judge?—it could be exactly the right thing for you, like a special father-son thing. A little better sense of life on the spiritual plane never hurt anybody—might even make you a better musician. Lots of musicians, you know, are very religious people—like they're tuned in to a whole other frequency than the rest of us. You need to expect that about him, and do your best to believe him. I don't want to spoil it, telling you anything else—giving you ideas and telling you he's got it all wrong. What he has to say, you need to hear it from him without my influence or say-so. You understand? It's for him to tell you about, not me." He moves the phone from his ear a moment, registering the bug noise again, the zing and crackle of bug zappers in the trees.

"I hear you, Mama. Before Vermont, where did we live? There was another house, right?"

"Your aunt's house in Newburyport?"

"No—that, I remember." Briefly he pictures the high ceilings in the room where he usually slept at his aunt's—the wainscot walls and four-poster bed and windows shut, with the steam making patterns on the glass. "I'm thinking back, like further back than that."

Her voice is distant now. Cooler. "All different houses, Jesse. Your father and you and I, together—we must've moved half a dozen times, you ask *him* about it . . ."

"But what happened? Like why did we go?"

"You were sick, honey, and there was no one to care for you full time. You've heard this before. I had to work, and your father wasn't around. So we went—first to your great aunt's, then to Wendy's in Newburyport. Then here to Vermont."

"But before that, did you and Dad, like, play and sing together? I just—I was trying to remember this."

She breathes into the phone. "We did. For a time. Sure. When we could. You wouldn't remember, though. It's a long, long time ago, and it was never anything much to him, the music—I don't think he was ever taking it seriously anyway. Your musical gift is all from your dad, I'm afraid. Can't claim any responsibility there . . ."

It's the first time he's ever heard her openly refer to it as a gift, and the effect on him is startling. His blood rushes, and he's aware of every molecule in the air around him, as if it were constricting purposefully to contain him and give protection.

"What did you say?"

"I said it's all him—your interests in music."

"My *interests*," he repeats.

"What'd I say something wrong again? Oh—before I forget. Genny wanted me to say—she also wanted me to make sure, if I spoke to you, that you know she's holding your money for you."

"What money?"

"She didn't mention that part. Just said, if you called to make sure you know she's holding your money. All's forgiven, and you're not to think you're in any kind of trouble. You'd best call her so there's no more misunderstanding."

"I'll do that." He stands, gets ready to hang up. "OK, Ma," he says.

A gushing wet breath into the phone, something between a sob and a snort: "I've been trying *real* hard these last few weeks and months to be gracious and courteous, Jesse. Just so you know. I realize I needed to let you go—give you what you want and not stand in your way. But it ain't easy. If you had even the slightest inkling how your actions affect others—Genny, me, Michelle—if you could act as if you cared even the slightest bit about that . . ."

"Please. Michelle could care less."

"You're not listening."

"She dumped me, Mama, like months ago."

"It's not about Michelle, it's about—it's about showing the people who love you a little kindness and respect in return."

"I called you, didn't I? I'm right here talking to you on the phone, aren't I?"

"Your father's words exactly. You be careful, honey—don't get so close to him you become him. It wouldn't be good on you."

"For Christ's sake."

"I'm not saying you will. I'm just saying sometimes I get a little scared, how you're turning out."

"News flash. Tell me something I *didn't* know."

"Just you be careful. That's all I'm saying."

Back at the campsite he kicks out his stakes and collapses the poles, knots the nylon back into its sack, slapping bugs off his neck and bare arms, and throws the tent half-packed into the bed of his truck. Gets in and heads out to the road, bumping fast over the ruts, still enraged, but pleased with the sensation of forward movement. Bugs swarm the headlights and burst over his windshield—moths and June bugs and long-bodied green things with translucent wings. "We'll see what's what," he says aloud. Sings a note or two. *Lack, lack, a-lack a-day, and whack fal the daddy*-o. He has only the dimmest of plans: see the house again, wake him up, club him to death, talk to him, throw himself on him, sing him a song. He doesn't know what. He can't understand what he's driven toward any better than he can understand what's driving him—the complex of pictures and memories and emotions he has no name for except maybe the one word—*lack*—and the fact that it won't let him sleep, won't allow him the release from himself into dreams anymore.

This time he leaves his truck at the end of his father's road and walks in grass at the edge of the gravel to muffle his footfalls. A few houses in, a dog slips from the shadows at him, growling. Some kind of shepherd mix, he thinks, as it comes into the light, black and brown with crooked ears and a pincer-like muzzle. "Easy," he whispers, and "Hey there—hey boy." His hands curl to fists, and sweat burns under his arms, yet he has the presence of mind to keep talking easily, as if he were a Southerner. "Hey, all right. It's all right." The dog edges closer and to one side, and Jesse turns, keeping it in front of him, until suddenly another dog slips from the shadows, this one plumed around the hind legs and friendlier seeming. It goes straight to Jesse to sniff a leg and cowers the moment he lowers a hand to touch it. The dog that had been growling sits abruptly to scratch, stands again, and barks once, hackles still stiff. "Come on," Jesse says firmly. "Come on."

The rest of the way they're with him. They circle ahead and back again, coming out of tree shadows and vanishing, collars jingling. He sings softly in a rhythm with his footsteps and his breaths in and out, and each time one of the dogs reappears in the road ahead, nose twisting to catch a scent, it's like seeing his own voice made material. He stops then, wondering if he whistled or sang a note too loud. "Go on," he says, "go," and waves his arms. He turns back to see his progress, and when he faces forward again the road is empty, moonlight silver on the bushes and undergrowth.

The porch will give him away, so he heads around back,

shadow to shadow, up the drive and past a sedan like a Lincoln, finally crouching in the eaves of the outbuilding at the side of the house to allow his eyes time to adjust. A streetlight from the next road over shines against one windowpane, and there's a swath of shadow he can't see through covering the yard, the moon on its way down over the other side of the house, stretching the shadow closer, thicker toward him. Dimly he makes out some shapes—the back end of a junked car, garbage pails at the side of the house, a lawn chair, a table. He snaps one knuckle, then another and tests his calluses against the edge of a thumbnail. Sweat builds under his hair. He mops it away and stands.

The weeds cling around his ankles, and a few steps before it takes his sight he's covered in the shadow of the house. The earth here feels lumpy and pocked through the soles of his sneakers, and he has to step carefully not to lose his balance. His heart races, and saliva is thick on his tongue, making him want to spit. Something catches under his foot, and he struggles a step, regaining balance, both feet slapping onto concrete now, close enough he can feel heat from the house and hear a fan buzzing somewhere above him. Again he kicks into something and this time falls, palms grating against stone, the kicked thing skittering ahead of him with a coarse end-over-end spinning noise, hollow plastic on concrete. It's a moment before he can match the sound with understanding: of course—the girl's tricycle. He sees it in the shadows now—front wheel cranked at an angle so one pedal almost touches the ground, plastic tassels dangling from the handgrips.

Moving to the side of the house, he hunches along with both hands out in case he should trip again. Here's the window he saw before, from across the yard—his way in. He feels for the sill—one hand, then the other; the window is propped open with a piece of wood, screen sagging, torn and patched with tape, and separating from its frame along the bottom. Just beyond that, inside, is the back shoulder of a couch. Slowly he rips up through the mesh, burst metal ends biting the pads and joints of his fingers, until there's a big enough gap and he can pull himself up headfirst over the sill, inside.

A wire mobile spins overhead, screws and washers and pieces of hammered tin, like a wrecked solar system, though as far as he can tell, the air is not moving. Baseboard safety night-lights glow in two corners of the room, casting pink and orange winglike shadows up the plaster board. Against one wall is the black square of a television screen; against another, a table cluttered with electronic equipment, effects pedals and other junk, a row of amplifiers piled underneath and another bunch of them massed to the side of the table. This must be the room his father emerged from and went back into earlier, carrying the girl. Beyond it and through another doorway is the girl's room, he guesses, from the shadowy mess of toys on the floor and the faint glow of another nightlight. To the left an arched doorway leads into the living room. Through it he sees the table where the men had been sitting, lit from the front window now, and one corner of the doorway where the woman had leaned. He

rolls to his feet, and more baseboard safety lights, motion-
sensitive, flicker on and back off. The floor is strewn with bits
of plastic and wood—game pieces, darts, and parts of a puzzle
or construction set, which prod the soles of his feet as he steps
over and around them.

Mixed in with the electronic equipment on the table is a
pile of small boxes, most of them covered in a foreign scrawl
Jesse can't decipher. He lifts one, blowing away dust and grit.
The thin cardboard compresses easily under his fingers—something bulblike and round inside. Amplifier tubes. *Buying and
selling restoration tube amplifiers,* the man in the recording studio had said all those years ago. Jesse remembers. *What was it he
told me? Some new scheme to get rich and quit the music business
. . . Why don't he sit his ass down and write another God damn
million-dollar song, if that's what he does the best?* From what he
can see, the amplifiers are all different sizes and types, some
without grates, others missing knobs and panels, a few showing
bare wires where a speaker cone should sit. He drops the box
back where he found it and moves away a step, momentarily
disoriented, a memory of something else stirring through
him—dim rainy light and ice on mulching leaves.

At the other end of the house he finds the way up—a steep
stairwell with ragged walls close in on either side. He goes fast,
slipping up them two at a time, leaning hard on the banister to
avoid making the boards creak. Pulls through to the top and
leans a moment, sweating. Low sloped dormer ceilings; acidic
scent of heat seeping up through floor paint and a cinder smell

of old stovepipe. Like home, almost. He ducks through an open doorway to his left, touching walls for a light switch, papered and buckling with heat, and moves back out to the hall. Nothing there.

Now he hears them: the fan and his father's snoring. Almost simultaneously he sees the door at the end of the hall—a narrow wooden door—and knows it's theirs. A key hangs in the keyhole, but there's no doorknob. He pushes in, and hot air blows over him with fan noise and the smell of sleep. Another moment and he sees them in the farthest corner of the room, shadow-shapes humped in the bed, naked and striped with light from the window blinds, chests moving in time to the noise of their snores. The sheets are mostly pushed off them through rails at the foot of the bed. He goes closer, stepping over shed clothing—pants yanked inside-out, legs knotted, shirts and glimmering sequin-heavy dresses and cowboy vests. His father's boots are arrayed under the windowsill, some on their sides, others lined up neatly with the tops nodding down.

At the foot of their bed he stops. He waits to see if they'll wake or register his presence, but they go on sleeping—the woman with her mouth open, hair bunched around her on the pillow; the man with his legs wide and hands at his hips as if in midjump, sweat gleaming in the folds of his neck. His belly jiggles abruptly full of breath and heaves it back out. Lips twitch open and shut and fingers curl. On and on, they sleep. His father makes a noise as if he might speak; yawns and turns slightly, clicking his teeth together, and resumes snoring. He's not sure what he'll say if they wake up—what he'll do. Most likely it won't matter. His father will never recognize him; he'll fear for his life and think no further than that—how to save himself.

Once, years ago at the Craftsbury fiddle contest, he saw a drunk biker fall headfirst from the roof of a parked school bus, killing himself. The man was huge, like his father now, and the instant he hit ground Jesse had known he was dead from the difference in the way he lay there. And then how the other bikers had jumped down after him, five or six of them, their hair floating up and legs wide, braced for the impact. No one else seemed to be noticing. And later, on his way to play his final rounds, passing by again, Jesse saw them all still crowded at the side of the bus, drinking, the dead man propped against a bus tire as if he were asleep. Topless hippie girls in skirts and open buckskin vests danced and swayed around him, and someone had woven flowers into his hair, encircling one ear. A half-smoked joint was stuck in the corner of his mouth. The way Jesse felt then, seeing this—so alive and pleased with the world, its strangeness, and the pale sky and singed smells of coals and cooking meat, fried bread and popcorn and marijuana smoke, and the sound from the stage blowing first one way at him then another, surrounding him, then gone—he knew it wasn't right: not the way you were supposed to feel about someone's death. But it was impossible for him to feel anything else, and moments later when he heard his name called to play, he knew he would win. He pictured the man falling and then the way he'd lain there, and the thousands of people around him who didn't notice or care. He ripped into the notes like he was the one falling. He glanced up at Dix over his shoulder, accompanying him on guitar, and watched his head jerk back subtly, his mouth twisting to one side with surprise or admiration.

His father whimpers and makes a clucking noise at the back of his throat, as if he wanted to swallow. He rolls on his side toward the woman and hangs an arm around her waist. Hairless from midshoulder up, the arm looks dipped in paint—no hair on his wrist or the back of his hand either. By contrast with the rest of him, his father's fingers seem almost dainty, tapering to nails all hooked and pointy as a bear's claw, not the way Jesse remembers. There's something almost appealing in this; also in the way his gut swells against the woman. She sighs once and the man shifts from her, onto his back, legs wide, and resumes snoring. Air ratchets harder at the back of his father's throat now, scraping in with such force Jesse can't see how he doesn't wake himself or rip a hole in his throat. The breaths come harder and closer together, as if he were growing enraged, and Jesse wonders again how they stay asleep through this or if they aren't pretending, when suddenly the air snags and stops.

In the silence he leans closer, waiting. Ten seconds, twenty seconds. His father's hands open against the bed sheets, stiffen, and grip down. Still no air moves. There is a faint shuddering through the bedrails, the frame chattering against the wall, and finally the man gasps a breath, slamming the headboard to the wall behind him with his weight.

Just in time, Jesse stands back. From the opposite corner he watches as the woman rolls toward his father and strokes sweat from his forehead, flops an arm over his stomach. "What's the matter?" she says. She clears her throat. His father says a few words back, more like a chord, and there's the sound of him lifting the clock from the nightstand, and one of them yawns, and his father says, "But most likely not."

Jesse lowers himself out of sight beside his father's boots and waits. He watches them turn and finally lie still. Presses his face to his kneecaps to stay awake. And when he's sure they won't hear him, he stands and drifts out of the room again, back down the hall, the stairs falling away like something in a dream, and out through the window he came in. In the cab of his truck he sprawls. He watches the sky glisten brighter through his windshield, pale gray to blue, and thinks, *Just a minute here, then I'll leave.* He closes his eyes and tips his head up, air buzzing in his sinuses, and pictures his father—remembers the damp look of his skin and the crease in his forehead just above the eyes, his belly heaving. His skin sticks under him against the seat, but he no longer feels it. *Only a few minutes,* he thinks, his eyes easing up further against his lids until he feels as if he were afloat. He pushes his face to the seat back, wrist pinned under his hip, seatbelt buckle hitting him in the ribs—each pressure a point of annoyance and a thing to remind him he's awake only until he can fall through it, out of himself, asleep.

Face numb and mind a white blank from the sun and heat, he wakes, and for a moment can't remember what he's doing or where he is. Then it comes back—the walk up the moon-silvered road, the dogs, the ripped back screen, his father snoring. He pulls himself upright by the steering wheel and bends the rearview mirror for a look at his face. There are no outward signs of the disorientation he feels—his eyes are a little swollen and red-edged, nothing more. Nine-thirty, his watch says, so it's only a few hours he's been lying here. He starts up and lets the engine warm, tapping the accelerator once to smooth the idle. Now he's stood so long at the foot of their bed watching them sleep, he feels oddly detached about what will happen next. He'll go right up and knock. He'll tell them who he is.

Just beyond their house he parks in a rubbed-out patch of oak shade and tire-worn roots. Sunlight stings his arms and face, and he wishes he had a hat. It would make him more like his father—always showing up when he felt like it, when his schedule would allow, bag in one hand, guitar in the other, hat tilted low; always the look on his face, anticipating their joy and excitement at seeing him.

The front screen door appears locked from within; beyond that the door is open, and through the screen comes a smell of bacon cooking, coffee, and something else Jesse can't place—a pungent smoky smell he's sure he knows but can't recollect. He stands a moment peering in through the screen blur. No one is in sight. The table is clear, and there's a sound of dishes moving, the *skirring* noise of a pot stirred and somebody speaking—a man's voice followed immediately by a woman's.

Jesse raises a hand and knocks.

The voices continue a moment and go silent, and his father steps out from inside the kitchen door. He's barefoot, in overalls with no shirt underneath. His chin jerks up, and he rolls his weight from one foot to the other in a way that seems oddly athletic, as if he were getting ready to pounce. Beyond the cooking sounds, Jesse realizes there's music playing, low—more gospel singing. In his hand his father has a plain white cup of something steaming that he brings to his lips and sips from and lowers again. He holds it with the points of his fingers, the fingers themselves possibly too thick to fit through the handle.

"Can I help you?" he asks. He sounds more puzzled than wary.

Jesse jerks at the door, but it won't open.

"Hey-hey, easy there. Wait just a second. That door . . ." His father comes quickly across the room, stopping only when they are face to face through the screen mesh. "Say," he says. His expression seems to soften a moment. "You're the one," he continues, "—didn't I see you parked out front yesterday? Drive a little Chevy four-by-four?" Still he sounds more curious than accusatory—as if he's determined ahead of time that whatever Jesse says next will be exactly the thing he wants to hear.

Jesse nods. "I was here last night, too," he says. It is not like seeing himself in a reflection, nothing that directly aligned, though parts of his own face are there in his father's—the eyes and mouth.

"What can I do for you?"

"Come on out here a second, I'll tell you."

"What?" He looks harder at Jesse and away again. Slips a hand in his pocket and seconds later lifts it out again to begin fooling with the latch on the other side of the door. "OK," he says, and a moment later, "Shit. Look out there. Just—if you don't mind stepping on out of the way a second." The door swings suddenly free of its hinges, right at Jesse, and his father has to come quickly around to catch it, easing it onto one side against the wall. "Damn thing. Ought to fix it one of these days, hey?" he asks, straightening again. "Drill out some new hinges? Well." He dusts his palms together and extends a hand. Jesse takes it. The skin is hard across the palms and knuckles but soft through the fingers. "Henry Stockton," the man says. "Glad to meet you."

"Jesse," Jesse says. He watches his father's expression slip against the emotions he must wish to conceal—lips tightening.

"Jesse," his father repeats.

"Jesse Alison."

Now his father staggers back a step, hands on his hips. "Holy smoke . . . !" he says, and Jesse knows without understanding exactly (the feeling passes for annoyance at first—the sensation of heat ticking through him, from his spine to the top of his head) that his father is overacting in order both to demonstrate and hide whatever it is he really feels. "Criminy. You're kidding! I thought . . . the things your mother must have said, I thought for sure I'd never see you . . ." He lifts his hands to cover his face a moment and returns them to his hips. "Holy Mac, it really is you, isn't it? I can see it now, almost. Yes." He peers harder at

Jesse, and Jesse blinks back, trying to make him come better into focus—hair curling over his forehead and gray-black stubble hazing his jaw so he appears as if in a faded print.

His father heaves a breath. "Well, I hardly know what to say. Ma!" he calls over his shoulder, through the open door. "Grace, come on out here—I'd like . . . someone I'd . . . I'd like you to meet my *son.*" He moves closer suddenly, placing a hand on Jesse's shoulder and then pulls him hard against his chest, chin in Jesse's collarbone. A sound like a sob bursts from him, and warm air gusts against Jesse's ear and neck. *Charmer,* he remembers his mother calling the man once—*Make you think anything you want to believe is true. Sell you your own soul, if you let him.* Her latest advice to him, as well: *Believe him without my influence or say-so.* Jesse stands stiffly, allowing the embrace.

$(f^{\#})\text{--}V^{7}$

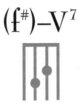

Almost everything his father knows about him is wrong or out of date, exaggerated, lacking in particulars, or plain made up: fiddle contests he won years ago, ones he never won at all, subjects he didn't study in school, interests he didn't have—fly fishing, stamp collection, a pet rabbit. It's all so distorted, Jesse hardly recognizes himself or knows where to step in with corrections. "Don't blame your mother," his father says. "Can't be all her fault. I was hitting the booze pretty bad then for a time and doing just about anything I could get up my nose—not that she's the world's most reliable source either, as you probably know." He shrugs. "Just the way it is." Nothing Jesse considers important and no news from the last five years of his life has reached him—not Genny, his stint in junior college, Michelle, bluegrass music, his guitar and mandolin playing, Nashville, or his desire to be a Bluegrass Boy.

"Bill *Mon*roe," his father says, squinting slightly, when Jesse comes to it. "I've met him a few times at the Opry backstage." He rubs a strip of bacon in yolk at the edge of his plate and rolls it in half to fit in his mouth in a single bite. "Wouldn't say I know him to speak to particularly," he continues, chewing, licking fingertips. "Just a hello in passing. There was a song of mine, had a line about being a heartbreaker, and the old man must've liked it, 'cause whenever he saw me around he'd say something to reference it. 'Oh no-o, there goes that heartbreakin' man.' That sort of thing. 'You watch out there—don't let any of the womenfolks near that man, he's the heartbreakin' kind.' Meant it kindly enough, I presume." He laughs and tips back in his chair. "Funny thing, hey, for a guy with a woman in practically every state, but you know how that is."

They rest forearms and hands on the sticky metal-topped table, plates between them smeared with breakfast remains— fish bones and pork gristle, eggs, cornbread, and traces of greens in a peppery white sauce. His father's plate is considerably better wiped than Jesse's, the bones picked bare, hardly anything remaining. He still wears a napkin stuck in the bib of his overalls and bits of egg white are caught in the coffee soak on his mustache. All throughout the meal, whenever Grace would pass them, coming in and out of the kitchen with new plates of food, pitchers of juice or milk or coffee, his father would pause in what he was saying to follow her with his eyes and touch her lightly on the shoulder or hip as if in apology— as if he couldn't bear for her to be in another room or in any way removed from him. "Ain't she the best?" he asks once, catching her against him and pulling her to his lap, arms folded around her. She laughs and leans back on him, a look on her face to make Jesse think it must satisfy more than aggravate her, having his father so dependent upon her, and sated. The food is good beyond belief, too—so good Jesse's eyes burn with the pleasure of eating, and at times he almost forgets what he's doing and where he is.

At the opposite corner of the table from him is the girl he saw the night before, Josephine, propped on two phone books, her chin slick with food, her feet swinging. He knows she is mostly deaf—nerve damage from a high fever, early on; it was the first thing they told him about her—though he doesn't feel this exactly, what it means or how it makes her who she is. She watches them with a consuming gravity and murmurs to herself continuously at the edges of their conversation. On her plate is a heap of shredded potatoes, which she eats from the center out, picking at it with her fingers and scattering what she doesn't eat around her on the floor and table and on herself. Whenever there's a pause in conversation or when her murmuring becomes too loud to ignore, his father and Grace will focus their attention back at her, as if she were the thing they'd been talking about all along. They'll face her full on and say things slowly, in a deliberatingly inflectionless tone of voice. There's an explanation for this that Jesse begins catching on to—something about her age, five now, and the school she'll be attending in the fall, and how important it is for her to become better at lip reading. In her ears are overgrown skin-colored hearing devices like plastic embryos, which she occasionally pokes at or covers with her wrists, causing them to beep and shrill. "Mama," she says then, laughing, apparently tickled by the sound.

When Joey's done eating, Grace is there beside her almost before she can signal a need. She wipes the girl's face with the edges of her apron and lifts her down from the chair and lets herself be pulled along to the room with the window Jesse broke in through the night before.

"Didn't think you'd find me such a family man, hey?" his father asks. He rubs his stomach and leans back in his chair, shooting his eyes wide as if he thinks this is a startling thing to have said. "You can probably see why."

Jesse shrugs and says he doesn't know if he can or not. From the other room come the sounds of a box being turned on its side, shaken and dumped out, contents spilling over the linoleum. The woman says a word or two with a kind of staged enthusiasm, and the girl says something back. The girl's voice is unsettling to him, caterwauling, too loud for speech and mostly unintelligible—like words pulled backward through their meanings. His father glances once at him and away again, frowning, and Jesse stares between his father's legs to have something to look at. He tries to remember what it might have felt like sitting on his lap—the heat and coarser texture of his clothing and hard weight of his muscles and bones beneath.

What he wants badly to tell him about now is the fiddle contests: the summer weekends he and Dix would ride out to contests all over Vermont and New Hampshire, sometimes for hours, strategizing all the way—which tunes to enter with, who would be judging, and who was likely to show up for competition, and so on. Always, there was the building excitement (trees falling away to either side of the road, brown and silver, leaves overlain with sun), and then the feeling he liked best, once they arrived on the contest grounds: the bright jittery hopefulness that made his teeth ache to the roots and sped his breathing. Waiting in the backstage area, or farther off somewhere with Dix, the grass would be trampled and slick underfoot with mud showing through if it had rained recently, and everywhere was the stream of noise around him he loved: other contestants warming up, music from the stage, applause, conversations between old friends who hadn't seen one another in years. Sometimes, playing through his rounds with Dix beforehand and together trying to imagine how best to present things for the judges (*Leave off that last set of high variations—too wild for here—just play it clean and straight, like on the record,* or, *You know how Gale Carter's going to rile up the audience with that "Listen to the Mockingbird"—you better rip it up and throw in some of them flashy chromatic licks at the end—applause is valid here*), if they played together long enough or Jesse's excitement was high enough, he'd begin having the impression Dix had transformed to a demonic cut-out figure of a man with a guitar, a two-dimensional puppet lurching side to side, overmuscled hands beating out a rhythm Jesse knew only to follow, though it no longer sounded much to him like music. He didn't mind this feeling and even came to recognize it as a good omen or a way of determining the depth of his concentration on a given day. Later, after winning or taking second or third prize, there was always the disappointment, getting back into Dix's car—realizing all over again that victory, by itself, is nothing. If he could slow the feeling enough to look deeply into it, he might realize, sometimes, what he really wished for was his father's presence—just one time, maybe even the next time— his father there to watch and see him win and make it matter.

All of this he wants to tell, and about the dead biker and the last time he played with Dix—every contest he won, summer after summer, and the tunes he played—but already he senses it will not mean enough; it will be endless rambling that gives the man no sense of what it was really like, growing up alone, and makes him too significant anyway.

"We heard how you got married, but we didn't know anything about these other two," he says. "Grace and Josephine."

His father blinks, giving away nothing. "Yeah," he says. "Funny how things work out." He recrosses his legs, and they go back to watching each other. Already Jesse's begun memorizing things in this room—the dents and patterns in the dirt on the tabletop, the piles of papers and the taped-over window screen and cracks in the window glass and the gaps between the few books on the shelf beside him, where the blond Hondo and the arch-top Gretsch lean. For now it all seems part of his father, the other side of an equation defining him, though Jesse's sure as soon as he leaves here he'll forget most of it, remembering only the man himself.

Jesse leans from his chair and lifts the arch-top guitar by its neck, first thinking to play it, then holding it out for his father to take. The strings pull sideways against his grip. From their slackness and the sticky grit of rust and dirt beneath them, he knows the instrument will be badly out of tune—probably months since anyone's touched it.

His father shakes his head and laughs once, palms raised. "Oh no," he says. "Not me. Not anymore."

Jesse persists. "Play," he says.

"Why don't you? I can show you a couple—"

He shakes his head. "You first."

The man relents. He takes the guitar in both hands, peering over its face as if in a mirror, and a moment later bends to tune it. High E and B. He cranks the tuners. "You realize . . . ," he begins but never completes the sentence. He plays with the pads of his fingers for lack of a pick—open-position chords, stopping again and again to tune. Even so, there's no mistaking the sound: the jump in the edges of the beat and the crooked clusterings of notes and the tone, that binding force between and inside each note that his father can never know is his and that Jesse would identify anywhere. He even sits in the same way, his shoulders rounded forward and neck craned, one foot lifting crookedly up and down against the floor, not quite in time. "Sure haven't missed it," he says. He shakes his hands out and continues. His fingers pop and squeak against the strings, and the sound honks in the f-holes. He hums and sings a bit, and their eyes meet, and his father shakes his head again, eyes wet now, smiling as if it were not his own fault he can no longer do this well—as if it were somehow beyond his will.

"Huh. Well," he says. A corner of his mouth tucks into a frown, and he fakes another little crappy melody, gliding three fingers up the neck, then laughs and again shakes out his hands. "Guess you can't tell I haven't been at it a while now." The guitar knocks against his leg.

"Let me," Jesse says, fishing in his pocket for a pick.

"Sure," his father says. "I'd like that." His eyes have a shielded cast now, lustrously shiny, as if they will no longer absorb light, only reflect it. "Let's see what you got." He rubs his hands up and down against his thighs, and his eyes droop shut, lids faintly purple and red. He makes a pleased mumbling noise at the back of his throat. Jesse almost remembers that—his occasional affectation of the Vermonter's nasal *mms* and *ah-yuhs* as preamble to whatever else he meant to say. Glancing once behind him and jingling change in his pocket, his father tilts back in his chair, and another shadow of memory crosses Jesse with it—wet earth and trees rolling against the sky. Always he had thought on his way home from school, there must be a way for him to know in advance if his father would be there—if today was the day he'd come into the clearing and find his father's car there with the out-of-state plates parked next to his mother's car, wood smoke winding heavily from the chimney and his favorite foods cooking inside, his music on loud. There were never any signs for it, yet Jesse was convinced and remained on the lookout, bending whatever he saw or felt or heard against the possibility of foretelling his father's presence—new tracks in the dirt, icy leaves, knocking sounds of cold in the woods—the same way the trees made the shape of the wind visible.

Jesse shoulders the strap and breathes once deeply to open the muscles in his arms and chest and to calm himself. *Easy,* he thinks, and starts in playing—jazz chords, the three or four sequences he remembers from watching and playing with Red. The strings flop against the neck, dead and sticky with rust—low action and everything flat by at least a half-tone, slipping flatter. He can't stop to correct the tuning now, though; that would be too obvious an insult to his father's sense of pitch. Instead, gazing just past him, out the window, and hooking an ankle over his knee, he lets his fingers move with the first thing that comes to mind: something mellow and soft to suit the thick-topped woody tone of the Gretsch—"How Great Thou Art," the way he remembers a guy playing it recently at Red's, brushing and pulling strings with his pick and using the tips of his right-hand second and third fingers for the additional voicings. He keeps glancing out the window and back again at his father, notes blowing through him.

His father smiles and rubs his hands up and down against his thighs; at times he seems on the verge of a yawn or tears, his eyes wet, sleepy, unreadable. "You got the gift!" he says, when Jesse quits playing. "You hearin' that, Gracie?" The woman's voice drifts in to them from the other room, *Some kind of angel,* followed by the sound of her footsteps, and the man talks over it. "That's my boy. Takes right after the old man, though, don't he?"

Jesse snorts. "Don't know about that," he says.

"It's a figure of speech, son, a bit of sarcasm." He blinks, draws a breath and looks earnestly at Jesse—too earnestly. "The apple never falls far from the tree—that's a known fact. But it ain't the point. The point is I wouldn't wish my luck or bad temperament on you for all the gold in the world. I mean that."

It's disconcerting: his sincerity is so overt Jesse can't possibly believe him, but neither can he disbelieve him—in fact, there seems no good way to respond to or register these words.

Jesse turns the guitar face-down in his lap and rests his forearms on its back. He picks at a callus, then stands and replaces the guitar against the shelf and just outside the dustless trench in the carpet where it had formerly sat. In his head is one of the tunes that woke him up the night at Genny's, after playing with Red—just the shadow-outline shape of the thing at first, like something reflected in water and reminding him, as it gains dimension, of everything he's ever forgotten and recollected— the feeling as it comes through him again, more a mood or impulse toward music than anything melodic. Then there are the notes themselves and the itch in his fingers and in every corresponding nerve. He shoves his fists into his pockets and pushes against his leg muscles to control the feeling.

"Something else I'd like to play for you," he says. "If you don't mind."

His father squints and opens his arms. "I'm all yours," he says.

Faker, he wants to say. *Liar.* And anyway, it will never be enough.

A violin case under each arm and instruments in either hand, he comes up the back plank steps and into the kitchen. Grace leans to one side with the door held open for him, arms wet up to the elbows with soapy water; his father stands at the refrigerator, a carton of orange juice tilted up, the muscles in his throat working. He drags a breath through his nose and lowers and crushes the carton, shoving it into the trash under the sink, and belches. "Got the whole band there," he says. He runs a finger beneath his mustache. Wipes the finger against his leg and swallows back another belch. "One little second here," he says. "Gotta see a man," and he ducks out of the kitchen. Jesse watches after him. For all his weight he's surprisingly quick and light on his feet, telltale shivers in the walls and floorboards giving away the force of his footsteps.

"A second," Grace says. She laughs. "Better make yourself comfortable. Could be half the afternoon in there."

Jesse goes back to the green-carpeted room (it seems to be both living room and dining room) and sets his instruments in a row beside the crooked woodstove. Eyes the table momentarily—it's already cleared and wiped—and heads back into the kitchen.

"You done the right thing," Grace says, from the sink. She

turns in his direction, nodding, but not looking right at him. From this he supposes she'd like for him to stay where he is, leaning just out of her sight, at the counter by the refrigerator—close enough, but also removed so they will feel free saying things to each other they might not ordinarily speak about. "I know it ain't easy. My own daddy, he didn't have nothing to do with us the whole time I was growing up. Funny thing, I always thought it was Ma's fault—like she drug us off somehow or done something to scare him so *he* didn't want nothing more to do with us." She laughs.

"It's not how it happened with us," Jesse says. This is not what he wants—consolation, understanding. He wants to be known. "Dad sold some songs, got a bunch of money and bang, he was gone."

Grace shakes her head and runs the water a while, turning plates back and forth under the stream and stacking them in the rack against one another. "I'm not going to tell you otherwise or say anything to defend him," she says. She closes the taps. "You won't get that out of me. The man can be a sonofabitch. No one knows better. But I will tell you one thing—" Here she turns, shaking water from her hands and burying them in her apron. The water stains gray through the white of the fabric, and her eyes fix on his. For the first time he notices how one eye is green with brown flecks, the other solid brown. "Your ma . . . ," she pauses, biting her lips a second. "Well, maybe I shouldn't be the one to tell you this, but—she mighta thought herself the only one to love that man, but there was girls like her all over, everywhere he played practically. Sure, she was his first, and he did what he could to get back and see y'all when he could—but that other one? The one he eventually married?" She makes a noise, crinkling her eyes. "He'd been off and on with her *six years* before they finally tied the knot. Had a whole other family going."

Jesse stares between his feet, thinking alternately, *What? What?* and, *Who the hell cares?* He lifts his weight from one foot to the other and waits for the dizziness of alarm to pass so he can speak again. The feeling he has is almost like what he gets playing or hearing a sequence of diminished chords—something that comical and hokey-spooky: the pressure between the notes spiraling ever up and up as the masked man makes his escape; the same pressure between his fingers, notes squeezed one into the other, tri-tone upon tri-tone. He remembers the winter his mother was so sick, and that last day by the fire, when she drew him to her, saying his name and forcing him closer as if she wished to press him back into her. He'd been so sure then he would have to separate himself from her for the rest of his life in order to survive—had even thought this might bring him closer to his father, allowing him to align himself with some part of the man's distance and mystery. Now he has to consider it all differently. It was nothing his mother had control of. The man had families all over the South, probably.

Despite his importance to them, they had never mattered to him.

Again he pictures his mother under the blankets, the cloth

over her eyes and the sweaty smell of her—then her lying beside him, her arms locked behind his head, and for the first time he understands it had not been just desperation and need. There was always something else—an element of protection.

"Did my mother—did she know?"

Grace draws a breath, releasing air up over her sweating face so strands of her hair move and lie still. She shuts her eyes and nods. "I believe so, but then it's hard to say. There woulda been two boys by then—Shawn and William, couple years younger than you." She pauses. "I don't see how he coulda *not* told her. But then, what she heard and what she wanted to hear, that's anyone's guess. He wasn't in his best form at the time, either—as I understand it. I'll tell you another thing." She clears her throat and widens her eyes slightly, looking up but not meeting Jesse's gaze. "You shouldn't be thinking to yourself like your daddy had a clear choice in any of this. I mean, he did, but he didn't. His trouble's his own making, and don't nobody know that better than yours truly. But it wasn't like he figured the one family was better than the other and he'd just go on over there instead of with you, if you follow what I'm saying. It was all a lot more complicated. Most of your daddy's money still ain't even his—it's all tied up in investments and such he can't touch on account of that woman . . ." She makes a guttural noise. "Just let's say she got her hands on him pretty well every which way."

Jesse's father fills the doorway beside him, an arm out against either doorjamb. Jesse wonders how he got there so suddenly—how he didn't hear him or feel his approach in the floorboards. "Don't you believe a word of it," his father says. He winks and makes a snuffling noise at the back of his throat, not exactly a laugh. "Whatever it is she's telling you, it's all nonsense." His gut sways suddenly closer, arms spreading wider. The wisps of hair in his bare armpits seem superimposed there to Jesse, accidentally stuck in the flesh that swells so white and unveined from underneath. "It's a scientific fact anyway, you know—how we can't hear half of what they say, women. Just don't register that high a frequency. A lot of aggravating high-pitched noises is all." He tugs at one of his earlobes and laughs. "Bad for your blood pressure, too. Might as well not even get started, it'll only mix you up." He turns and heads back into the living room.

"Was that a joke?" Grace asks. She smiles and shakes her head. "That was supposed to be *funny,* Henry?"

"I heard that," his father says. "You said something about me being funny."

They both laugh.

"Joey's in her room?" he asks.

"On the porch. You left that door open." Grace stares straight ahead, waiting for a response. "She got tired of coloring. Can you check on her?"

"Yeah-yeah."

Muttering to herself, she lifts the griddle from the stovetop with a corner of her apron and dunks it into the sink water, gray-black with fish bones and bits of food floating in the soap scum. The griddle bumps to the bottom of the sink; her elbows dimple and the muscles in her forearms shiver with tension as she goes after it, scrubbing. From the next room Jesse hears his father unlatching the catches of his guitar case. There's the snap of metal against metal as each one's unsprung, and then the creak of the top lifted back and dropped open. "Nice little piece," he says, and something else Jesse doesn't catch as he drags a fingernail hard over the strings—*ping ping ping ping ping ping.* He hears him drop the case cover back again, closed, and snap down one button before lumbering onto the porch, already chattering about something to Josephine.

Now he understands: his mother had not wanted him to hear this from her, because she didn't want any of Jesse's rage or indignation directed back at her. She didn't want his feelings to be diffused by indirection but rather to go directly to their cause: his father. And yet she'd failed here as well. Here was this woman whom he did not know at all giving him the corrected version of his life story while his father stood aside making dumb jokes, impervious as ever. No, as much as he can, Jesse will resist what he feels is the role scripted for him to play—the outraged, embittered, long-lost son. He'll surprise them all. He'll stand aside some, too. He'll take another page from his father's book.

"How about you?" Jesse asks Grace. He watches her forehead bunch and wrinkle. "When did you and him hook up?"

"Six years ago this past spring." He waits, but for the moment she says nothing further. She pushes a forearm against her hairline and goes back to scrubbing. "He used me on a couple of sessions, singing backup, you know, and I guess you could say we hit it off." Here she smirks in a way Jesse can't read.

Prideful or abashed—he doesn't know. "Didn't have much to do with each other though, really, till just about a year ago." She tucks her chin. "He's my producer now on a new project we ain't quite done with yet."

"Gospel singing?"

The woman nods and slides her eyes at him. "Some. You heard?"

"Last night."

She nods again. "We about got it mostly in the can now. You sing any parts? Sound like you must be around a high baritone."

"That's right. You want me to put down some parts," he says, "I'll be glad to give it a go. Maybe sometime if I'm back visiting again . . ."

Grace shakes her head. She stacks the griddle back behind the other dishes and reaches in through the water to pull the drain. Runs a dishrag around the bottom of the sink as it empties, wrings that, and shakes water from her hands, drying them again in her apron. "Ain't any singing left on that project, to speak of. Not much, anyway. Just, I'm always on the lookout for someone I can sing a good harmony on. Maybe later, after we put Josephine down, you and I could go outside and sing a few." She hangs her apron from the refrigerator door and tugs once at the neckline of her shirt. "Phew—must feel to you about like you died and went straight to hell, in this heat."

The rest of the morning and afternoon his instruments remain in their cases; no questions get asked or answered; nothing at all happens until Jesse's father goes to put Josephine down for her nap. By then the living room and front porch are strewn with her toys—puzzle pieces and construction sets, drawings, books, dolls. One moment his father is standing beside Grace and him, eyes shut and chest swelled with breath—a hand on one of each of their shoulders, then both hands lifted together, between them, palms up—asking a blessing. The next moment he's crouched and chasing Joey room to room, brandishing a rubber yellow snake between his thumb and forefinger, saying, "I'm a git you! I'm a git you! It's the 'Little Girl and the Dreadful Snake'!" And glancing once at Jesse, "Not one of Monroe's finer moments, you have to admit."

Now Jesse and Grace sit at the table mostly in silence, drinking sweet tea. He watches her lift a lemon wedge from the glass and pop it into her mouth, sucking away pulp from the rind and laying the rind on the table. She begins speaking, and Jesse tries to focus on the words—to hear them without feeling so much as if she's in the way, taking up time he's meant to spend with his father. *Why are you here?* he wants to ask, though the question could more easily be put to him.

"I swear it sometimes, that girl's got a musical gift too. You see her talking to herself and dancing, tapping out a rhythm, and you just gotta wonder what else goes *on* there, in that head of hers." She expels a breath and lifts her drink, tilting it until there are only ice cubes in the glass, then refills it from the blue glass pitcher between them. "One of these days maybe they'll figure a way to rebuild the human ear for people like her. She's got about twelve percent the normal hearing range with her, you know," here she touches her own ear, "her thing in. Almost nothing without it. All the parts are there—you can see on the ultrasound, her little eardrums and whatnot—just none of it's right." She lifts out another wedge of lemon, squeezes it into her glass and pops that rind into her mouth as well.

"Must be hard," he hears himself saying. Watches his hand move across the table for his glass, lift, and bring it to his mouth.

"You know what?" She smiles once looking just beyond him. "Let's go on outside while we got a half a moment and see if we can't make some music."

"Good idea." Jesse stretches his hands under the table and rubs them together, out of sight, realizing the ache and frustrated hunger he's felt all morning and still feels, wishing he could speak to his father alone without Josephine continually interrupting, tugging on his father's shirt or rubbing her face on his leg, chattering at him; it's almost the same as longing to play: another way to express that longing, anyway, will be through music. "Sure," he repeats.

Grace's eyes flash over his. She's already pushing back her chair, standing, collecting their glasses to bring outside. "I'll just tell your father that's where we're at. Joey's probably almost to sleep by now."

They sit across from each other on the back concrete patio, both of them on upended logs, like stumps, Grace with her ankles splayed and hands pressed between her bare knees, rock-

ing and singing. The heat is almost as unbearable here as
indoors, and every so often Jesse has to pause in his playing to
swat away flies and mosquitoes. He does his best to accompany
her on guitar and, when he can, to take the melody from her so
she can harmonize, though their voices are not ideally suited.
After a while his father joins them, sitting on one of the torn
lawn chairs and eating peanuts, shells and skins scattered
around him on the ground and broken in webby shreds on his
chest and belly. His fingertips shine with grease. Now and then
he'll stop to listen or to brush himself off, swig from the sweating glass of tea beside him, or grab a new handful of peanuts
from the bag, and Jesse will look at him then for any indication
of what he's thinking. Any sign he recognizes what he's hearing.

Grace's voice is like nothing Jesse's ever heard. He watches
her to see how it's done—how her chin raises and her throat
tremors slightly—as if any of the physical evidence for it could
explain the sound. So many layers and variances of tone inside
each pitch that, almost without thinking, Jesse wants to mimic
it in his own playing. He damps and chokes strings with his
right wrist and moves suddenly up the neck to strike a note,
then back again just as fast to hollow it—changing, breaking,
layering each tone as thickly as he can. Again, he watches her
mouth; he leans an ear to the side of his guitar, fingers spread
and squeaking over strings—*dreek, drr-eek*—remembering
suddenly how that sound had once seemed to him a secret word
for music, or an instruction—*drink, drink*—a picture of cups

and chalices and bowls brimming with sound that went with it. Her throat swells, eyes close and open, and he leans up again to be sure he's not missing anything. At times something in her voice is so edgeless and unrestrained, all spit and bone and breath, he can hardly stand hearing it, and then he looks away from her at his father again, still picking peanuts from their shells. Jesse watches him nod and scuff his feet and brush shells and skins from his lap, breathing and chewing.

What Jesse and Grace know in common is almost nothing—a few hymns and old gospels. The scales and chord patterns and the form of verses and choruses for most of what she sings is familiar enough, though, that he has no trouble following. Occasionally she'll stop him. "You got a minor chord to go right there," she might say humming root notes for him; or, shaking her head, once laughing, "No, no, you don't go up like that for them high cracker notes, just stay right—hmmn, hmmn—real simple, like on the pedal tones." He listens again and does as she tells him, though he can't always see how it will work until it happens.

When it's too hot on the concrete they move farther into the yard, following shade until none is left, and she says it's time to quit. "That little girl's gonna be getting up from her nap any minute now, and I ain't done a thing to see about starting supper." She squats next to his father a moment, speaking softly. Then, "Might be nice to cook out tonight."

His father nods and cracks another peanut.

"I'll make you a list. You can go to the store." She stands again, brushing the front of her skirt straight, and heads across the yard, Jesse and his father watching after her.

"Man, she can sing," Jesse says. His father nods and pops a peanut into his mouth. Light seems to be streaming across the yard after her; everything appears frayed with heat and wetness to Jesse, and he's suddenly overwhelmed with sleepiness. How many days now since he slept fully? He yawns and the light shoots into him, catching and refracting through his sweaty eyelashes and the corners of his eyes, and he staggers upright, dizzy. Stoops to fold shut the top of his guitar case and lifts. "Sure could use a nap myself, about now," he says.

"Take that couch in the spare room, if you like," his father says.

Floating at the edges of sleep, dozing and waking again, Jesse imagines he can almost make sense of Josephine's babbling—a story about Sinbar the bad girl with blue skin—though it won't stay fixed long enough or clearly enough to take shape outside his partial dreaming. She chatters in a monotone at one of her dolls, moving its arms back and forth, then sets it aside for the yellow snake, still chattering. "Brudda brudda brdda daz a essy? Ees a hessy brrda?" Mostly he wishes she'd just leave or be quiet. He kicks his feet one way and another and rolls abruptly onto his side. The couch is too short for him to stretch over it fully. Once, feeling the touch of her breath on his ear, he opens his eyes to find her there inches from him—her tiny upturned nose and depthless, expressionless, miniature brown eyes. He smiles at her and says, "Hey," and when she doesn't smile back or respond in any way other than to poke a finger into his cheek, her fingernail digging at his skin, he rolls from her again, facing into the back of the couch. *Sister,* he thinks. *My new baby half-sister.* None of his feelings about this are recognizable: her little hands and arms, the smooth curve of her forehead, the milky crust of food around her mouth—none of it seems connected with him. There is only this prickling, vague annoyance. He'd like for it to be silent, but she won't go away. Ever. The last time she wakes him she's standing at the arm of the couch, half wailing in a monotone and tracing imaginary lines in the air with her fingertips as if casting a spell. He reaches for her hands, understanding as he does, one of the words she's been repeating: "brudda," "brdda," would be *brother.* Her eyes shoot wide, and she runs from the room. He turns in more tightly against himself—lets the smells of dust and patchouli, sweat, mildew, and food leftovers, thick in the cushions under his cheek, carry him back down to sleep.

He wakes up thinking: *Genny—gotta call Genny.* The house is quiet, their voices reaching him from outside, through the window, and he goes for the telephone where he saw it earlier, hanging on the wall in the kitchen. Dials her number and waits, watching his father and Grace and Joey through the screen in the backyard. They're playing a game that involves a set of plastic golf clubs and the junked car, chasing each other around, waving the clubs in the air, and hitting the car and the ground. *Snakes,* Jess thinks, and wonders how many might live under there, in the hood or the rotted-out tires or in the weeds growing under and right through the car. Black snakes, coral snakes, king snakes, water moccasins—no, there wouldn't be any moccasins. Probably just garter snakes. Probably nothing dangerous. Or they wouldn't be doing that.

". . . can't get to the phone right now, but if you leave your name and number after the tone . . ."

"Gen—Genny," he says, once the outgoing message runs out. "If you're there, pick up. It's me, Jesse. I—"

There's a click and her voice. "Jesse!"

He pictures her ear—her hair falling over it, over her shoulder, her neck. There's such palpable comfort to him in her physical presence, her smells, her manner and appearance, even just envisioning it, all at once he knows how much he loves her— not in the sexually in-love sense of the word, either, which has always confounded him because of her attractiveness to him as well. He would not be the same person without Genny; he would not be half of what he is without her.

"Where are you calling from?"

He fills her in, briefly. Describes the house, the room he's standing in, Grace, Joey, his father. "He's fat! I mean really—like huge. I almost wouldn't have recognized him. Half my life I thought he was one thing, and he's this other guy. It's just like— weird." He speaks softly and in a rush, though for the moment there's no risk of his being overheard. And in everything he describes, he wants his feelings for her revealed—wants his descriptions to stand in for or contain all his new fondness and gratitude.

"I owe you an apology," he says, finally. "For the fiddle."

"Yes." She's silent a moment. "I was wondering if you'd bring that up."

"I don't know why exactly—like why I took it. I just had this feeling. Like it was mine. Pretty stupid, I guess."

"Lots of things that aren't ours can seem like they'd be nice to have, Jesse. Especially when you're deprived a long time. That's why we have laws—"

"But this was different, Gen. I know it was wrong and stupid, I realize that, but it just seemed like . . . oh, whatever. The way that fiddle *sounds*. I can't explain."

"Try."

"I can't. Anyway, if it's all right, I'll just bring it back, and we can forget it ever happened, OK?"

"Jesse." Her breath flutters into the phone. "Look, I've been over this more than a few times in my mind since you left, let me tell you. I've made my peace. So I'm just going to say this once, short and sweet. Even though I hate to seem to be the one rewarding such regressive and socially fucking retarded behavior on your part. That fiddle was always going to be yours. It was *meant* as a surprise, you know, for your twentieth. I was going to work on it some more, make those f-holes a little more respectable, bush the pegs, and refine the scroll—in fact, I hope you'll still let me do some of that. But I *want* you to play it. Both

Verlinda and I want you to play it. I think I knew that the first time I heard you on it. Just, took me a while to figure it out, and then you beat us to the punch—and not in a way I'm particularly fond of either, but, well, considering what you're going through, I guess it's not such a big deal."

"I don't deserve that."

"No, you probably don't. But it's an emotional time for you. Seeing your father—no doubt it stirs up all kinds of emotion. Makes you a little unsteady. So why don't we just set this one aside. Talk about it more when you're here. OK? You've got enough on your plate as it is, so let's just put it aside."

"If you say."

"It's the truth, Jesse."

She conveys a few other messages for him—two from Red, one from Steve about a low-budget recording session, another from Duncan. Apparently the band Duncan wants to recommend Jesse for will be gigging at the Station in two nights— Saturday; Duncan will be playing fiddle, but he thinks it's a good idea for Jesse to show his face, meet them, maybe sit in part of the night. "You're on your way, kiddo," Genny concludes. "You got people lining up here to see you when you're back."

"You've heard of these guys?"

"Sure. They're great. I mean it. She'd be great for you to work with."

"You mean . . . Wynne—that's a girl, not a guy?"

She laughs. "I swear it, Jesse, sometimes I think you really did just fall off the back of a wagon."

In the end she says it for him and provides some of the explanation as well: "I always wondered what it was about you—that kind of frightened, rabbity thing about you. Now I understand. You *couldn't* tell me what you were doing, or anything about your father really, because of what he'd done to wreck things for you and your mother—your relationship with your mother. I had to get to know you on your *own* terms and love you for who you were, not because of feeling sorry. And now you've managed to reconnect with your father, there's no more of that, whatever it was . . . the obstacle's been removed. I don't know how to explain it. Just, you can be yourself, which is—well, it's a huge relief to me anyway. It's a great thing, Jesse."

The explanation is too simple by half, but it is close enough to the truth—a kind of truth, anyway—he isn't going to argue.

"I'm gonna hang up now before I start bawling," he says.

"I love you, Jesse."

"Thanks. I appreciate it . . . and everything." He watches out the window as his father scoops Joey and spins her over his shoulder, around and around, and lowers her again. He still can't bring himself to say it.

After eating, they lie in the grass together, all of them on a single blanket in the backyard—chicken bones, greasy paper plates, napkins, bowls, and corncobs in a pile beside them. What his father tells him is so much like dreaming or being in a reflection that after a time Jesse hardly hears any of the words for it, only the story itself. Red firelight from the grill shadows their hands and faces, making it easier for him to slip from the scene this way and forget himself. From the distance comes the occasional, percussive *boom* of fireworks and the whining ratchet of bottle-rockets released in a cluster. The sky is faint lilac-blue still, a lone jet trail unfurling at the far northern edge of the horizon, thickly iridescent as a scar. *Fourth of July,* he thinks *Independence Day*—only it isn't yet; sometime next week. His father sighs once, and there's the sound of him scratching a finger in his hair, and he goes on; meanwhile everything else he's said so far continues in its own current of images and associations beneath the words, in Jesse's imagination. Met too early on, he and his mother—as soon as he came down from Ontario, his second to last year of high school. "Going on my third attempt to finish school in my seventh school district in as many years—I guess you'd say I had about as much as a fool's chance of finishing, hey? Till I met your mama, that is, and I knew then I'd be hanging around at least as long as it took to convince her to go with me, which turned out to be shortly after we both graduated." Everything about them had seemed matched or the same, he says—same hairstyle, same music, same classes, and clothes, and tastes, and the same arrogant dislike of being kids in a high school—like they were fated to be together. "The way our voices blended," he says, "people used to say sometimes back then it'd give you a real bone-shiver."

Jesse pictures them after school in empty classrooms, singing, and in some of the other places he and Michelle had always met up—late springs at the boarded summer camp by the lake; their favorite south-facing slope on the mountain behind Jesse's mother's house, the sycamores there that sheltered and hid them, and the pocket of sun-warmed rocks they'd lain on; study carrels in the farthest corner of the basement of the public library: Michelle's skin in all of those different lights and temperatures, and the imprint of wool, cotton, or elastic denting her underarms and the tops of her breasts; her smell, too—something peculiarly sweet and pungent in her hair, like a taste he could never experience, and the streaks of lighter hair mixed with darker blond, which were also a desire maddeningly confused and thwarted no matter how much or how often he touched and stroked and sifted the strands. He pictures the boat—her parents' boat, rocking in its berth, sails furled, paint buckets, tarps, and brushes strewn over the deck. He remembers the sound of her feet hitting as she jumped down from the gangway next to him, and the moonlight continually shifting in the water around them with the soft lapping sound of lake waves, and her mouth tipped right at him, suddenly, so he understood what she wanted and had been waiting for all this time.

"I had a girlfriend like that," Jesse says. It's the first time he's put it this way—a thing from the past. "Haven't seen her since spring now," he adds. Then after a moment, "College."

His father grunts. "Just as well. You wouldn't want it to last. Believe me, there will be others." He continues. "We had our troubles, for sure, your ma and I. Things was good enough, though, and neither of us knew any better—couple of kids—so we took our show on the road. Settled a ways outside Nashville, fighting all the time. One of them quaint little Southern towns with the houses all in a square and sleeping porches and wrought iron everyplace, dirt roads going out into the country. Pretty as a picture. We hired bass players and percussion to add to our little act, if we could afford it. If we couldn't, or if there wasn't anyone good enough in the town we were playing, it'd be just the two of us." He pauses to lick his lips and suck a breath, making the pleased mumbling sound at the back of his throat. "I guess you'd call it country music, though mainly we didn't. Slip in a few old folk ballads and protest songs and you'd have said we were in the wrong town—should've been in New York, not Nashville, though that scene had mostly dried up and blown away by then anyway. *The answer, my friend, is blowin' in the wind . . .*" he sings jokingly. Something rustles, and Jesse lifts his head to see Josephine standing at the edge of the blanket with her back to them, fists clenched. Grace circles a hand around the girl's ankle and says nothing. "Hank and Janelle," his father continues, making his voice like a radio announcer's. "Or, Hank and Janelle and Hearts Afire. Played our last gig just a few months after you were born. Johnson City, I believe it was. Might've been twelve people in the audience. Couldn't hardly get us to stand on the same stage together by that point—but, hey, work is work."

"I'm gonna see about getting her to bed," Grace says. She rolls to a seated position. "You two stay on out here as long as you like—got some catching up, I'd say."

She leans to kiss his father, and Jesse looks away. Again he remembers the room they'd lain in, before Vermont, and the rough carpet against his skin. He's no longer sure which details are embellishments, new ornaments laid in—there are too many to be certain: the nippled cover in the ceiling where an overhead fixture had been; night in the curtains towering at the foot of his bed, breezes moving through them; his mother's voice coming from down the hall; her in a nightgown or slip, hair undone, shaking and spinning him in a circle so her face was the only fixed thing in the world. Something else, too, he hasn't thought of for years now: the drawings he made before he could remember making them—knots and mazelike skeins of lines scrawled over the page, all saved in a folder by his mother. Each one, according to her, titled the same: *Map to my daddy's house.*

"So what happened?"

His father doesn't answer. He lifts a hand and turns it one way and then the other, as if inspecting for something, then lowers it to his mouth to bite back a hangnail. "You were pretty sick a while there, and your mama decided it was time to go on back North. I could tell you otherwise, but it'd just be lying. I've always been the kind of a guy who can't be alone for more than a day or two. Women sense that and tend to respond—you know, give you whatever it was you seemed to be needing. Leastways that's been my experience. I could've run after you, I suppose, and maybe a part of me really wanted that—sure, a part of me wanted that, but it wasn't in the cards. I don't know's she would have had me at that point anyway, after all we'd been through." He pauses a moment, draws a breath. "After all I'd put her through."

The stars are out now, flickering through the heat and wet air, and soon the bugs will become unbearable. Jesse remembers pulling himself from the basement hatchway only the night before and can hardly imagine anymore how that was also him, and now here he is, lying beside his father in the grass. Moonlight bends up from the lower northern corner of the horizon, making steps of the few clouds there hanging in scalar streaks like a ladder or the broken outline of a woman. He raises himself on his elbows and hears again the endless buzzing racket of insects he's grown so accustomed to he hardly thinks of it as sound anymore, but as something driven into him— some inward formulation of the constant heat and his loneliness and confusion, dislocation and missing home.

"And then you met that other woman."

"Denise?" his father says. His voice is mostly neutral saying it, though as he goes on there's a kind of defeat and self-criticizing sadness in it Jesse's not familiar with. "Like I said, I've never been the type to want to live alone for very long. Kinda makes you a walking target—for a woman who notices that sort of thing in a man."

"That why you quit?"

"Quit?"

"Music."

"Let me tell you. You stay in this business long enough, you

don't *get* to quit. You might try some different things, say, pro-
duction, engineering, marketing, whatever—you might put on
a few different hats like that. Your luck might take a turn. But
you can't quit it. It's got to be in your *blood*. I know that ain't
what you're asking, though. What you're . . . you look down the
road and you see a guy like me—had some family trouble, trouble with women, so on, so on, and you wonder, how'd it happen? What's gonna turn a guy from thinking that songwriting
was the only way to get a leg up in the world? Hell—I remember. Ain't nothing to make me forget how it was when I was hot.
I'll tell you. I was *hot,* man—I was so hot, nobody could put a
stop to me. Give me a line, I'd write you a song. Look at a girl
standing there on the street corner—hell, there goes *ten* more
new songs. Damn! Pop cans on the side of the road, bacon fry-
ing in the pan—whatever. You name it, gimme a line, I'd make
you a song. A *good* song. Where all that went . . ." He opens his
hands again in the air above him, lets them fall. "Hell, I don't
know. I don't suppose it went anywhere. It's all still right here."
Thumps a hand on his chest. "Somewhere. Just right now, anyway, it don't seem the most important thing. Just—maybe a
person's needs change. Maybe a person gets sick of repeating
himself so many times and starts to think maybe the whole
enterprise is gone just a little stale. A little bit fraudulent. The
gift can be a trap, you know. The music gift. And then maybe
you start with the drinking and the drugs—change your perspective, see things a little different, and maybe the songs will
come, hey? But they never do. Not that way. Not for me."

Jesse will never tinker with words and chords, or walk around with a target on his back. He knows this. The *gift* for him is a simpler thing: there's nothing else he can do but play.

The silence between them fills again with insect noise.

"One more question."

"Shoot."

"Was I born here?"

"Maringo?"

"This house."

"Ha! No—I didn't buy *it* till about four, five years ago. My little hideaway. My *love grotto*." He laughs. "Actually more like a secret tax shelter. You woulda been fifteen by then." He stretches and flops an arm over to where Jesse had been lying.

"Sixteen."

"Sixteen—heck. I wish there was something I could do to ever make it back to you, being gone all those years. But there just ain't, and I know it. As a friend of mine used to always say, 'Wish in one hand, shit in the other, see which one fills up first.' You make your choices and you get on with it, and I don't think there's any other way the good Lord would have us think of things." He pauses a moment. "Wish I had some better thing to say to you about all that, but I just don't. I was a sonofabitch, I know I was a sonofabitch, and I'm sorry for it, but ain't nothing I can do for you to change it."

"Then was I born in Nashville?"

"Nashville? Not exactly, no. I'll be honest," he pauses. "I wasn't there at the time, so I don't know for a fact. I was gone somewheres, probably on the road or chasing women." He turns his head so Jesse hears him clearer, closer now, the spit moving in his mouth as he speaks. "I ain't proud of it, son. You know that." Again he pauses a moment. "It'd be on your birth certificate, where you were born, I reckon. If you got one. Sure you got one. So far as I know your mother never made it to any hospital, and I don't know if she was on her way there or just laying up at home. She didn't say. We weren't on the best of terms right then. You'd have to ask her."

"But it was the South."

"Oh yeah—it was that."

Jesse draws his knees under his chin and locks his forearms around his shins. He feels the moisture in the ground wicking through his jeans. *Home,* he thinks. *This is my home.* It's the first time in his life he can't say anymore what that means. He digs his hands in the grass and stands, slapping bugs from his arms and neck.

"I'm going in," he says and heads across the yard, up the plank steps, inside.

(g)–I

Josephine will not sleep. They sit in the too-bright living room, talking music and hearing Grace's cassette—rough mixes from her last session, two weeks ago now. Every few minutes the girl runs out again carrying one of her toys—a stuffed yellow monkey, a dog with blue ears. His father pushes laboriously from the couch each time, smiling and joking, scoops her up and goes back with her to the bedroom. Grace hardly bats an eye. It's as if, now that the clock has finally run down past Josephine's bedtime, she has relinquished all responsibility. From here on, the business of keeping Josephine in bed and getting her to sleep is plainly up to Jesse's father. Grace will do nothing more to help.

She's deep into herself, listening back, and though Jesse knows she wants his opinion—"Tell me where you hear it getting funky, some of the timing's out, I know"—she is too absorbed in the music to pay him much attention, really. There's no doubt in Jesse's mind, the only good thing happening on the recording, so far, is her voice. The musicians his father has hired for the cuts (two of them the men Jesse saw through the window the night before—a keyboardist named Frank, and a bass player whose name he doesn't catch—all of them guys from a white country-rock band his father also produced) are clean enough players, but their timing does not match up with Grace's or in any way flatter or give her support. The way she leans back on the beat and runs her phrases together, sometimes syncopating the starts and ends of lines, she needs a more fluid backing. A more jazz-influenced backing. She needs the kind of accompaniment that would make her voice float—not this rocky, clattering, bump-along beat that keeps squaring up too soon, ending phrases under her in a way that makes it sound as if she's lost or doesn't know what she wants to emphasize. There's no fixing the tracks he's heard so far, and no single cut that's better than the others. He won't say so, though he's fairly sure, watching Grace, she knows this too.

"All my life it's been my dream—having this record. Just me, singing," she says. The second version of the third cut has just finished. Her face brightens, and she goes on. "I'm proud of it, too, and what your daddy's done to help me out—getting the right people to play and booking the studio and making sure everything's just so. But it's a lot of work." She laughs. "I mean, I've sang some backup and whatnot on other people's projects before, but this whole . . . this is something different. Guess you could say I had some illusions about how a record gets made."

"We've got distribution lined up even if we can't get a label to sign," his father says from the door at the other side of the room. "I think it's hot. Don't you think it's hot?" He looks anxiously at Jesse and goes right on, not waiting for an answer. "You're a little too close, is all, honey. You can't hear anything for what it is. That's normal. Trust me, when we make our first million, you'll be thinking it was a pretty sweet deal after all—pretty well worth all that work."

"Ain't saying it ain't worth the work, Henry. Just—I didn't how much it was going to take. Singing this note over and over to get the feeling right, and that one to fix the pitch—you know—till it don't hardly feel like *music* anymore. Like me *singing*." Josephine peers around Jesse's father's leg at them, the blue-eared dog clamped under her arm. "Go put that child to sleep, please," Grace says. She leans her forehead in her hand. "Please, Henry? She'll be wound up and cranky all day tomorrow if she don't get to sleep soon, and you know who's going to be the one to deal with that."

The tape reverses then; there's the count in, and music comes from the speakers again—an up-tempo rock ballad with Grace's voice out front more, and a horn section working in counterpoint swells to the keyboardist in a way that offsets his rhythm—and all of a sudden Jesse thinks he can understand his father's musical vision. He wants these interlocking rhythms and styles to reflect and heighten everything mismatched and eclectic in Grace's own character and singing voice—her strident tone and loose phrasing; her different colored eyes; her affection and sympathy always offered and taken back simultaneously—like a platform of broken levels beneath her that somehow coalesces at the same time it refuses to be any one thing.

"This one's closer to finished," his father calls to them over the music. "Don't you think?" He looks to Grace and then back at Jesse. "This one's our number-one hit."

"I can tell," Jesse says. He watches his father there in the doorway still, stooping now to within inches of Joey and nodding at her, then laughing and lifting her over his head and swinging her back and forth with the music, mouthing words to her and catching her back in his arms again.

"She wanted to dance," he says, whisking closer to Jesse and Grace, then away again. "How can I say no?"

"You can say no," she says, but she's smiling too, and Jesse knows she'd never have him refuse this. The song ends with all of them laughing, and the next track starts—a slower, modal, blues-influenced number—*the Lord is my Shepherd—he leads me into green pastures—there are no evil shadows*—D with a flatted seventh. Grace hunches forward on the couch now, eyes shut as if she were in a trance, singing softly over her own vocal. Jesse feels he's heard this song before, though he can't say where or when—possibly it's one of his father's own.

He gets up from the couch and crosses quickly to his instruments, beside the stove where he left them. Turns the fiddle cases on their backs and pops them open both at once, drawing his bow from the old case of his youth and the red fiddle from under its ancient strip of velvet that still smells faintly of a woman's perfume and Genny's shop. He turns the fiddle around in his hands once to admire the figure in the back wood, and stands, fiddle under his arm. He twists the thumbscrew, flicks the strings, and lowers an ear to the side of the fiddle to hear how far out of tune he is with the track. Close enough.

He waits and listens more and finally slips the fiddle under his chin, still listening, then runs a line in under her vocal—two notes together, two more. Where the vocal line constricts at the ends of phrases, he pushes through, outlining the chord-voicing in the electric guitar backup to smooth the transitions; when it drops open or floats up he goes with it, echoing her flourishes, then vanishing back into the chords on her longer legato notes; and when nothing at all is happening in the track, he fills with the bluesy chromatic runs and slower off-time double-stops he's always loved lining up against a vocal. There's a coil-reverb-drenched electric guitar solo ending with some drier, plucked-out-sounding notes followed by nothing—a hole left for some-body else's overdubbed solo, bass pulsing and drums thumping, piano throwing up fans of arpeggiated notes—and Jesse floats in here with the melody line up high, then lower, thinking of Duncan, and trails into what he presumes will be her vocal entry back into another chorus, bringing it in with some under-stated dissonances and falling away again. He can't hear where his fiddle separates from the track or where her voice breaks against the rhythm anymore. The feeling in his throat is one like he's lining the inside of the song with skin and, standing aside from that, caressing the skin at the same time. He watches her mouth and eyes—open now and locked on his—and waits for the feeling between his shoulder blades and along the ridge of his neck, his skin tightening from the pleasure of this music.

"You," she says, when the song is finished. She points at him. "You done *saved* that track. Henry—did you hear that?"

His father grunts, moves back a step in the doorway.

"If we can get you in the studio, can you play it again exactly like that?"

"Not exactly," he says. "Something like it."

The song starts again. *Take three,* someone says, *you're rolling,* and there's the count in.

"Henry? Can we book in some time at the studio? Are you *listening*?"

His father slips from inside the doorway altogether, almost quick enough, almost deep enough into the shadows that Jesse doesn't see him touching the back of a wrist to his cheeks, his eyes, and coughing once to clear his throat. "Huh," he says from there. "Sure. Why not." His voice sounds thinner and broken. Then, "Well, no, honey—. The studio's booked until next month."

"Get them to *un*book! This is your *son* we're talking about. He ain't gonna be around . . ."

There's the sound of his father's footsteps retreating; he says something else Jesse can't catch, and he and Grace meet eyes.

"How long are you staying for?" she asks.

He shrugs. "Thought I'd probably leave tomorrow."

She gets up, goes to the tape player, and brings the volume down to a whisper. "Can we get you to stay a little longer?" She makes a hissing noise and stops the tape. "I can't stand hearing that even one more time right now."

"Sounded OK to me," he says.

"Yeah," she says. "*OK.* That ain't the point, though, is it?"

He presses his fingers to the strings of the red fiddle and lowers his head, focusing all his attention on the sound of his father's voice in the next room, talking to Joey, as if by listening he will draw the man closer again. Nothing emerges distinctly to Jesse, none of his father's words, though there's pattern enough in his vocal inflections—a call and response that correlates with something Jesse only dimly remembers now. The voice fades to inaudibility and returns, and there's the sound of insects outside, a lone cricket on the hearth. He lifts the fiddle under his chin and draws open notes, adjusting the pitches, then crosses to the front window, where he stands, continuing to play. The tape player off now, he can hear the red violin more clearly; it's not exactly how he remembers—the sound is closer under his ear and more focused, as if the new fingerboard were applying a weight to every note, hardening the edges toward the middle and flattening away overtones. He doesn't mind, though it makes him play somewhat more inwardly. The sound is still as even, warm, and clear as before, only now, playing, he feels as if he were standing beside the music and not surrounded by it. The notes come back at him off the glass, and there's his own hazy reflection against the black outside, the fiddle cradled against his shoulder like a second head, bow angling back and forth, blue string-tails. *My fiddle,* he thinks. *Mine.* Behind him, in the reflection he sees his father come back into the room to stand beside Grace, talking softly, an arm around her shoulders. She curls closer against him, smiling, and finally turns him to face her so their hips almost touch, feet moving independently but together. They sway and step, mostly staying in one place, always talking, and Jesse turns from his reflection to see them as they are. *Me and your ma . . .*, he remembers the man saying all those years ago. *So me and your ma can take a turn around the room. That'd be something, hey?* He drones the open strings and watches his fingers bump up and down against the fingerboard and shifts his wrist one way and another to release his thumb and catch it again differently against the neck, feeling in his own neck and temples and solar plexus how those adjustments draw him in closer and closer to the heart of each note: air, wood, molecules in vibration. The shoulder pad pinches against his chest bones. Nothing is more satisfying, he thinks, adjusting again, watching them dance, listening.

His father brings pillows from upstairs and a set of worn yellow sheets with clowns printed on them. Together they pick up and sweep together handfuls of Josephine's toys, game pieces and marbles, pens, Tinkertoys, dolls, dropping them into a green plastic container like a washtub. The house is silent except for the sound the toys make hitting the bottom of the container and the floorboards squeezing and popping under his father's weight as he moves quickly one way and another, hunched, a hand on his knee, picking things up, breathing hard.

"Should be good enough," his father says. He kicks a few last items—crayons, a plastic figurine, miscellaneous wooden pieces—some back behind him, some in under the couch, out of the way. His face is shiny with sweat; he blinks slowly, his eyesight seeming engaged as if from a distance, though he continues working quickly and efficiently. He pulls cushions from the couch and kicks them into a row, stretches sheets over the top, again moving crablike and with surprising agility, hunched, with a hand on his knee. "That should do her," he says, and they face each other. He puffs in and out a few times.

"Ought to get that fixed," Jesse says, indicating the window behind his father, the one he broke in through the night before. "Practically waltzed right in here last night."

His father nods. "Lots of things I ought to do," he says.

In the silence the bug noise from outside seems suddenly multiplied.

Jesse knows the answer; Grace already told him, but he wants to ask anyway—wants the words from his father's mouth: *Why did you leave us? How come you didn't want to come back?* He can't say it though, and the longer he waits, the more the silence seems composed of his inability to bring the words out. They beat in his brain and throat, caught like the bugs in the window screen: *How could you never want to come back?*

His father yawns and lowers and opens his eyelids again, slower this time. "Say you wanted to get an early start tomorrow?" he asks.

Jesse shrugs.

"Well, you be sure and wake us up." He turns as if to leave and swings back again toward Jesse. "Couple little things I wanted you to have—wanted to give you."

"It can wait."

"Nothing much. Pictures and whatnot. Couple old recordings of your dad so you can think of him once in a while."

"Set them at the foot of the stairs then, in case."

"Nah." He shakes his head. "You wake us up. We'll get you fed and ready for the road."

Again there's the silence, the two of them facing each other, nothing to stop him. Still he can't bring himself to ask. He clears his throat as if there were something else he intended and watches his father to see if he'll guess—if he'll come out with the answers himself.

"I already told you how sorry I was," he says. Then, "The other thing—I guess I can't tell you this in such a way you might ever actually believe it, but you were always . . . you always had my best wishes. There wasn't a time I quit thinking about you— you and your ma, ever. You see her and tell her I said so. Tell her." He blinks again, this time leaving his eyes shut. Jesse is surprised at the length of his eyelashes against his cheeks; more surprised, still, when the eyes open again and he sees his father is crying, silently, with no other facial animation. Jesse lifts a hand toward him and lets it drop at his side as his father's mouth falls open, the lips caved inward. "I woulda liked to *been* there, you know, all those years—you know that. But I'm a dog and a coward, and you might as well know." He leans again, a

hand on his knee, catching his breath quickly in and out—
"Jesus!" he says—and straightens, scrubbing the backs of his
hands under his eyes and sniffing. "OK, OK. I'm OK. Ha. You
just take care of yourself," he says. "Hear? And stop back any
time. Any old time you need anything."

"I will," Jesse says.

He sniffs. "Knock 'em dead in Nashville, too, OK? Tell 'em I
sent you."

"I'll tell them."

"There's a million good pickers there, but don't let it . . .
don't get caught up trying to sound like anyone but yourself.
Just stay true to yourself. Shit. There's a subject I could write you
a book on."

They fall silent again, and his father pulls the string on the
light to keep from drawing more bugs into the room. He sniffs
once more and coughs, lifting his weight foot to foot. "Better get
on up to the little woman."

He's himself again.

"You should be comfortable enough here, hey?" He nudges
the cushions with his foot.

"Sure," Jesse says. "I could sleep about anywhere right now."

"Then I won't keep you. Take care, son." He brushes by, a
hand on Jesse's arm momentarily, moving higher to his shoulder, then gone. "Sleep well."

Jesse watches after him. The moon is bright in the next
room, through the front picture window, and he sees his father
coming in and out of its light, his image silver-edged as if he

were part of a film negative. He breathes once sharply and waits for the feeling to pass—the feeling he's once again about to lose his father. He hasn't felt it in a long time.

In his last dream he and his father are in the truck, driving somewhere. Each road seems the same—trees flashing by alongside them and overhead, catching the glare of his headlights. There's a new rattle to the insects, bright and zipping, almost tambourine-like. It makes his skin crawl. "Hang a left here," his father says, and Jesse could swear they're on the same road again, heading back the way they just came. "Slow up," he says, and Jesse does. Now his father leans toward the windshield as if he were listening or watching for something outside. The bug noise increases, and the air in the cab seems to thicken as they slow. "OK, take this little right here." Again, Jesse does as he's told, coasting off the road onto an overgrown sandy track barely wide enough for a car. Where it isn't sandy the road surface looks slick and soft with moss. Moss hangs from the trees alongside too and muffles the sound of his exhaust. And suddenly blooming out of the darkness on a hill above them is a house like nothing Jesse's seen before—some kind of chateau or multileveled villa with turrets and balustrades and elaborate wrought-iron grating everywhere. Ground lights follow the S-curve of a paved drive, milk-white in the moonlight, ending somewhere just beyond where they can see. There are lights on in every wing and window of the house, burning pink and purple and yellow against the black. "Pull up here," his father says.

He speaks without facing Jesse, points to a spot where the hill overhangs the track steeply. "Kill them headlights and cut the engine." From here the house is invisible again, only a faint radiance against the bright night sky. "Wait here," his father says. "Won't be but a couple minutes. If I ain't back in less than twelve minutes, you just get on out of here. Keep going straightaways and you'll come to the main road. Use the turnout at the next crossroads, and I'll catch you there."

"Twelve minutes," Jesse hears himself say. The number seems significant.

"Time it." The door groans out, and his father swings to the ground.

"Wait a second," Jesse says.

Again the door groans out and this time shuts, and his father leans back in, grinning. "If it takes any longer, you know what to do."

Before he can answer, the man has vanished around the bed of Jesse's truck, scrambling up the rise, his jeans and the soles of his boots flashing out of the dark momentarily, then gone. The engine clicks as it cools, and Jesse stretches back against the seat, waiting. He leans one way and then another to make out the time on his watch. His knees are already stiff from sitting, and the next thing he knows he's gotten out of the truck to stand beside it. Still, his knees hurt. There's a smell and a softness in the air here, almost as if an ocean were close by, and he listens for a surf, catching instead the tinny, distant pulsation of music, too faint to identify—then bell-like voices and glassware clinking. A party. A party for him and his father! He works the sounds together into a surf-sound of unmarked tones droning over the grass, then turns them back again to voices, music, and glassware.

A few minutes more and he jumps up the bank after his father, following his footsteps across a sunken grassy space and through hedges, onto a lawn. The man is coming toward him now with something huge over one shoulder, a sack of objects loosely wrapped and clinking. For a moment, seeing him, Jesse thinks the whole lit-up house and the sky beyond it are balanced on his shoulder—like he's hauling it all back for them. Then his perspective inverts, the stars stop moving, and he sees it's his father moving after all, not the sky or the house unmoored. There are cars parked up the lawn behind him, steel and chrome catching the moonlight, and a man like his father standing beside each one with a woman on his arm. The thing on his father's shoulder clatters to the ground, and Jesse realizes he is attempting to hide now—crouching and still creeping closer, a shadow bent into its own shadow, jogging and clinking and puffing and headed slightly to the right of Jesse. "Over here," he hisses and waves, and his father falls flat, vanishing. "It's me," he says, "over here," and then he's running to him. But when he gets there, his father is on his back, apparently unconscious and drenched in sweat, neat circles of it under his arms and winglike crescents to either side of his stomach and darkening each buttonhole. The sack of things is gone or never existed. *Heart attack,* Jesse thinks. But no, his father isn't dead. He mops his forehead and sits up, the curls sticking to his skin.

"I told you to wait," he says.

"You did," Jesse says. "I waited." But his voice doesn't seem to have any sound or impact with the man or any way of reaching him.

Searchlights spool the lawn in their direction, and a voice comes over an intercom telling them not to move. His father looks older now—his face shrunken against the bones with hatchet-shaped, white sideburns cutting the width of his cheeks, and Jesse realizes then it isn't him anymore. It hasn't been him all along; it's Bill Monroe.

"Come on, let's get," the man says, standing, and just as the lights find them, sweeping his face, Jesse knows it's all a dream. He wakes in time to feel his legs jerking and teeth clicking open and shut in anticipation of being shot down.

He will never be a Bluegrass Boy. He wakes up knowing it. There's no point pretending otherwise or imagining it could turn out another way for him: he came too late into the world. Five years earlier, ten years earlier, it would be another story. Eventually, he will meet Bill Monroe and play with him, but he won't wear the hat and suit and tie. He'll remember how he dreamed him—sweat-soaked on the ground, hatchet-shaped sideburns, half merged with his father; all his other overblown fantasies, too—and he'll know none of this shows in his face, except as a kind of muted awe and yearning: a thing he once felt strongly and had to abandon. He'll hang on to the neck of his mandolin, look right back at Monroe, and nod—give away nothing more. For a moment, anticipating this, Jesse feels as if he were able to see straight through himself to the root of his personality. But the feeling doesn't last. Just as quickly it's supplanted with new pictures and thoughts, sounds and textures from the world around him creeping in, and giving him ideas about his future. He'll go wherever the music takes him, east, south, north, west, and try not to regret it.

Just before leaving, he looks in on them. He stands at his father's side of the bed in the overcast light, hands loose at his sides—*liar, faker, fraud,* he thinks; *my father.* He tries to commit each detail to memory: the man's smell, musty, and a little like cooked eggs; the folds in the flesh around his neck; his eyelids and the shape of his mouth under the mustache. Right now it doesn't seem as if he's struggling to breathe, though Jesse supposes, from the tilt of the mattress, half off its frame, and the sheets flung down and knotted between their feet, that at some point in the night he must have slept himself close to death again.

He rocks on his feet but doesn't move any closer. "Goodbye," he whispers. Grace's eyelids flutter but don't open, and she makes a popping noise in her mouth.

"Bye," he whispers again.

He goes back out the hall to the stairwell and down, then through the green living room, the kitchen, out the back door, and down the plank steps, outside. His truck is where he left it, the keys in the ignition, his instruments already stowed in the cab and under the tarp in back. All he has to do is get in and drive.

The air is so wet he isn't sure at first, going across the road, if it's rain on his skin or his own breath blowing back over his face. Then a few drops spike in through his hair and splash his cheeks, and there's no mistaking it. Rain. There's the sudden rushing sound of it through the trees—wind gusting so the trees appear momentarily turned inside out—and just in time, he pulls himself up into the cab of his truck. He watches it run over the windshield, mixing with the dust and grime; hears the wind lift and bring it slapping over the roof of the truck, carrying electric and acidic scents of earth, clay, and sky through his open side windows. He leaves them halfway down and turns his key in the ignition. Eases the clutch in and pulls the gear lever toward him, but there's some way he feels held here. What he wants, still, is for his father to come around the back walkway or out onto the front porch to see him off, wave at him or even convince him he should stay a while longer—breakfast and something else after, music and more conversation about old times. He tilts his head against the headrest and shuts his eyes, willing himself to feel this and let it go at the same time. Nothing's left for him here, he's sure of it, and yet he can't leave—not yet, maybe not ever. In his head is the song he didn't play for his father—the one that woke him up and that he has no name for. He feels it in his fingertips and in the ache between muscle and bone, nerve and tendon—a feeling like the way the rain splashes back off the earth and soaks into everything. Even this close, parked outside his father's house and ready to leave him again, he's full of longing. He'll just count to ten, and if no one comes to stop him, he'll be on his way. He leans over the steering wheel, eyes closed, hearing the music and counting. *One, two, three, four . . .*

About the Author

Gregory Spatz is the author of the novel *No One But Us* and a story collection, *Wonderful Tricks*. His stories have appeared in many publications, including *The New Yorker, Iowa Review,* and *New England Review.* The recipient of a Michener Fellowship, an Iowa Arts Fellowship,  and a Washington State Book Award, he teaches at Eastern Washington University in Spokane. Spatz plays the fiddle in the acclaimed bluegrass band John Reischman and the Jaybirds.